"You don't need to be a dog lover to enjoy Steven Rowley's new book, *Lily and the Octopus*, but if you've realized you like your dog more than most humans you encounter, this is one you won't want to miss."

—*Newport Beach Independent*

"A joyful book; it is also a sincerely written tragedy that invoked the purity of friendship between animal/human family members."

—*EDGE Media*

"Steven Rowley strikes a chord in a moving book about heartache and friendship."

—*Portland Press Herald*

"The connection between man and dog is loud and clear in this sweet novel. . . ."

—*Fort Worth Star-Telegram*

"Philosophical and introspective, *Lily and the Octopus* also looks at the transformative power of love, the importance of forgiveness, and the beauty of really living."

—*The Free Lance-Star*

"[*Lily and the Octopus*] isn't simply another 'boy and his dog' story. It is a profound exploration of grief—how we find ourselves lost, how we search for reason, how we sacrifice ourselves for our loved ones. . . . In the magical, hopeful world of *Lily and the Octopus*, we will learn to live—and love—again."

—Garth Stein, bestselling author of
The Art of Racing in the Rain

"Singular, spectacular, and touchingly tentacular."

—Chris Cleave, bestselling author of *Little Bee*

"A bighearted, inventive, funny novel that also happens to be a profound meditation on love and forgiveness. *Lily and the Octopus* is a delight."

—Christina Baker Kline, bestselling author of *Orphan Train*

"My favorite book of the year: Steven Rowley's *Lily and the Octopus*. Hilarious, heartbreaking. You will absolutely cry and you will love it."

—Patrick Ness, bestselling author of
The Rest of Us Just Live Here

"A quirky and deeply affecting charmer of a novel, *Lily and the Octopus* is funny, wise, and utterly original in its exploration of what it means to love any mortal creature."

—Sara Gruen, bestselling author of *Water for Elephants*

"Intelligently written, finely observed, and surprisingly moving, this is a book you'll find hard to put down."

—Graeme Simsion, bestselling author of *The Rosie Project*

Lily and the Octopus

STEVEN ROWLEY

Simon & Schuster Paperbacks

New York   London   Toronto   Sydney   New Delhi

Simon & Schuster Paperbacks
An Imprint of Simon & Schuster, Inc.
1230 Avenue of the Americas
New York, NY 10020

First Simon & Schuster trade paperback edition June 2017

SIMON & SCHUSTER PAPERBACKS and colophon are registered trademarks of Simon & Schuster, Inc.

For information about special discounts for bulk purchases, please contact Simon & Schuster Special Sales at 1-866-506-1949 or business@simonandschuster.com.

The Simon & Schuster Speakers Bureau can bring authors to your live event. For more information or to book an event contact the Simon & Schuster Speakers Bureau at 1-866-248-3049 or visit our website at www.simonspeakers.com.

Book design by Ellen R. Sasahara
Cover design and illustration by Na Kim

Manufactured in the United States of America

9 10 8

The Library of Congress has cataloged the hardcover edition as follows:
Rowley, Steven, 1971-
Lily and the octopus / Steven Rowley.—First Simon & Schuster hardcover edition.
pages cm
I. Title.
PS3618.O888L55 2016
813'.6—dc23   2015027647

ISBN 978-1-5011-2622-2
ISBN 978-1-5011-2623-9 (pbk)
ISBN 978-1-5011-2624-6 (ebook)

For Lily

The Law for the Wolves

Now this is the Law of the Jungle,
  as old and as true as the sky;
And the Wolf that shall keep it may prosper,
  but the Wolf that shall break it must die.
As the creeper that girdles the tree-trunk,
  the Law runneth forward and back;
For the strength of the Pack is the Wolf,
  and the strength of the Wolf is the Pack.

—Rudyard Kipling

The Octopus

It's Thursday the first time I see it. I know that it's Thursday because Thursday nights are the nights my dog, Lily, and I set aside to talk about boys we think are cute. She's twelve in actual years, which is eighty-four in dog years. I'm forty-two, which is two hundred and ninety-four in dog years—but like a really young two hundred and ninety-four, because I'm in pretty good shape and a lot of people tell me I could pass for two hundred and thirty-eight, which is actually thirty-four. I say this about our ages because we're both a little immature and tend to like younger guys. We get into long debates over the Ryans. I'm a Gosling man, whereas she's a Reynolds gal, even though she can't name a single movie of his that she would ever watch twice. (We dropped Phillipe years ago over a disagreement as to how to pronounce his name. FILL-a-pea? Fill-AH-pay? Also because he doesn't work that much anymore.) Then there's the Matts and the Toms. We go back and forth between Bomer and Damon and Brady and Hardy depending on what kind of week it has been. And finally the Bradleys, Cooper and Milton, the latter of whom is technically way older and long dead and I'm not sure why my dog keeps bringing him up other than she loves board games, which we usually play on Fridays.

Anyhow, this particular Thursday we are discussing the Chrises: Hemsworth and Evans and Pine. It's when Lily suggests offhandedly we also include Chris Pratt that I notice the octopus. It's not often you see an octopus up close, let alone in your living room, let alone perched on your dog's head like a birthday party hat, so I'm immediately taken aback. I have a good view of it, as Lily and I are sitting on opposite sides of the couch, each with a pillow, me sitting Indian style, her perched more like the MGM lion.

"Lily!"

"We don't have to include Chris Pratt, it was just a suggestion," she says.

"No—what's that on your head?" I ask. Two of the octopus's arms hang down her face like chin straps.

"Where?"

"What do you mean, where? There. Over your temple on the right side."

Lily pauses. She looks at me for a moment, our eyes locked on each other. She breaks my gaze only to glance upward at the octopus. "Oh. *That*."

"Yes, *that*."

I immediately lean in and grab her snout, the way I used to when she was a pup and would bark too much, so excited by the very existence of each new thing encountered that she had to sing her enthusiasm with sharp, staccato notes: *LOOK! AT! THIS! IT! IS! THE! MOST! AMAZING! THING! I'VE! EVER! SEEN! IT'S! A! GREAT! TIME! TO! BE! ALIVE!* Once, when we first lived together, in the time it took me to shower she managed to relocate all of my size-thirteen shoes to the top of the staircase three rooms away. When I asked her why, her reply was pure conviction: *THESE! THINGS! YOU! PUT! ON! FEET! SHOULD! BE! CLOSER! TO! THE! STAIRS!* So full of ebullience and ideas.

I pull her closer to me and turn her head to the side so I can get a good, long look. She gives me the most side-eye she can muster in annoyance, disgusted with both the molestation and unwanted attention, and my gaucheness as a big, stupid human man.

The octopus has a good grip and clings tightly over her eye. It takes me a minute, but I gather my nerve and poke it. It's harder than I would have imagined. Less like a water balloon, more like . . . bone. It feels subcutaneous, yet there it is, out in the open for all to see. I count its arms, turning Lily's head around to the back, and sure enough, there are eight. The octopus looks angry as much as out of place. *Aggressive* perhaps is a better word. Like it is announcing itself and would like the room. I'm not going to lie. It's as frightening as it is confounding. I saw a video somewhere, sometime, of an octopus that camouflaged itself so perfectly along the ocean floor that it was completely undetectable until some unfortunate whelk or crab or snail came along and it emerged, striking with deadly precision. I remember going back and watching the video again and again, trying to locate the octopus in hiding. After countless viewings I could acknowledge its presence, sense its energy, its lurking, its intent to pounce, even if I couldn't entirely make it out in form. Once you had seen it, you couldn't really unsee it—even as you remained impressed with its ability to hide so perfectly in plain sight.

This is like that.

Now that I've seen it, I can't unsee it, and the octopus

transforms Lily's entire face. A face that has always been so handsome to me, a noble and classic dog profile, betrayed only slightly by a dachshund's ridiculous body. Still, that face! Perfect in its symmetry. When you pulled her ears back it was like a small bowling pin covered in the softest mahogany fur. But now she looks less like a bowling pin in shape and more like a worn-down bowling pin in occupation; her head sports a lump as if it had actually been the number-one pin in a ten-pin formation.

Lily snorts at me twice with flared nostrils and I realize I'm still holding her snout. I let go of her, knowing she is seething at the indignity of it all.

"I don't want to talk about it," she says, tucking her head to gnaw at an itch on her stomach.

"Well, I *do* want to talk about it."

Mostly I want to talk about how it could be possible that I've never seen it before. How I could be responsible for every aspect of her daily life and well-being—food, water, exercise, toys, chews, inside, outside, medication, elimination, entertainment, snuggling, affection, love—and not notice that one side of her head sports an octopus, alarmingly increasing it in size. *The octopus is a master of disguise*, I remind myself; *its intent is to stay hidden*. But even as I say this silently in my head I wonder why I'm letting myself so easily off the hook.

"Does it hurt?"

There's a sigh. An exhale. When Lily was younger, in her sleep she would make a similar noise, usually right before her legs would start racing, the preamble to a beautiful dream about chasing squirrels or birds or pounding the warm sand on an endless golden beach. I don't know why, but I think of Ethan Hawke answering the standard questionnaire inspired by Bernard Pivot that ended every episode of *Inside the Actors Studio*:

"What sound or noise do you love?"

Puppies sighing, Ethan had said.

Yes! Such a wonderful juxtaposition, sighing puppies. As if warm, sleeping puppies felt anything lamentable or had weariness or exasperations to sigh over. And yet they sighed all the time! Exhalations of sweet, innocent breath. But this sigh is different. Subtly. To the untrained ear it might not be noticeable, but I know Lily about as well as I think it's possible to know another living thing, so I notice it. There's a heaviness to it. A creakiness. There are cares in her world; there is weight on her shoulders.

I ask her again. "Does it hurt?"

Her answer comes slowly, after great pause and consideration. "Sometimes."

The very best thing about dogs is how they just know when you need them most, and they'll drop everything that they're doing to sit with you awhile. I don't need to press Lily further. I can do what she has done for me countless times, through heartbreak and illness and depression and days of general uneasiness and malaise. I can sit with her quietly, our bodies touching just enough to generate warmth, to share the vibrating energy of all living things, until our breathing slows and falls into the parallel rhythm it always does when we have our quietest sits.

I pinch the skin on the back of her neck as I imagine her mother once did to carry her when she was a pup.

"There's a wind coming," I tell her. Staring down the octopus as much as I dare, I fear there's more truth to that statement than I'd like. Mostly I am setting Lily up to deliver her favorite line from *Elizabeth: The Golden Age*. Neither of us has actually seen the film, but they played this exchange endlessly in the commercials back when it was in theaters and we both would

collapse in fits of laughter at the sound of Cate Blanchett bellowing and carrying on as the Virgin Queen. My dog does the
best Cate Blanchett impression.

Lily perks up just a bit and delivers her response on cue:
"I, too, can command the wind, sir! I have a hurricane in me
that will strip Spain bare if you dare to try me! Let them come
with the armies of hell; they *will not pass!*"

It's a good effort, one she makes for me. But if I'm being
honest, it isn't her best. Instinctually she probably already knows
what is fast becoming clear to me: she is the whelk; she is the
crab; she is the snail.

The octopus is hungry.

And it wants to have her.

Camouflage

Friday Afternoon

My therapist's office is painted the color of unsalted butter. Sitting in that office on the couch with the one broken spring that made it just maddeningly shy of comfortable, I have often thought of shoving the whole room into a mixing bowl with brown sugar and flour and vanilla and chocolate chips. I crave cookies when I'm annoyed, when I feel I know better than those around me. Crisp on the outside, chewy on the inside, fresh-baked chocolate chip cookies warm from the oven, with the chocolate soft but not melted. I don't know the derivation of this comfort craving, but there's a quote from Cookie Monster that's always inhabited my head: "Today me will live in the moment, unless it's unpleasant, in which case me will eat a cookie." While I don't take all of my mantras from goggle-eyed blue monsters with questionable grammar, this one has taken root. Lately I've been craving cookies a lot.

My therapist's name is Jenny, which is not a name you should accept for a therapist. Ever. A gymnast, perhaps. Forrest Gump's wife, sure. A worker at one of those frozen yogurt places where you pump your own yogurt and all they have to do is weigh it and they still think their job is rough. But not a therapist. I just don't think people take Jennys seriously. Case in point: My name is Edward Flask, but people call me Ted—something I insisted upon after the unfortunate nickname "Special Ed" followed me through grade school because I was so shy. I can see my name scrawled in Jenny's handwriting across the top of a legal pad on her lap, but the *T* in *Ted* is bolder— clearly an addition she made after remembering no one calls me Ed. And I've been seeing her for months! Still, Jenny takes my insurance and has an office that is adjacent to my neighbor- hood (at least by Los Angeles standards). The conclusions she draws are always the wrong ones, but I've gotten good at taking her dimwitted advice and filtering it through the mind of an imaginary and much smarter therapist to get the insight into my life that I need. That by itself sounds dysfunctional, but it happens to work for me.

I entered therapy after I ended my last relationship eighteen months ago, six years in and maybe two years after I should have. It started out strong. We met at the New Beverly Cinema after a screening of Billy Wilder's *The Apartment* and we argued about its merits. Jeffrey was smart—scary smart—and passion- ate. When I blanched at *The Apartment*'s themes of infidelity and adultery, Jeffrey pressed me on my professed love for another of Wilder's films, *The Seven Year Itch*.

At first, his charisma made it addictive to be around him. But over time, I recognized it was also a façade; there was a wounded boy inside of him. He had grown up without a dad, so it made sense to me that he sought constant validation. I found it en- dearing. Humanizing. Until he started to indulge that little boy. There were tantrums. There was acting out. There was his need to control things that he had no business controlling. But he was still that boy, and I loved him, so I stayed, thinking it would get better. And then one morning I woke up to one of life's clarion calls: I deserved better than this. That night I said I was leaving.

After more than a year off from dating, I'm finally putting myself out there again. Dipping my toes in old waters from which I thought I had long since sailed downstream. Jenny asks me about this.

"How is that going?"

"*That?*"

"Yes."

"Dating?"

"Uh-huh."

It's the last thing I want to talk about. The octopus has almost as tight a grip on my head as it does on Lily's. And yet I can't bring myself to tell Jenny about our unwanted visitor. At least not yet. I can't show my hand, expose the fear that the octopus brings and have her say all the wrong things, as she's all but guaranteed to do. Jenny. I can't do her work for her—not on this. I would rather do her work *without* her, which means, for now, holding this one close to my chest.

I shouldn't even have come, shouldn't have left Lily alone with the octopus, but the sunlight was streaming through the kitchen windows in the exact way that she likes, and the long beams of late afternoon would provide her ample warmth for a long nap. I couldn't get an appointment with the veterinarian until Monday, and something in me thinks the sun could be healing. That it might irradiate our visitor, desiccate our fish out of water.

"Are octopuses fish?" I ask it out loud without meaning to.

"Are octopuses what?"

"Fish. Are they considered fish."

"No. I think they're cephalopods."

Figures Jenny would know that. She was probably one of those girls who wanted to grow up to be a marine biologist before she went off to college and fell for a psych major with big, masculine hands and a name like Chad. I wish I was curled up on the floor in the sun beside Lily. I wish I could lay my hand on her like I did when she was a pup, to let her know that all that worried her would be okay so long as I was there. It's where I belong instead of here.

"What about dating, though?" Jenny snaps me back to attention.

"Dating. I don't know. It's fine. Uneventful. Soporific."

"Juvenile?" she asks.

"Not sophomoric." God, I want cookies. "Soporific. You know, tedious. Tiresome."

"Why is it tiresome?"

"Because it is." *Cookies*.

"It's always interesting to meet new people, isn't it? Couldn't you look at it that way?"

"I could." I say it in a stubborn way to make it clear that I don't and I won't. I don't know if it's me—maybe I'm not ready to date. I don't know if it's them—maybe the good ones are already taken. I don't know if it's my age. Los Angeles is a Neverland of Lost Boys who preen and crow far too often and demonstrate substance far too seldom. I started dating with enthusiasm and put my best foot forward in the task. But soon I found myself on a string of first dates where I couldn't remember if the story I was telling was one I had already told, or if it was a story I had told a previous date a night or two earlier. In an effort not to be boring, I had concocted a string of my best anecdotes, a highlight reel of witticisms, and in employing them over and over again, I ended up boring myself.

All of this I should be saying out loud, if only because my insurance company is paying for this time and I am paying for my insurance (as a freelance writer it's no small expense), but instead I offer an anemic "I just . . . I don't know."

"Tell me," Jenny implores.

"No."

"Come on. *Tumor me*."

The octopus swooshes its powerful arms in front of me, and in a chaotic flash exposes its hungry beak as it leaps for my face.

I flinch, swatting my hands in front of my nose. "What did you just say?" It comes across as accusatory.

Jenny looks at me, concerned. She has to see the sweat forming just along my brow line. I look frantically around the room for the octopus, but as quickly as it appeared, it is gone.

"I said, 'Humor me.'" Her concern melts into a smile.

Did she?

My butter prison is closing in; the walls seem closer than they did five minutes ago. This is usually a sign of an oncoming panic attack. They used to be rare, but lately I've had several. The best way to stave off a full-blown meltdown is to do the one thing I don't want to do—talk about dating. To remember life continuing. To not give in to that which causes the panic. So I relent. "There's this one guy. Handsome. Smart. Funny. Handsome. I said that twice, didn't I? Well, his looks merit it. I just can't tell if he's that interested."

"In you."

"In the art of puppeteering." I cross my arms protectively. "Of *course* in me. We went out a second time. And it was good." This is stupid. I should be talking about the octopus, but I can't think about the octopus. I can't feed the panic. "But still,

I didn't know. If he was interested. *In me.* So, I thought when we say good night the second time, if he tries to kiss me, that'll be some indication. And if he tries to hug me, I won't break the hug first." Pleased with that plan, I point to my head—like it's more than just a hat rack. Then I realize perhaps the octopus is hiding on my head, heads being a place he seems to be fond of, and I give myself a top-to-bottom pat down. Jenny looks at me like I'm experiencing some sort of debilitating seizure, but forges ahead.

"Smart. Then you could see if the hug was a friendly hug or a romantic hug. So, what happened?"

"I broke the hug first."

Jenny looks at me, disappointed.

Defensively: "Well, he didn't break the hug, either, so we were just standing there like two stroke victims propping each other up!" The walls are now so dangerously close that I wonder if they will crush me or if I will be pressed into their buttery softness, creating a perfect mold of my form after I suffocate in clotted cream.

"That in itself should have told you something." Jenny makes a doodle on her notepad, darkening the *ed* in my name to match the bolded *T*. She's being *paid* to listen to me, and even she finds me boring. But it's not her fault. Less than twenty-four hours since the arrival of our . . . *cephalopod* houseguest, I already recognize a trait we share: I, too, am hiding in plain sight. I am walking through life invisible, skulking like a failure, hoping few people notice me. I've been doing that since things went south with Jeffrey.

"I think you need to allow for the fact that some people have difficulty expressing themselves," Jenny muses.

Jenny always employs the phrase *some people* when she's talking about me. But once again, this is the wrong conclusion. This guy did not have problems expressing himself. I do not have problems expressing myself. This guy just didn't know if he liked me, and that made me anxious. Even if it was my fault he didn't know. Even if I was not letting myself be seen.

C is for cookie, that's good enough for meeee. Cookie cookie cookie starts with C.

I filter her analysis through the voice of my preferred, imaginary therapist and he comes up with sharper advice: It has only been two dates. Why do I need to know how this guy feels about me? Why does everything have to be settled? Do I even know if I like *him*? I mean, beyond his looks? I have to be better about living in the not knowing.

And suddenly it's not about dating, it's about the octopus. *I have to be better about living in the not knowing.*

Friday Evening

June in Los Angeles is the opposite of June everywhere else. Here, it means only one thing: gloom. The sun disappears behind clouds and fog and smog and haze and doesn't reappear for weeks. Normally, I like it. Normally, I'm fine with it being the price we pay to have sunshine the rest of the year. But tonight there's no sunset, and it bothers me.

Trent calls and proposes dinner and I say no, but Trent doesn't take no for an answer, so I say yes to save us from going twelve rounds. I feel bad about leaving Lily for even another hour, but I also know I need to talk to someone, and if it's not going to be Jenny it might as well be Trent. He knows how to get through to me and always has, ever since we met on our first day of college in Boston. He was a loud Texan and I was a quiet Mainer and I was immediately captivated by his southern charm, much as he was fascinated with my northern chill. It was a friendship that worked from the moment he knocked on the door of my dorm room and asked if I wanted to walk to 7-Eleven for cigarettes; he was the Ferris Bueller to my Cameron Frye.

From the time we were twenty-two, Trent would tell me not

to worry. He said it was all going to happen for us when we were twenty-nine. Bad breakup? Who cares. Dead-end job? It wasn't a waste of time. Any other stress? Why waste even a moment caring—it was all going to happen when we were twenty-nine. I questioned him at first. Why twenty-nine? Why not twenty-eight? And then I started to panic. What if it didn't happen for me until I was thirty-one? I didn't know how to use swear words correctly until the seventh grade, or what the Internet was until 1995. I worried about falling behind. Still, the bravado of the statement, and the confidence with which he delivered it, eventually made me a believer. I never bothered to ask what "it" was—the *it* that was going to happen for us. I'm not confident he entirely knew.

And then, in the very waning hours of my twenty-ninth year, I found Lily. The day before my thirtieth birthday.

Trent is already inside the restaurant when I get there. It's our usual place. We like it because when you order a martini it comes in a chilled martini glass, and then, when you're halfway through the drink, they bring you a *fresh* chilled martini glass for the rest of it. They even transfer the drink for you and bring you fresh olives. Astonishing, right? Service.

"Hi, friend. I ordered you a martini," he says.

"Thanks. Do you have the other thing?"

"Teddy," he says, scolding me for even thinking he might have forgotten. He slides a single Valium across the table. I put the pill into my mouth, chewing it slightly before I press it under my tongue. It works faster if you press it under your tongue. Trent gives me a minute to make it happen.

"Are you going to tell me what's the matter?"

I hold up my finger for him to wait as I carefully massage the pill fragments between my tongue and lower jaw until they dissolve.

"Lily has an octopus." The words taste chalky and raw, and they're out of my mouth before I can stop them, which means I really do need to talk about this.

Trent looks confused. "What?"

"An octopus. On her head. Above her eye." Spelling it out does nothing to alleviate his confusion. He's giving me a look. So I sum it up and say, "Kind of like yours."

Trent is the only other person I know who has had an octopus other than, like, on a salad. His came in 1997. We were roommates then, here in Los Angeles. I found him one night on the couch rubbing his calf and looking bewildered. "My leg is numb," he said.

I don't know if it's my imagination, or my anticipation of the Valium's effect, but I exhale and ease into a Diazepam vision of Trent and me at twenty-six, our old, dilapidated apartment as real to me as when we lived there.

Turns out the left side of his body had been growing numb for months, and a doctor-ordered MRI revealed an octopus still in its infancy. Within weeks he was in surgery, and although it was traumatic at the time, his recovery was quick and we soon put it behind us. Later I wondered why it took him so long to say something. We routinely spent hours analyzing every last one of life's events and details: That time we broke up a lesbian fistfight. The proper thread count for sheets, and what made Egyptian cotton so great. How many celebrities could we realistically get to come to one of our parties. Why we always burned oatmeal. Was it okay to ask out a male nurse I met on fifty-cent drink night at The Apache. Why did we go to a bar called The Apache in the first place? (Fifty-cent drinks.) There was plenty of time for it to come up before I found him on the couch looking confused.

Trent taps me on my arm and I look up. The restaurant is busy tonight, busier than usual.

"You drifted," Trent says. The Valium must be kicking in. "How is it like mine?"

"Well, not exactly like yours, because you couldn't see yours, but Lily's is just sitting on top of her head for all to see."

"Her . . . octopus."

"Yes."

"I never had an octopus."

"Yes, you did! And if you didn't I'd like to know what the hell they took out of you at Cedars when they cut open your skull."

"They took out a t—" he starts, before stopping.

"What the hell do you think we're talking about?"

"I thought we were talking about an octopus."

"Exactly."

Our martinis arrive. Three olives each. We sip our drinks in silence. The vodka is a cold salve on my throat and a welcome way to wash the powdery aftertaste from under my tongue. It burns as I swish it around my mouth.

"Do you want to get the deviled eggs?" I don't know why he's asking me this, because I always want to get the deviled eggs. He flags down a waitress and puts in an order. I don't even have to say yes. "Did you call the vet?"

I nod. "They can't see her until Monday."

"When did you first notice the . . ."

". . . octopus? Last night. It just showed up. If it was there before, I didn't notice. It's weird, though. It doesn't really move, it just sits there with its arms hanging down the side of her face. I think it's . . . sleeping."

Trent muddles two of his olives into his martini with his

fingers and I pull one of mine off the toothpick with my teeth. I can see him doing math in his head.

"How old is Lily again?"

"No."

"What?"

"*No.*" I am firm. "I can see what you're doing, weighing the probative value of my options here. One, I haven't been to the veterinarian yet, and I don't know what's involved in removing an octopus that's clinging to her head."

Octopusectomy.

"Two, I am not letting that thing have her. I won't allow it."

In my twenties, I had another terrible therapist (therapists!) who concluded that since my mother never says "I love you" (at least not in the same way that other mothers do), there was going to be a limit to my ability to feel love. Love for someone, loved by someone. I was limited. And then on the very last night of my twenties, when I held my new puppy in my arms, I broke down in tears. Because I had fallen in love. Not somewhat in love. Not partly in love. Not in a limited amount. I fell fully in love with a creature I had known for all of nine hours.

I remember Lily licking the tears from my face.

THIS! EYE! RAIN! YOU! MAKE! IS! FANTASTIC! I! LOVE! THE! SALTY! TASTE! YOU! SHOULD! MAKE! THIS! EVERY! DAY!

The realization was overwhelming—there was nothing wrong with me! There were no limits to what I could feel!

And just as Trent had predicted, with only moments left to go on the clock, it all happened for me when I was twenty-nine.

I slam my fists on the table and the silverware jumps and the vodka sloshes to the very rim of our glasses and I grit my teeth and glare. "*It cannot have her.*"

A chill runs down Trent's spine. I know this, because a chill runs down my own. He puts his hands over mine to calm me. He has a dog, a bulldog named Weezie. He loves her like I love Lily. He knows my heart. He understands. He would fight this fight.

The waitress comes with our deviled eggs and with two freshly chilled glasses and transfers the rest of our martinis. She smiles at us awkwardly and disappears.

I watch as ice sluices down the side of my new glass in slow motion.

It.

Cannot.

Have.

Her.

Friday Night

Friday nights are my favorite nights. You wouldn't think a twelve-year-old dachshund would be good at Monopoly, but you'd be wrong there. She can stack up hotels along one side of the board like nobody's business and usually does so with little commiseration for others who might not be able to afford her upscale rents. Me, on the other hand, I like the first side of the board. The one with the deep purple and light blue properties with vaguely racist names like Oriental Avenue. Something about the color palette on that side of the board calms me. Lily is colorblind; she doesn't undertake any such considerations when buying property. Also, I never feel too aggressive building hotels on those properties if I'm lucky enough to get the monopoly. The rents are reasonable and people are usually flush from having just passed Go. I guess I just don't have the killer instinct.

Lily always makes fun of me when I want to be the wheelbarrow or the shoe. She considers these the game pieces of weak, feckless players. She always wants to be the cannon or the battleship or the "shot glass." (I haven't had the heart to tell her she's been playing that piece upside down and it's actually a thimble. She would be furious if she ever found out.)

Tonight our hearts aren't really in it, but it's what we do on Friday nights, so we go through the motions. I might have suggested we just skip it and do something less involved, like watch a movie (although Saturday nights are usually Movie Night), but I'm feeling some guilt from having left earlier today for therapy and dinner with Trent. As always, I have to roll the dice, move her game piece, conduct the transactions, buy her houses and hotels, and be the banker—because, well, she's a dog.

Double fours.

"That's doubles two times in a row. One more time and you go to Jail," I say. She lands on one of the green properties. "North Carolina Avenue. No one owns it. Do you want to buy it?"

She shrugs. She is a shell of my usual Monopoly partner, both of our minds elsewhere. But while I'm putting on a brave face (maybe it's the vodka and Valium), she's just warming a chair. I look across at her. As always, I put a pillow on her seat so she can see above the tabletop, but tonight she looks smaller to me. Maybe she was always that small—I don't think she's ever weighed more than seventeen pounds—but her presence in my life has always been outsized.

"Do you not want to play? We don't have to play." She sniffs at her pile of money. When she bows her head I can see the octopus, so I look away. I've decided not to engage it, to look at it, to talk to it, to even acknowledge it, until our vet appointment on Monday.

We'll see how long that lasts.

"Tell me again about my mother." This is something Lily likes to hear from time to time. It used to bother me, her curiosity about where she came from. I guess maybe I was feeling some remorse about tearing her away from her dachshund family when she was only twelve weeks old, away from her mother and father and brother and sisters who later came to be called Harry and Kelly and Rita. But now it's a story I like to tell. It's a story about beginnings, and heritage, and our place in the greater world.

"Your mother's name was Ebony Flyer, but people called her Witchie-Poo. Your father's name was Caesar, after a great Roman general. I only met your mother once, on the day that you and I were introduced."

"My mother's name was Witchie-Poo?"

"It was a beautiful day, the first week of May. Spring. I drove hours into the country to this old white farmhouse with clapboard siding and peeling paint, my heart in my throat the whole way. I was so nervous! I wanted you to like me. The place sat a ways back from the road and the lawn was almost yellow; we hadn't had much rain that spring, which was good for you and bad for just about everyone else."

"I hate the rain."

"Yes, you and every other dog. Anyhow, there was a little wire pen on the front lawn and inside were you and Harry and Kelly and Rita tumbling all over one another like noodles in a pot of boiling water. It was hard to even tell where one of you ended and the next one began, you were just a pile of paws and tails, so the lady who lived there picked you up and set you gently on the grass. The four of you ambled and tumbled and stumbled and bumbled, and I stood there thinking, *How on earth am I ever going to choose?*"

"But you did. You chose me!" Lily picks up a little red wooden hotel and chews it enough to put a few teeth marks on it before spitting it out onto a railroad. Normally this is not behavior I would allow, but she does it quite gently, sort of nonchalantly.

"No. No, that's not true, exactly," I say, and she looks up at me, startled.

Like any good adoptive parent, I have always fed her that line of horseshit: A mommy and daddy who have a baby get stuck with whatever baby they get. But adoptive parents *choose* their baby, and so they love them that much more. Of course, in most cases, it's blatantly untrue. Adoptive parents are lucky to get the call whenever and wherever they do, and so they get the baby they get just the same as parents who actually give birth.

"No?" Lily sounds offended.

"No," I repeat, because it's the truth. Then I pause for dramatic effect. *"You,* in fact, chose *me."*

And she did. While Harry and Kelly and Rita carried on in a game that involved rolling and somersaulting, Lily broke free from the group and wandered over to where I was standing talking to the lady who bred them.

"I was thinking of keeping the boy one myself, unless you have particular use for him. He's high-spirited, but I think he can be trained to show."

I hadn't given much thought to whether I wanted a boy or a girl. Not wanting to appear sexist and get on the wrong side of the woman who had the sole say in whether I'd be taking one of her puppies home, I said, "No, I'd be glad to choose from among the girls."

I studied the pups, looking for the girls, and was at a loss to tell which one was male. I would have to pick each one up and make a subtle determination; worse than appearing sexist would be to come off as a pervert.

It was then that I noticed the puppy who became Lily gnawing on my shoelace. She clamped down and put herself in reverse until the lace had been gently untied.

"Hello, you adorable . . ." I crouched down and made my inspection. "Girl."

"That's the runt, that one there," the lady replied, just this side of dismissively.

I picked up the runt and she snuggled under my chin, tail wagging like the pendulum of the smallest, most fragile grandfather clock.

"I'm Edward. People call me Ted," I whispered into her ear before lowering my own ear to the top of her head. I heard her speak for the first time.

THIS! IS! MY! HOME! NOW!

And so it was.

"I choose this one," I told the lady.

"You can have your pick of any one. The male, even, if you really want. I'm not sure this one will show all that well."

"All the same, I'm not really interested in showing her. So I choose this one."

I worried for a second she was going to try to discourage me further from choosing this puppy. She studied us both for a moment as I held the runt protectively, and eventually her face softened and relented. I wondered if she wasn't just relieved to have someone take the runt so she could charge more for the rest of her flawless litter.

"Seems like she kind of chose you." And then, after a beat, "I suppose that's how it works." She finished with the off-center smile of a car salesman who's just sold a lemon for nearly full price.

I tell Lily this story over the Monopoly board and she seems satisfied. Touched, even. I smile at her, but sideways so I don't have to acknowledge the octopus. She shakes her head and her ears flop back and forth and the familiar chime of her collar and dog tags jingle the room alive. It's only after she stops that I realize I've been gripping my chair so tightly my fingers are white. I suppose I was hoping she would shake her head so violently that the octopus would lose its grip, sail across the room, and splat against the wall, dying instantly.

For the first time tonight I look at her head-on, and the octopus is still there, still holding on tight, only now (and I kid you not) the son of a bitch is smiling at me.

You motherfucker.

Lily looks at me, confused. "What?"

I compose myself as quickly as I can. "It's your turn," I say, hoping to reengage her in the game.

"No, it's not."

"Yes, it is. You rolled double fours so you get to roll again. Do you want me to roll for you?"

"Does it look like I've suddenly grown hands?" She's learned that sarcasm from me, something I used to be proud of but now find abrasive.

I roll the dice. Double twos. Lily and I look at each other for a few long seconds—both of us know what it means. I reluctantly pick up her battleship and move it directly to Jail.

Saturday Late Afternoon

There are times when Los Angeles is the most magical city on Earth. When the Santa Ana winds sweep through and the air is warm and so, so clear. When the jacaranda trees bloom in the most brilliant lilac-violet. When the ocean sparkles on a warm February day and you're pushing fine grains of sand through your bare toes while the rest of the country is hunkered down under blankets slurping soup. But other times—like when the jacaranda trees drop their blossoms in an eerie purple rain— Los Angeles feels like only a half-formed dream. Like perhaps the city was founded as a strip mall in the early 1970s and has no real reason to exist. An afterthought from the designer of some other, better city. A playground made only for attractive people to eat expensive salads.

I'm flipping through a menu of such salads, overwhelmed with the ridiculousness of it all. Do I want a dressed array of greens with pickled yardlong beans? Perhaps I am more in the mood for sautéed beetroot and chicory. Or do I go all in with the fifty-ingredient Guatemalan salad? This is the city I live in.

Can I even name fifty salad ingredients? I purse my lips with indecision. They feel dry.

"I think I'm addicted to ChapStick." I look up. Did I just say that out loud?

"How can you be addicted to ChapStick?" he asks, tossing back the last of his drink. His forehead is dripping sweat, but I don't think it's nerves. I think he's just the kind of guy who sweats a lot.

"Someone once told me they put trace amounts of ground-up glass in ChapStick. That's how they get you addicted to it. The little shards of glass give you hundreds of microscopic cuts that dry out your lips, making you need . . . more ChapStick. I seriously looked at the label one time, as if in addition to 44 percent petrolatums, 1.5 percent padimate, 1 percent lanolin, and .5 percent cetyl alcohol it was going to say 4.5 percent broken glass. It doesn't." He looks at me, stunned. Not knowing what else to do, I continue. "It's a cover-up. The Whitehall-Robins Healthcare Company of Madison, New Jersey, which distributes ChapStick, is probably owned by The Altria Group, which is a made-up name for what used to be Philip Morris to make people associate them less with tobacco." And then, to punctuate the sentence: "They own a lot of stuff."

I reach for the last piece of our jicama appetizer and shrug. Everything inside me told me I should have canceled this date, and now that I'm on it, I'm furious at myself for not listening. I should have held out for another date with the handsome hugger. But instead this is me living in the not knowing, and I hate it. This is a waste of our time. I know it. He knows it. He's not saying it (or anything, really), so I'm babbling to fill the silence. But seriously, I'm coming off like an idiot. And a bit of a conspiracy-theorist. Not even the fun kind who believes in little green men—the other kind, the kind who writes manifestos and Priority Mails them with explosive devices. I wouldn't date me and neither should he.

We had decent email chemistry, this new guy and I. But that happens sometimes in online dating. A few zippy emails, some decent back-and-forth, and then in person? Nada. Nothing. Zilch. I should be better at detecting when that's going to happen by now, but I'm not. It's still a roll of the dice. That's why I don't get excited anymore by a few zippy emails and some decent back-and-forth. It doesn't necessarily mean you'll have any real desire to see that person naked. Something like profuse sweating doesn't usually show up in pictures—especially if the pictures are of them being active. You think, oh, he's sweating because he's hiking Runyon Canyon, or tossing a Frisbee at the beach. You don't imagine them sweating like this sitting at a table reading a menu of salads.

"Are you addicted to anything?" I realize I'd better bring him into the conversation before I launch into my monologue about Robitussin.

"Sex."

I have no idea if this is a joke or not. If it is, it's kind of funny. If it's not, I might get raped. I play it off like it's a joke and move on.

"What do you do?"

"I'm a flight attendant, but I'm quitting that to become a professional dog walker."

Fucking L.A. *Professional* dog walker. Is that a thing? Are most dog walkers maintaining their amateur status to compete in the Dog Walking Olympics? I guess that's what I am. An amateur dog walker. It's where I should be now. Enjoying a walk with Lily in the early evening. The gloom has parted just enough by five o'clock that there's some soft light streaming through that would make a walk with her seem nice. It could be the only sunlight we see for days. Suddenly I want to be here even less.

"That sounds like a . . ."—how do I phrase this politely?— "lateral move."

"It's kind of a step up, actually."

"That makes me feel bad for flight attendants." I cringe, imagining him handing me a ginger ale with his sweaty mitts.

"Well, here it's a step up. In L.A., people will pay anything for their dogs. Do you have any pets?"

"No." I try to remember my dating profile (how much is on there about Lily?) and weigh the chances that he actually *read* my profile and would remember it well enough to know that I'm lying, or if he just flipped through my photos to find the one shirtless one. I shouldn't have written that thing a bottle deep in one of New Zealand's finer white wines and I certainly shouldn't have posted a shirtless photo. That was the wine's fault.

"Me, neither. I want to, though. Have a pet."

This (aside from the maybe sex joke) is the most interesting thing about him. I don't even know what he means by a pet—dog, cat, reptile, bird, one of those chirping key chains that Japanese children used to carry, hamster, fish, rock—but he wants one.

I try to think of how to tactfully cut this short. If it's not going anywhere (there's so little connection here there's not even interest in sex), there should be a socially acceptable way to just get up and walk out. I mean, if there's nothing obviously wrong with the other person—they are "as advertised," but you're just not, for whatever reason, feeling it—there should be a way to get up and leave. If there *is* something obviously wrong with them, you can say so right up front. Maybe not in those exact words, but you can say something like, "I'm sorry, I don't think this is going to be a match." Once I got a particularly creepy vibe from a guy just from his handshake, and we weren't meeting in a sufficiently public place, so I said just that and left. Another time, I wish I had said that up front but instead suffered through dim sum while having to answer questions like, "Do you think you're the kind of person who could perform an emergency tracheotomy?" (For the record, no, I do not.) But once you're in the middle of a date, you're kind of committed to seeing it through to its natural conclusion. My first date with Jeffrey lasted two days—there was just so much to say! I suppose that sets a very high bar.

Lily was asleep when I left, and I felt like one of those new parents who wanted to wake their sleeping baby to see if it was still alive. But while she normally sleeps on her left side, this afternoon she was on her right, octopus side down. Good. Maybe it will suffocate in her paw-print blanket. Otherwise she was curled up in her usual way, the way that made me call her Bean. I'm already looking forward to whatever movie she and I may watch together when this interminable date is over. On Saturday nights we watch movies. I hope she's well rested. Maybe we'll order Indian; the place up the street has these chickpeas in a tomato and ginger sauce that are really something. I think again about how to end this ordeal. *Well, since you're not really that interesting in person, I think I'll head out.* If only it were that easy. I should just go ahead and make a third date with the hugging guy. At least I was interested enough in him to want to know if he was interested in me. Why did I break the hug first?

"What about kids?" I ask. "Do you want kids?" I like kids well enough—I have a niece that I'm crazy about. But I'm already too old to be a young father, and I don't particularly want to be an old father, and I'm single and it's not something I would do on my own. Nor do I have a particular drive to change my relationship status just to have kids, despite my being on a dating website. So I don't really think kids are in the cards.

"No. Definitely not. I don't get kids."

"Oh, well, there you go. I want to have kids. Need to have kids. Lots and lots of kids. We'll form a singing group and tour second-tier European cities like Düsseldorf." And just like that, there's my out.

On the way home, I have a sudden craving for ice cream. I stop at the grocery store and head right to the frozen food aisle and select a pint of Ben & Jerry's Karamel Sutra for me and an individual cup of vanilla for Lily, because what the hell. One summer when she was young we were driving somewhere together, and I pulled over to the side of a road when I saw an ice-cream place with one of those walk-up windows. We got out of the car and marched together across the gravel parking lot and I ordered a mint chocolate chip ice-cream cone because the mint chocolate chip ice cream they had was green and it always tastes better to me when it's green (even though the dye they use is probably carcinogenic). We sat at a picnic table on some grass and I scooped Lily up into my lap.

WHAT! IS! THIS! CLOUD! THAT! YOU'RE! LICKING! I! LOVE! TO! LICK! THINGS! WOULD! I! LIKE! TO! LICK! THAT!

Even on my best days, I always wished life excited me as much as it excited her. So I lowered the cone to let her have a lick. The response was immediate.

THIS! IS! AMAZING! WE! MUST! HAVE! THIS! TO! LICK! EVERY! SINGLE! DAY!

It was impossible, eating the rest of that cone. She stood on my lap and put her front paws on my chest, her tail ticking on its fastest setting. And then the back paws tried climbing, looking for footholds in my abs, anything to hoist herself closer to her minty prize.

"Hey, hey, hey!" I objected. "Sit!" She did, steadying the paws on the right side of her body on my left leg and the paws on the left side of her body on my right leg while trying to maintain a semblance of balance. Her eyes looked up at me lovingly and with great anticipation.

Someone once said give a dog food and shelter and treats and they think you are a god, but give a cat the same and they think they are the god.

We shared the rest of that ice-cream cone, for I am a god.

Sunday, 4:37 A.M.

My legs jerk in that way that they do when I'm half-asleep and dream that I'm falling and about to hit the ground. I wake up in a cold sweat, prop myself up, throw the covers back, and reach for Lily all in one fluid motion.

The octopus is rattling the bed. Its limbs have come alive, all eight, and they swarm around Lily, gently but with purpose, and I just know that its dormancy is ending.

I put my hand on Lily's chest. Nothing. I press down harder while my own heart stops. And then it comes, the familiar rise and fall of her muscled torso. She's still here. She's okay. The octopus's arms slow and then stop and the terror becomes less immediate and things go back to more or less the way they have been since I first noticed the octopus on Thursday.

I try to remember if I was dreaming just now, just before I awoke. Something about standing on a boat, and maybe Lily was there. Or maybe she was both there and not there, in the way that in dreams things can happen on several different planes. I think I was chasing something. Not chasing, hunting. I can't even be certain there was a boat or a dream at all. It all feels less like a dream and more like a memory, albeit a memory just out of reach.

Lily's chest rises and falls again. Her breathing is deep, sonorous.

For the first three months that she was mine, she did not occupy my bed. She slept in a crate beside me. It started out across the room, but the first several nights she whimpered and whined, unable to sleep away from the warmth of her litter-mates. Each night, my judgment increasingly affected by my own inability to sleep, I moved the crate a little closer to me, until I could lie with my finger between the bars of the swing-ing door. We slept like that—side by side, me in a bed, her in a crate, sometimes my finger and her paw touching—until it was time to spay her. After the surgery to remove her uterus she refused to wear the cone that would keep her from picking at her stitches. *THIS! IS! THE! DUMBEST! THING! I'VE! EVER! SEEN! AND! I! WILL! TAKE! NO! PART! IN! WEARING! IT!*

Without the cone, she helped herself to licking at her wound whenever I was not there to stop her. So during the day I took her everywhere with me, and at night I brought her into my bed and slept with one arm stretched across her. I don't know that I physically prevented her from pulling at her stitches, but it was an emotional comfort. Enough at least that it allowed her to sleep through the night, undistracted by the discomfort of her incision.

She never again slept out of my bed unless we were apart.

When her stitches were removed and her wound had healed, I no longer slept with my arm across her. Free to roam the mat-tress, she immediately burrowed beneath the covers to the very foot of the bed to sleep alongside my feet. Two nights I battled her, convinced of her imminent suffocation if she insisted on sleeping so burrowed. She would tunnel down to the bottom of the bed and I would drag her back up for air. Then she would tunnel back down to the bottom of the bed and I would drag her back up for air. We did this for hours ad nauseam, and late in the second night I hit my breaking point.

"Fine. You want to sleep down there? Then you will suffocate. You will cease being able to breathe. And the last thought you will have in this life is that I was right and you were wrong and you will go to your grave regretting having a brain the size of a walnut."

I lifted the covers and stared down at her and I could just make her out staring at me. By then I had all but given up trying to outstubborn a dachshund, an exercise in futility if there ever was one. All I knew was that I was tired and I needed sleep. I would dig her corpse out of the bed in the morning.

Of course when morning came she was fine. She trotted up to the covers' edge to greet the daylight, stretching her front legs in some complex yoga pose and yawning the sleep away.

Tonight it is me who wants to burrow to the foot of the bed, to find the safest spot under the covers, where I can feel small and protected and warm. A spot away from the nightmare of the octopus, away from the reach of his quivering arms, away from what I know is coming next.

Sunday Night

On Sundays we eat pizza, the one ritual Lily and I have that stems directly from my childhood. When I was a kid, Sunday night was always pizza night. My sister, Meredith, and I would take turns making pizzas with my dad and it was the one night we were allowed to drink soda. It was something we looked forward to even though the weekend was drawing to a close. My mother enjoyed it because it was the one break she got from overseeing our endless feedings, something we never fully appreciated. (It was not in her nature to put her feet up, however, and she spent the time doing other thankless tasks like ironing our bed sheets or using the odder vacuum attachments to clean under the fridge.) My sister and I enjoyed it as something we could do with our dad. Making the pizzas was half the delight, and we had to claim Sundays on the calendar in the kitchen to stake out whose turn it was to help assemble the pies. The event was scored by the game-ending plays of football or the familiar ticking that starts *60 Minutes*. (I'm Mike Wallace. I'm Morley Safer. I'm Harry Reasoner. And I'm Ed Bradley. Those stories, plus Andy Rooney . . .)

Lily and I continue the tradition, although we usually order pizza to be delivered so Lily can bark at the deliveryman like a crazed townsperson accusing Goody Proctor of being a witch. I think she looks forward to it, too, even though it's the end of the weekend, the end of the concentrated time we spend together before the craziness of a new week begins.

I'm asking Lily if that's what she wants to do, order pizza, when the octopus tightens its foul grip and the first seizure begins. I can tell something is wrong almost immediately, as Lily gets a confused look on her face and starts to back away. And then without further warning she stumbles and falls on her side, just tips over, unable to catch herself, and her legs go rigid and she seems to stop breathing.

"Lily!"

Her legs jerk and her body shakes and she stares somewhere far off in the distance and I drop the pizza menu and run to her side.

"Lily!" I shout again; if she hears me, she can't respond. I kneel and stroke her neck and try to support her head so that it doesn't slam against the linoleum. After a few beats of this, her legs start to run, stiffly, without bending, and she foams a bit at the mouth. The whole thing only lasts about thirty or forty seconds, but it feels like an eternity, and when it subsides I am hot with sweat.

"Shh, shh, shh," I manage, worried that she will try to come out of it too quickly. I pet her gently, in the way I do when she's restless at night and I want to lull her to sleep. Eventually she is able to focus on me, and I do my best to smile so that she won't be overly alarmed, but I oversell it, looking more than a little bit creepy.

"You look weird," she says.

I help her to her feet, but I don't let go in case she falls again. She tries to take a few steps and I feel like an anxious father teaching his child to ride a bicycle without training wheels, holding on to the seat as they wobble awkwardly into balance. Lily takes three steps into a wall and falls into a seated crouch.

"Take it easy, will you?"

She shakes her head and her ears flop. "That was . . . different."

"Yeah. It was." *Don't do it again*, I want to add, but I know she's not the one who did it.

It was the octopus.

It's a toss-up to say who's more shaken by the whole experience, her or me. I fluff the paw-print blanket that lines her bed, get her settled, scratch her neck the way that she likes it scratched, and beg her to try to sleep.

"What about pizza?" She seems exhausted, like a boxer who just went twelve rounds instead of getting knocked out in the first.

"You take a nap and I'll order the pizza and when you wake up you'll smell it and it will be here."

She yawns and her jaw squeaks like a rusty hinge and the only protest she makes is to remind me that she likes sausage. As if I could ever forget.

"I know. You're a sausage dog."

She falls asleep quickly and soundly. Her chest and soft belly rise and fall with each subdued breath. I sit next to her on the floor, my legs tucked close and my arms wrapped around them, and I make some of the eye rain she likes, but not too much. I don't know where the rage first takes root—my heart, my gut, my brain, my soul—but it has been metastasizing over the four days since the octopus first came calling. I look it directly in the eye.

"*You*." I surprise myself with how guttural it sounds.

There is no reply.

"YOU!" This time I intentionally snarl.

The octopus stirs. Its arms swoosh around Lily's sleeping head like they did late last night and sluggishly it opens an eye. Horrified, I feel myself digging into the linoleum so as not to retreat. Holy fuck. What is this thing? It blinks at me drowsily as I advance, slowly, as close as I dare, neither of us making any sudden moves.

It speaks. "If you're talking to her, she's asleep."

I jump back. Did I expect an answer? I don't know. I'm alarmed and disconcerted and yet not at all surprised that he can articulate. He? He is a he, I think, with that voice. I think I knew this was coming. That one chapter was ending with another about to begin, that a foe this formidable would make himself heard.

"I'm talking to you." Since this is the first time I'm openly addressing the octopus, I should have given more thought to what I want to say. But this is all gut, all emotion; whatever is going to come out is going to come.

"What can I do for you?" His tone is bored, verging on annoyed.

"Fuck you, that's what you can do." I stare at him to wait for a reaction.

The octopus feigns offense. "There's no need to be vulgar."

I stare the octopus down. "Leave."

The octopus looks for a moment like he's considering my directive. His gaze swoops up to the ceiling, hangs there for a beat, then falls back down to me. "No."

I stand, drawing myself up to my full height of six feet two inches, and outstretch my arms, making myself as large and as intimidating as possible. You're supposed to do this with bears, I think, and other frightening things. As a final sign of my physical dominance, I puff out my chest. "Leave. Go. *Now*."

"I'm sorry, I can't."

"However you came, *leave*." There is an icy coldness to the exchange that chills the room ten degrees.

"I'm afraid it's not that simple," he says. I hate his smug posturing. *I'm sorry. I'm afraid.* As if he wants to leave but can't, and the reason he can't is beyond his control.

"I won't let you win."

"Win what, exactly?"

"*You shall not pass!*" If I could strangle him, if I could get my arms around his eight and wrench him from her skull, I would. I would eviscerate him and tear his flesh, rip his pieces into tinier pieces and lay his guts bare. But I don't dare, not knowing how he's attached.

"Are we playing a game?" I hate that I'm not getting a rise out of him. His placid tone is making me more irate.

"What do you want from me?" I yell.

"Nothing."

I turn and I punch the cabinet where I keep the baking pans. Inside they rattle and clang. "What do you want from *her*?"

Pause. "I'm not sure I've decided."

"I will do everything in my power to stop you."

"It would disappoint me if you did anything less."

The only words I have left are Cate Blanchett's, and I say them with all the gusto of Elizabeth the First standing tall in the face of the advancing Spanish armada. "I have a hurricane in me that will strip Spain bare if you dare try me!"

The octopus lethargically blinks again.

"Do you hear me, octopus?" I gnash and growl and spit. My face is hot and my fists are clenched. *I have a hurricane in me!*"

"*Do* you?" The octopus is unconvinced, enraging me to full boil.

"I'm serious, you prick. We're going to the vet in the morning and I will do whatever it takes to stop you. I will max out every credit card at my disposal. I will beg, borrow, and steal. I will order every test, every pill, every measure, every treatment."

The octopus blinks, but doesn't retreat. Skeptically: "Will you?"

I would pull the walls of this house down on top of him if he weren't attached to the fragile skull of my deepest love. In my whole life I've never been more angry.

Mostly because he is right.

The Invertebrate

Five Years Earlier

Stuck

Come to San Francisco." It's my sister, Meredith.

"When?" I ask.

"Day after tomorrow."

I look across the chaotic airport terminal at Jeffrey, who is trying to trade our two tickets for seats on an earlier flight out of JFK. I'm sitting thirty yards away on the grimy airport floor, our phones plugged into the only available charging station. We have been on the East Coast for eight days; Christmas with his family, and then several days in the city, just the two of us, to wander and explore and eat. But now the snow that was so beautiful just days ago is falling harder and harder and people are trying to rebook their flights to get out ahead of the advancing storm. "I don't know. We might be stuck."

"Then get unstuck!" Meredith is uncharacteristically emphatic.

"What are you doing in San Francisco?" An announcement blares over the airport speakers, but I can't make sense of it.

"Where are you? I can barely hear you," Meredith says.

"New York. Trying to get a flight home. Why San Francisco?"

Silence at the other end of the line.

"Meredith?"

"I'm getting married!"

My mouth drops open and this kid sitting across from me, ignored by his own family, stares. Meredith explains how her boyfriend, Franklin, proposed on Christmas while they were visiting his parents in San Francisco. How they just decided to forego any period of engagement and tie the knot at city hall before returning home to D.C. Technically they're eloping, but since his parents are local, they are coming to bear witness, and since I live in Los Angeles, she wants Jeffrey and me to be witnesses for her side. When she's finished she asks, "How was New York?" as if nothing else has just happened.

"Good. It was good," I say, my voice swallowed by another announcement and a family pushing a mountainous pile of luggage on a cart with a rattling wheel. I can't tell if I'm lying or telling the truth.

"I can't hear you," Meredith exclaims.

"You're not inviting Mom?" I ask.

"You know Mom."

"Yes, we've been introduced." The boy across from me lifts up his nostrils and sticks out his tongue. I make a face in return.

"She's not one for ceremony. She probably didn't even want to go to her own wedding."

"I'm not so sure that's true." Although I wonder which wedding my sister is referring to—the one to my father (which I can't picture because there are no known photographs), or her second, the one to her current husband, which Meredith and I both attended.

"Ted? Can we count on you?"

More noise. "Sure."

"I can't hear you!"

I raise my voice. "I'll see you in San Francisco."

A woman dressed like the Statue of Liberty stands in the middle of the terminal and I'm curious how she'll get through security. I wonder if she's the same Statue of Liberty we saw just yesterday handing out pamphlets when we impulsively hopped in line at the TKTS booth in Times Square. We refused whatever she was selling and were rewarded with front-row seats to the Broadway revival of *Hair*. At curtain they called up the front few rows to dance onstage to "Let the Sunshine In"—our Broadway debut. As someone who struggles at times not to be seen, it was exhilarating to stand onstage and feel the hot lights on my face, the audience still in darkness (but out there), waving my hands in the air.

> *Life is around you and in you;*
> *Let the sunshine;*
> *Let the sunshine in.*

I could still feel the white heat of stage lights as we exited the Hirschfeld Theatre onto Forty-fifth Street, spilling into Times Square. I could *see* the sunshine, even though it was dark and had started to snow the lightest, most magical, movielike flakes. Street vendors selling chestnuts, buskers banging on pickle buckets, dancing tickers with holiday stock prices, workers preparing Times Square for New Year's Eve—everything seemed touched by light. Everything, that is, except Jeffrey. Jeffrey stewed under his own cloud, worried by the snow and the forecast for more. I convinced him to grab a slice of pizza with me by agreeing that we would eat it back in our hotel room. I ate mine perched in the window watching the city receive its gentle dusting. Jeffrey paced and checked the weather. He tried to call the airline, but after forty-five minutes on hold he gave up. I finally got him to come to bed by agreeing we could head to JFK at the crack of dawn.

Now that we're here, I'm anxious to get home. I miss Lily. If we can get on this flight, we might even get home in time to collect her from the sitter's and celebrate a little Christmas together. I have a stocking for her at home filled with chews, a stuffed squeaky toy, and a new red ball. Jeffrey is downright agitated. His desire is not to get back to Lily (although I'm sure he misses her, too). His desire is for certainty, for a plan we can execute; his growing need to control every situation is kicking into overdrive. It's almost laughable, watching him scramble in the face of a storm—I mean, how do you control the weather? C'mon, Jeffrey. Life is all around you and in you. Let the sunshine in!

My phone vibrates on the floor and I look down, thinking it's Jeffrey texting me flight options. But there's no message. Then I look over at Jeffrey's phone. He has a text message from his friend Cliff.

When are you back? I want to play.

Cliff. Do I know a Cliff? I think he's a friend of Jeffrey's he met playing online poker. I look over at the airline counter, but Jeffrey is nowhere to be seen. I scan the terminal left and right. No sign of him. I feel almost panicked when a shadow falls over me. It's Jeffrey holding two coffees and smiling. "Success."

When we're in the air Jeffrey pulls earphones out of his backpack and plugs them into his laptop.

"Are you going to watch TV?" I ask, knowing he always has a few episodes of something downloaded for a flight.

I must say it with an accusatory tone because Jeffrey replies hesitantly. "I was going to."

We never used to watch much TV; we used to talk about our days—commiserate over the things that bothered us most and laugh about the happenings that struck us as odd—but lately it has become a crutch. Our upstairs neighbor pulled me aside at their holiday party to say how happy it made her that she could hear the sound of laughter from our bedroom late at night. How well suited for each other we must be. I bit my lower lip to keep myself from saying it was Jeffrey watching reruns of *Frasier*.

Jeffrey closes his laptop to appease me and rests his phone on top of it. "Would you rather talk?"

I stare at his phone and think of the text message I saw and suddenly it doesn't sit so well. *When are you back? I want to play. I want to play* means poker, surely. That much is innocent enough. But when are you back? Why does he have to be back to play a game that is played online?

"When are you coming back?" Lily would ask me those words every time I had to leave her. The first time was four months or so after I first brought her home. She was fascinated when I pulled my luggage out of the deep closet in the second bedroom. As soon as I had the suitcase unzipped she climbed pluckily inside, and since she wasn't yet fully grown, a few wrinkles of skin puddled around her seated butt.

WHAT! IS! THIS! COZY! BOX! THIS! WOULD! MAKE! A! GREAT! BED! FOR! ME! I! LOVE! ITS! SIDES! AND! THIS! ELASTIC! STRAP!

"That is a suitcase. I have to put my things in it so I can travel."

"Great. I'm already in it, so you're ready to go!"

"Sadly, I can't have you in it. It's for my clothes and shoes and shaving kit."

"Why can't I be in it? I am one of your things!"

I sat down beside the suitcase and scratched the back of her head, between her ears. "You are, in fact, my most treasured thing." She raised her nose in the air and squinted her eyes. "But you're going to stay nearby and have an adventure of your own."

Lily looked at me with her soulful, almond-shaped eyes. "We're going on *different* adventures?" She was tugging my heartstrings the way she tugged at my shoelace at the puppy farm when we were introduced—slowly, but with purpose.

"Your adventure will be fun. You're going to play with other puppies, the way you used to play with your brother and sisters, Harry, Kelly, and Rita."

"Harry, Kelly, and Rita?"

"That's right. But other puppies whose names I don't know, but I'm sure are just as nice."

The boarding facility I had selected was a ways outside the city and it was clean and welcoming and alive. Dogs roamed indoors and outdoors on their own whim, and there was a special place sectioned off for smaller and younger dogs. Inside, it smelled like pine.

A woman welcomed us and did her best to allay our fears; Lily and I were both apprehensive. "Is this Lily? Welcome, Lily. I think you're going to love the other dachshunds here. Their names are Sadie and Sophie and Sophie Dee."

Lily turned to me. "Are they the other puppies whose names you didn't know?"

"That's right. Except now I do know their names. They are Sadie and Sophie and Sophie Dee."

"They are not Harry and Kelly and Rita?"

"No, they are Sadie and Sophie and Sophie Dee."

Lily considered this for a moment before adding, "My mother's name is Witchie-Poo."

I scooped up Lily and balanced her on my arm. "They don't need to know that."

The woman took the canvas tote from my shoulder that held Lily's blanket and food. I repositioned Lily so her paws were on my shoulder and I could whisper in her ear. "I'm coming back for you. In a week. Don't ever think I'm not coming back."

"When are you coming back?"

"In seven sleeps. I am coming back for you."

I kissed her on the top of her head and sat her on the ground. I handed her leash to the lady, so that she was now in control of my dog. "C'mon," she said. "I'll introduce you to Sadie and Sophie and Sophie Dee." Then she turned to me. "She'll be fine."

I nodded. I knew this. But also not. Would she? Be fine? Lily stood and turned back to look at me and we both swallowed the lumps in our throats.

The lady opened the gate to the smaller dogs' pen and I caught a glimpse of the other three dachshunds. Two of them were long-haired, and one was short-haired like Lily. I imagined the short-haired dachshund to be Sadie because she had a dappled coat and looked most different from the other two, who just happened to look like Sophies. All three greeted Lily with wagging tails.

HELLO! HELLO! HELLO! I'M! SADIE! I'M! SOPHIE! I'M! SOPHIE! DEE!

Lily paused before her tail started to wag and she entered the pen. Once inside she disappeared in a blur of paws and tails and ears as the gate closed behind her. The last thing I heard was her distinctive bark.

I'M! LILY!

In my car I broke down in ridiculous sobs.

How does she know I'm coming back? How does she know I didn't just give her away?

Because she trusts me.

Just as I should trust Jeffrey. There's a perfectly rational explanation for that text. *I want to play* means poker.

I turn to Jeffrey and his laptop is back open with his earphones plugged in. I've drifted. I made a fuss about his watching TV and then promptly checked out.

I take a deep breath and try to reengage, tapping him on the shoulder, pulling the earbud out of his left ear. "We each have a few days before we have to be back to work. How would you feel about going to San Francisco?"

I wait for him to react. I wait for his body to physically reject the spontaneity. I wait for him to keep the sunshine out, to make an excuse as to why he has to stay in Los Angeles, something to cover this "playing" with Cliff.

But instead he simply smiles and says, "Okay."

Backbone

My cell phone rings in an ominous way, sounding almost flat, the way it does when you know something is wrong before you answer the phone. I fumble to retrieve it from my pocket and the call almost goes to voicemail before I can answer. There's no time for anything to be amiss; we leave for Meredith's wedding in the morning.

It's Jeffrey. "Something's wrong with Lily. You need to come home."

I look at my watch. It's a little past three o'clock in the afternoon and I am more or less on my way home anyway. I'm just leaving the grocery store and the last thing on my list is to pick up our suits for the wedding from the dry cleaners.

"Can it wait thirty more minutes?"

I think of all the things that might be wrong with Lily. Vomiting. Diarrhea. Neither pleasant, but neither the end of the world. Too many treats from her Christmas stocking. Limping? She once had a thorn in her paw, like the old fable involving Androcles and the lion. It took some gentle prodding to get her to sit still long enough to remove the craggly thing. Bleeding?

Bleeding is easy—just apply pressure. Jeffrey can be an alarmist. Whatever it could be can probably wait.

"She can't walk. You need to come home now."

When I burst through the door I find Lily in her bed in the living room with Jeffrey sitting on the floor beside her. Lily looks frustrated and concerned when she sees me, and she doesn't get up and her tail doesn't wag. The new red ball from her Christmas stocking sits motionless on the floor. Her inability to greet me in her usual way all by itself makes my stomach drop.

"What's going on, you two?" I almost don't want to know the answer. In eighteen hours we are supposed to be on an airplane again.

"Let me show you," Jeffrey says.

He gingerly lifts Lily out of her bed, in the heedful way he did the first few months we were dating, before they bonded, before he was confident in the proper way to do it. He places her squarely on the floor and the back half of her body immediately wilts, her hind legs splaying sloppily to one side. They just give way underneath her.

My heart sinks to depths normally reserved for my stomach, and it becomes difficult to think or breathe.

I kneel on the floor next to them and tuck one hand under Lily's muscular chest and one hand under her soft belly. I stand her up again, supporting her with both hands. I almost don't dare to let go.

"Stand for me, Lily." I say it like a hypnotist giving a directive to an entranced person under my command. When I let myself remove the hand under her belly, her toenails scrape on the hardwood floor as her legs once again slip to the side. "C'mon." This time I'm pleading. "Stand up for me, girl."

Again, when I let go, the awful slithering of toenails on wood and the total wilting of legs. She almost tips over entirely before I catch her at the last second.

"What happened?"

"Nothing happened," Jeffrey replies.

"*Something* happened," I insist before adding, "What have you done?"

"What have I *done*?" Jeffrey is shocked.

She was my dog long before we ever met, and while she has become his dog, too, over the course of our relationship, they don't have the same bond. He does not treat her with the same attentiveness (or, truthfully, the same permissiveness), and when he's displeased with her behavior he is always the stepparent absolving himself of responsibility by throwing his hands up and calling her "your dog." This can't really be Jeffrey's fault, but I wonder just the same.

"Are you accusing me of something?"

I stare at Jeffrey. Am I accusing him of something? Even in this moment I'm forced to wonder if my assertion is about Lily or the text message. I don't know. But I can feel Lily tremble in my hands, and I know immediately now is not the time. "No. No, of course not."

"I hope not."

"I'm *not*." I placate him while I place Lily back in her bed, where at least she's supported by the cushiony sides. "Just watch her while I call the vet."

When I get our veterinarian's voicemail it dawns on me that it is now four o'clock on New Year's Eve. I immediately dial the first animal hospital I can find a listing for, even though it's on the west side of town. When I explain the situation, they insist I bring her in right away. If they can do anything for her, there's a short window in which it can happen, and that window is rapidly closing.

I hang up the phone, grab an old blanket, and wrap it around my girl. I lift her carefully, and nod to Jeffrey. "Let's go."

In the car we hit a red light that I know to be a long red light and I burst into sobs. My choices now, as I see them, are either having a dog with wheels for hind legs or, possibly, letting her go. Without warning, without moving or standing or crouching, Lily poops into the blanket on my lap, and my sobbing becomes inconsolable. She's dying, my baby. Right here in my lap.

The light turns green. I yell at a distracted Jeffrey to "*Go!*" and he steps on the gas and in the chaos I find a doggie litter bag in my jacket pocket because doggie litter bags are in all of my jacket pockets—I have a fear of being caught without them. I clean up the blanket as best I can and drop the sealed bag near my feet. I know this bothers Jeffrey, but he doesn't say anything, and really, what other choice do I have? We both crack our windows for air.

Jeffrey makes decent time across the city, and when I see a sign that says Animal Hospital I make him stop even though the address does not match the street number I've scribbled down on the back of a Target receipt. I must have transposed some numbers in haste.

Inside, the waiting room is small and hot and chaotic and I worry about having a panic attack. The nurse hands us a clipboard with papers to fill out and I push it back at her and say, "There is no *time* for paperwork." Jeffrey apologizes for my outburst, which annoys me, and he takes the clipboard and a pen. There is only one free chair and he takes it so he can write. I lean in an empty doorway and cradle Lily in her tattered swaddling. Soon a doctor materializes for a consultation, and when I explain the situation she tells us that we actually want the surgical hospital that's across the street and two blocks down. *Tick tock, tick tock.* Precious moments wasted.

As we turn to leave, a woman who looks like the Log Lady from *Twin Peaks* (although I'm the one holding the log in the form of a paralyzed dachshund) grabs my arm and says, "Whatever they tell you, don't kill your dog." I want to tell her to fuck off, but I'm frozen speechless in my tracks and tears start to well. "She can still have a happy life if you let her." Instantly this woman is my everything.

I nod and my eyes overflow with moisture, but Lily does not attempt to kiss my tears and the part of my brain that knows I can't waste even another second unfreezes me and I'm out the door.

Jeffrey tears into the parking lot of the surgical center, cutting off several cars at my urging. Inside they are expecting us, the last doctor having called ahead on our behalf. A surgical technician pries Lily out of my arms and they rush her behind a swinging door. Before I can protest, she is gone. No one offers us paperwork. No one tells us to sit. No one tells me not to kill my dog. Lacking anything else to do, we stand in the middle of a large, sterile room, surrounded by anxiety and tragedy, with nothing to look at but our feet. There's free coffee, but it's probably awful, and I know that I can't drink black swill when the rest of the world is sipping golden New Year's champagne.

After a short but interminable wait we're ushered into a private examining room. Lily is not there. There are two seats, so we sit. We fidget until a veterinarian enters. She has blond hair and a kindly face and looks too laid-back to be a surgeon, but has such an authoritative air of command that I wonder if she served in the military. Based on Lily's neurological signs, she is most suspicious of a ruptured intervertebral disc and wants to perform a myelogram to determine the site of the herniation.

I don't know what a myelogram is, and I know I don't have time to educate myself beyond the context that it is some test to detect pathology of the spinal column.

"And then what?"

"And then, pending the results of the myelogram, Lily's best chance of walking again is surgery."

"Surgery." I'm taking this in as fast as I can.

"The sooner the better."

Apparently there is no time to think. "So, we'll know if surgery is the way to go after the myelogram?"

"In all honesty, I would make that decision now. She'll already be under anesthesia for the myelogram, and if it does indeed reveal a ruptured disc, it's best to perform the surgery right then and there."

"So you need a decision now."

The doctor looks at her watch. "Yes."

Decisions. Lately they're not my strong suit. I think of the ways recently in which I've felt paralyzed myself. Should I quit my job to freelance full-time as a writer? Should I talk to Jeffrey about the doubts I have in our relationship? About the suspicious text message he received? Could Lily and I start over again on our own?

"And how much does spinal surgery cost for a dog that is mostly spine?" The doctor crouches in front of me and offers a half-smile. She doesn't need to tell me things I already know: that this is always a risk with the breed. That purebred dogs come with these health issues, as they've been genetically mutated for purpose or show.

"All together, everything—anesthesia, myelogram, surgery, recovery—we're talking about six thousand dollars."

Now it's me who is left immobile. Six thousand dollars. I look at Jeffrey. I think of dwindling savings. Of having just paid off all my credit card debt. Of vacations that might not be taken, retirement accounts that won't get contributed to, of having to push my dreams of writing full-time back another year.

"It's your call," Jeffrey says. "I can't make this decision. She's your dog." *Your dog.*

I want to punch him. I want to punch everyone, except maybe the doctor who can save her.

"Why don't I leave you to talk it over for a moment?" The doctor stands, and before I know it I've grabbed the sleeve of her lab coat.

"She has a ball. It's red. Red ball. She loves it. She'll play with it for hours—tossing it, chasing it, hiding it, finding it. She'll play until she's out of breath, and even then she'll take it to her bed and fall asleep on top of it. She is alive when she's playing with that ball. If she . . ."

I can't even finish the words. Jeffrey places his hand on my shoulder as I'm reduced to tears again.

"If she can't . . . play with that ball anymore, then I don't know what kind of life there is left for her."

The doctor turns to me. She's not unmoved, but she's seen people wrestle with this decision before and there's nothing so special about me.

I continue through gasps and swallows of oxygen. "I don't want you to think I'm a horrible person. That I would let money even become a part of this decision. It's just I don't know what her life would be if she can't play with that ball."

I plead with my eyes. *Fix her! Save her!* One nod is all that I need, and she studies me before giving it. She has heard me, and she's trying to communicate something. "I'll be outside in the hall."

It's not even necessary for her to go. "Will you be the one performing the surgery?"

"Yes." Another nod. She's telling me Lily will walk again. She's telling me she knows this, but legally can't say it because of ridiculous reasons like malpractice insurance. So she's telling me without words, in the way that hostages blink secret messages in videotapes that evade detection by their captors.

I look at Jeffrey, who once again says, "I can't make this decision." At least this time he adds, "But I will stand by yours."

I look back at the doctor. My heartbeat is in my ears. The room is hot and smells like medicine. The fluorescents blink angrily, asking to be replaced. My head is spinning, but with adrenaline, not with dizzying thoughts. Now is when I have to start making decisions. Now is my time.

I stand tall with my hands by my sides and now I'm the one who speaks with authoritative command.

"Do it."

We'll Take a Cup of Kindness Yet for Auld Lang Syne

We leave the animal hospital as soon as I agree to the surgery. They almost insist on it. Since it's New Year's Eve, they are running with a limited staff and don't want to assign any of their already sparse resources to oversee a hysterical person in the waiting room. If the surgery goes well, they don't need me insisting on seeing her or overseeing her recovery. And I would. I would be like Shirley MacLaine in *Terms of Endearment*: "It's past ten. My daughter is in pain. I don't understand why she has to have this pain. All she has to do is hold out until ten, and IT'S PAST TEN! My daughter is in pain, can't you understand that! GIVE MY DAUGHTER THE SHOT!" If the surgery does not go well, I guess they don't want that scene to play out in their waiting room, either.

So we go home. Jeffrey stops to pick up Chinese for dinner and I stay in the car and call Trent. He is already at some New Year's party and I can't communicate the enormity of what is happening and I get frustrated and just hang up. Alone in the

65

car, and without really thinking, I call my mother. While the phone rings, I think about how every conversation with her feels incomplete. About how we talk around the perimeter of things, but never about the things themselves. What will this call accomplish? Why do I still need my mother? As soon as I hear her voice I start crying, and I hate myself for it because if she's not going to give me what I need, then why bother to call her, being needy.

"Well, of course you're upset, she's your baby."

Huh? I'm not surprised that she offers sympathy, I am just surprised at the "of course." Growing up, we had four dogs. Not all at once, but over the course of eighteen years. None of them were my mother's babies; she had two human children and that was quite enough. The "of course" is all I need, and I no longer feel ashamed. *Of course* I'm upset. *Of course* I'm feeling lost. *Of course* I have emotions. She's my baby. Even my mother can see that.

When we finish speaking, I call Meredith. It's hard when talking to my mother not to spill the secret, not to share the added stress of having to attend a wedding, but I keep Meredith's confidence intact.

Meredith is wholly supportive. "We'll change your flights, have you on standby, get you a return flight home right after the ceremony—whatever you need us to do. And, of course, we'll cover any costs." Hearing Meredith's voice makes it easier. "But if you think you can, please come."

I pick at some General Tso's chicken and poke at a steamed dumpling, but I don't have much of an appetite for anything other than vodka. We are supposed to be at a party thrown by our neighbors in the unit of our duplex above us; I send Jeffrey upstairs to give our regrets. The dull roar of the party is constant, and at times laughter bubbles over, reminding us that life is continuing outside of our anxiety, that seconds are ticking off the clock, marking the end of an old year and the start of a new one.

But in our apartment, time has stopped. There's maybe something playing on HBO. Even it seems to unspool in slow motion.

Until the phone rings.

I'm not even aware I've answered it until the doctor's voice is in my ear. "Lily came through surgery fine." I dry heave my relief. "The myelogram revealed compression of the spinal cord over the tenth through twelfth thoracic vertebrae. We took her directly into surgery and performed a hemilaminectomy over this area."

I'm nodding as if I understand exactly what this means. I'm nodding for someone who can't see me, trying to listen but also play back in my head the confirmation that all this went fine. I try to repeat *hemilaminectomy* in my head and it sounds like a child trying to pronounce aluminum: alumi-numi-numi-num.

"Basically, we make an incision that creates a window into the vertebral bodies and exposes the spinal cord so we can retrieve the herniated disc material." *Retrieve it and do what with it?* "Lily's procedure went without complication and she recovered from the anesthesia uneventfully."

Uneventfully. Like being put under and myelograms and spine windows and alumi-numi-numi-num surgeries are everyday phenomena in life.

"Is she able to . . . Was the surgery a success?"

I am suddenly aware that I'm standing, as if the doctor has walked into our living room. I have no memory of getting up, and now that I am up, I'm unsure of where to look or what to do with my hand that is not holding the phone. The news is what I want to hear, but somehow I'm ice-cold, the warmth of the vodka having drained out of my limbs.

"Animals that suffer this type of injury make most of their neurologic improvement over the first three months postoperatively. You'll notice some immediate improvement, but don't be discouraged if Lily's progress is initially slow. But I'm cautiously optimistic."

"Cautiously optimistic that . . ." There's a hiccup of laughter from upstairs and I give a death-stare at the ceiling.

"Cautiously optimistic. That she will recover."

"Fully?"

"Cautiously optimistic."

Stop saying that. Will she walk?

"We need to board her here for the next seventy-two hours to monitor her initial recovery and watch for any signs of complications. Our offices are closed tomorrow for New Year's Day, which means you can visit her the day after if you want to. But only briefly. It's not good for her to get too excited. Otherwise, you can take her home the day after that."

"Thank you, Doctor."

"It was our pleasure working with Lily."

She's not getting what I'm trying to say.

"No." I say it with import. "*Thank you.*"

I hang up the phone and collapse on the couch and relay to Jeffrey what I was told and when we can see her and when we can bring her home.

He looks at me, not quite knowing what to say. "I guess we have a wedding to attend."

I'm Afraid There's No Denyin' /
I'm Just a Dandy-Lion

EIGHT TIMES I WAS COWARDLY

1   When I was five and my father told me to walk in a more masculine way and I was so immediately overcome with shame that I did.
2   That time in the seventh grade when this popular kid with a French last name called me a faggot and instead of standing up for myself I thought of how *faggot* would sound in French (fag-oh) while wishing for the floor to swallow me whole.
3   When my parents divorced and people asked me about it and I pretended I was glad.
4   When this guy in high school performed oral sex on me and I told him afterward that it was not a big deal because even though he might be gay, I was comfortable with my heterosexuality.

5 Deciding not to major in creative writing because I thought that the broader and blander "communications" was the safer degree.

6 When I ended one relationship by becoming so distant and cold that after months of trying to reach me and discover what was wrong, he was left with no choice but to break up with me.

7 When I didn't immediately confront Jeffrey about the text message I'd seen.

8 Every time I don't tell my mother that I love her because I'm afraid she won't say it back.

AND ONE TIME I HAD COURAGE

1 When I left Los Angeles for my sister's wedding, leaving Lily behind, boarded, in recovery, trusting her to heal.

The Tonga Room and Hurricane Bar

I watch the low morning sun glimmer off the water as we take off over the Pacific; it's a short flight to San Francisco and we're still getting in on New Year's Day as planned. I ask the flight attendant for a ginger ale to pop an old pill I found in the bathroom drawer (which I'm hoping is Valium, but is probably Vicodin), otherwise I don't say a word. I'm grateful for my window seat. Normally I'm stuck in the middle, as Jeffrey refuses to sit anywhere but the aisle, but the flight to San Francisco is a smaller plane with only two seats in each row on either side of the walkway. If nothing else, I can stare out at the view below and not have to make eye contact with anyone. Eye contact is dangerous. Eye contact is a trigger.

When we land and I'm able to turn on my phone, I have two missed calls. The first is from Meredith, to see if we made our flight, and the second is the animal hospital calling to say that Lily has made it through the night and continues to exhibit good vitals. I listen to the second message four times for any hint that they are lying to me or glossing over an unpleasant truth, but I can't glean anything untoward and I end up not calling them back.

Meredith is waiting for us at baggage claim. She greets me with a hug, which I collapse into.

"You okay?" she whispers in my ear.

"Okay adjacent." I can be matter-of-fact with her, even today. We're only eighteen months apart, and while I sometimes joke that my first eighteen months were the best of my life, it's just that—a joke. "Did you call Mom?"

"We're eloping. Okay? If we invited everyone and made a big to-do it would be a wedding."

I don't know why there's a weird feeling in the pit of my stomach about this, but there is. Is Mom "everyone"? I tend to obsess over the ways in which our mother is like every other mother—and all of the ways that she isn't. "Okay." It's Meredith's decision.

"But I'm glad you're here!"

She and Franklin and Jeffrey and I manage lunch at a noodle house in Chinatown and check into our room at the Fairmont Hotel before I can't hold it inside any longer.

"I. Need. A. Drink."

It's almost five o'clock (if the give-or-take is three hours), and so we head down to the bar in the lobby. Some asshole is playing annoyingly plinky ragtime on a grand piano, but my aggravation doesn't trump my thirst so I order a double vodka on the rocks. Meredith agrees to an impromptu bachelorette party, partly at my urging (a bachelorette party sounds like a good excuse to drink), as long as she doesn't have to wear a tiara or carry a penis whistle or anything like that. I apologize to Franklin (he's not invited) and I call my friend Aaron, who now lives in San Francisco and who Meredith knows from years ago when we all lived in Maine. He agrees to join us for the revelry. Three gay men and a bride.

When Aaron arrives he's as handsome as ever (for some reason this is comforting—the beauty in life) and I fill him in on the Lily situation and the impromptu nature of both the wedding and this makeshift party.

"We all need some celebration and some fun," I say. The lobby bar is not fun.

"I know where we need to go," Aaron says, and he leads us to the elevator.

"We're already on the ground floor," Meredith offers. "The front door is that way."

"Shhh." He winks, taking Meredith's hand. "You and me— and I think they'll agree—are going down to the terrace level to take up residence in the Tonga Room and Hurricane Bar for tropical storms and Singapore slings."

Was that a poem? I wonder. It feels like he's using words from another language that I usually speak, but that now sounds foreign thanks to the double vodka and emotional exhaustion.

When the elevator dings, Aaron corrals us inside and presses the button for the terrace level, and the car lurches and our stomachs dip as we head down.

The Tonga Room is squarely underneath the Fairmont Hotel, and the Hurricane Bar is a Polynesian-themed marvel situated around what must once have been the hotel's swimming pool but is now a lagoon, complete with a rain forest–style thunderstorm every half hour. A barge floats on the lagoon, carrying a band that plays in between storms. The cane-and-rattan furniture and the tiki lights make it a tropical, tacky mess.

In short, it's perfect.

"Singapore slings for everyone!" I say.

Waiting for our drinks, I fidget endlessly with my phone as if the animal hospital will call. The battery is at 35 percent and I have only one bar of reception. It dawns on me that it's still New Year's Day and the hospital is closed except for emergencies and they're only going to call if something is drastically wrong, but it's only after Aaron eases the phone out of my hand and sets it upside-down on the table that I really understand that I don't want them to call. No news, it's true, is good news.

The cocktail waitress arrives, expertly balancing a tray with our four Singapore slings—gin concoctions the color of a tropical sunset, topped with a pineapple wedge, two Maraschino cherries, and a paper umbrella. Before we can even take our first sip, I look at the waitress and exclaim, "Four more slings!" like I'm at a presidential reelection rally clamoring for another term. Meredith starts to protest, but I cut her off. "It's either that, or a penis whistle and I tell everyone on that barge that you're getting married tomorrow."

Meredith nods her understanding, then confirms my order with the server. "Another round, please."

The server smiles at my sister with sympathy and whispers, "Congratulations."

As we drink our first slings, we grill Meredith about the wedding. Who proposed, when, and why elope. We do our best to make her the center of attention. While she's not consumed with bridehood, it is still her occasion, her day and not mine.

"Remember when you were six and got your head stuck in the back slats of a park bench and Mom freaked out and called the fire department?"

"What?" Jeffrey asks.

"You've never heard this? Turns out she could just crawl out the way she crawled in, but for some reason refused until two firemen pulled her out screaming."

"Why firemen?" Jeffrey asks. "Where was your father?"

"Working," I say. "He was always working."

Meredith smiles and turns the color of her drink. "What made you think of that?"

I don't know what made me think of that. "Are you stuck?" The words are out of my mouth before I can stop them.

"What? What does that even mean?"

"I don't know." I whisper, *"Pregnant?"*

Meredith nearly chokes on her drink. "I'm stuck here with *you* drinking this, which is like grain alcohol or something. I had better not be pregnant."

"Oh, relax," I say, and Meredith kicks me under the table, hard, like we used to do when we were kids and ordered by our parents to be quiet. I scrunch my face at her, signaling that she will get hers in return, and she laughs again. Aaron and Jeffrey ask something about her dress.

"What about Franklin being Chinese?" I blurt.

"What about it?"

"I don't know." I'm trying to stay involved, pull my thoughts away from Lily, to be in the moment. "What about kids? Does it change anything about how you will raise them?"

"Of course not. It mostly just means I can never wear heels." Meredith has always been self-conscious about her height.

As we drink our second slings, we press Aaron about single gay life in San Francisco and remain tuned to his every word like he's a telenovela—his stories are outlandish and addicting and we understand most of what's going on even if the concepts are a little foreign for the rest of us in longer-term relationships.

"You mean people just do that in the streets?" Jeffrey interrupts when Aaron is in the middle of a story about the Folsom Street Fair.

"What do you mean, naked?" I add. "Naked, naked?"

"What are chaps?" Poor Meredith.

By the third round of slings, we know what we're doing. We dispense with the pineapple and the cherries and the umbrellas and get down to the business of gin. Two rainstorms have showered the lagoon and we're due for a third, and the band on the barge has paddled by us several times playing what they bill as Top 40 hits, but which are certainly not the current Top 40 hits unless Kool & the Gang have made some recent cultural resurgence I'm not aware of. Some straight couples dance on the barge, but I'm not sure how they boarded or if they're even supposed to be there.

The conversation turns to Lily, and Meredith and Aaron ask questions and I let Jeffrey answer as I lower my head to my glass and chew on my straw. After a few minutes, my straw mangled beyond any ability to do its job, I finally speak.

"When Lily was a year old she ate an entire bag of wasabi peas." I laugh at the ridiculousness of that sentence, but no one else does. "She'd once eaten a bag of chocolate-covered blueberries that someone had given me as a gift, so I had been down this road before. Since chocolate is toxic for dogs, I called the vet and they suggested giving her some hydrogen peroxide as a way to induce vomiting—one teaspoon for every ten pounds of body weight, so one and a half teaspoons for Lily. Pretty effective stuff. To this day I don't know if wasabi peas are toxic to dogs, but to be on the safe side, I decided to pull out the old hydrogen peroxide. Only this time she was wise to the trick and wanted no part of it. So I grabbed her by the snout and pried open her jaw. At the last second she zigged left and I zagged right and the peroxide ended up going down the wrong pipe. So not only did she not throw up, but now in addition to wasabi peas burning her stomach she had hydrogen peroxide burning her windpipe, and she couldn't breathe without a horrible wheezing sound. I rushed her to the animal clinic, and a few hours later it was as if the whole thing hadn't happened, but I remember thinking I was going to lose her." I remember how much I hated myself that night, how I felt like a total failure if I couldn't keep her alive for more than a year.

Somewhere in my speech the rain over the lagoon had started again, and the patter of rain on water sounds like a gentle snare drum. I pause and take the disfigured straw out of my glass and replace it with another straw from an empty glass. I don't even know whose empty it was, nor do I care. "I don't know what made me think of that."

But I do know. I hate myself again, much as I did that night. Living things, maybe not barnacles or plants (although plants technically do bend their leaves toward the sun), need to move. And under my watch Lily was unable to retain what she was born with—the ability to move herself about. Even if it was an accident, or an injury that was breed-specific—just one of those things—it was my fault, just as every unpleasant thing that happened to her was a failure of mine to keep her safe.

On the table, hidden behind a standing cocktail menu, is a bowl of snack mix. I stick my finger in it and swirl the crunchy items around, taking a sort of inventory to see if there are any wasabi peas.

There aren't.

"*Ow!*" The kick comes swiftly under the table and I jump and the cocktail glasses rattle. I look across at Meredith, who is grinning broadly.

Enough with the self-pity.

"You're in trouble now," I say to Meredith.

"What did I do?" she says, feigning innocence while failing to stifle laughter.

I grab as many of them as I can by the elbows and pull them away from the table. "Let's dance!"

The rain stops and the barge sets sail again, this time with us aboard, and I'm already waving my hands in the air doing some sort of rhythmic snapping thing when the band starts to play "You Make My Dreams" by Hall & Oates.

The Vow

I'm not entirely sure what Franklin's Chinese parents think of their son marrying a tall white woman, but I'm pretty sure what they don't think the occasion needs is two six-foot-plus homosexuals. Still, they nod and smile and do their best to make polite conversation, and the judge who officiates turns out to be Chinese and that seems to go a long way toward making the whole thing more palatable.

San Francisco City Hall is a stunning feat of marble, ambition, and architectural chutzpah; a Beaux-Arts monument to government as beautiful as any cathedral. After Meredith and Franklin get their marriage license, we wait in the cavernous entryway at the base of the grand staircase for their turn to get hitched. The floor's marble inlay consists of circles and squares and I trace them awkwardly with my foot. Meredith looks stunning in a simple cream-colored backless wedding dress from J. Crew. It's perfect for both her body and her temperament. My sister is not someone whose wedding I ever imagined. She's not the kind of girl who grew up daydreaming of one, or playing bride in any fashion. But now that I see her looking radiant in this backless cream number against the ornate-but-not-ostentatious backdrop of city hall, I can't imagine it any other way.

When it's their turn, we climb the grand marble staircase, Meredith and Franklin first, Jeffrey and me and Franklin's parents silently behind them. I look up at the dome. It's supposedly the fifth largest in the world and it's a marvel to behold. At the top of the stairs we stand in a rotunda in front of two double doors. Behind them are the mayor's offices, where San Francisco Mayor George Moscone and supervisor and gay rights pioneer Harvey Milk were assassinated by a former colleague in 1978. I shudder when I remember this. The location seems solemn, but important.

The ceremony is simple, Meredith and Franklin holding hands in front of the judge, exchanging rings and vows. I try to manage being a combination of witness, photographer, family of the bride, and maid of honor. I take out my digital camera and snap as many pictures as I can without feeling disruptive, knowing the rest of my family will want to see them. I do everything I can to be present, even if my mind is 381 miles away.

To focus, I think of how dogs are witnesses. How they are present for our most private moments, how they are there when we think of ourselves as alone. They witness our quarrels, our tears, our struggles, our fears, and all of our secret behaviors that we have to hide from our fellow humans. They witness without judgment. There was a book once about a man who tried to teach his dog to speak a human language, to help him solve his wife's murder. It said that if dogs could tell us all they have seen, it would magically stitch together all the gaps in our lives. I try to witness this moment how a dog would witness it. To take it all in. For the rest of my family, this wedding will be a gap in their lives, and I need to do my best to fill it.

The ceremony is perfect for my sister and her new husband—all business, no flourish. Nothing about the bride as property. No one to give her away, no mention of them being man and wife, no mention of a Christian god that none of us really believe in. They are both attorneys. The law is their church. When the judge unites them he says, "By the power vested in me by the State of California, I recognize you as married." And just like that, as quickly as it began, the ceremony is over.

I wander to the third floor, with its peripheral balconies, to take some photographs from above. Really, I need a moment to breathe. I want to call the animal hospital, but I don't. They won't do what I want them to do, which is to put Lily on the phone. In her drugged-out state, on sedatives and painkillers, she won't talk much to me anyway. Below, Meredith and Franklin descend the central staircase and I capture a lovely shot of them holding hands. I snap another of Jeffrey leaning on a marble pillar looking relaxed and handsome.

After the wedding, we head back to the Fairmont Hotel and I excuse myself to the lobby bar. The same asshole is there, playing the same piano. I purchase a bottle of Veuve Clicquot from the bartender and get him to give me six glasses. We pop the champagne back in Meredith and Franklin's room and I toast the newlyweds and Meredith makes a round of phone calls to break the news to my family. They go down like this: everyone is shocked, everyone offers heartfelt congratulations, and after each call she hands the phone to me. And then I get the brunt of it.

"Did you know about this?"

"How long did you know?"

"Did you put her up to this?"

"You didn't tell me?"

"Why were you invited?"

"Is she pregnant?"

In everyone's shock, they forget to ask about Lily. I just sip my champagne and roll with it as best I can. But inside I'm wondering why on the day of my sister's union more people aren't thinking about me.

My mother is on the phone last. She's on the verge of tears; I can hear it in her voice. She would have liked to have been here. I think she's especially hurt that Franklin's parents were in attendance. She doesn't see my having been the ambassador for our family as adequate balance. And she's right. There is no one equal to a mother.

"Meredith looks really happy," I say into the phone, trying to defuse some of my mother's sadness. Should I have been more insistent with Meredith?

"I wrote a check for one thousand dollars and put it in the mail," my mother says, but I'm not sure she's talking to me.

"Excuse me?"

"For Lily's surgery. I'm sorry that I don't have more to contribute."

Now it's me on the verge of tears. "You didn't have to . . ." I start, but I stop. It's an incredible gesture and instead of protesting I should just be grateful. "Thank you." I think it comes out audibly.

After the calls I snap a few more pictures of the newlyweds in front of their enormous window. The top floor has a stunning vista of the city and the bay, and I frame them with Alcatraz far in the distance, just over my sister's shoulder. This is my silent statement about marriage. Or maybe about my own relationship with Jeffrey.

When are you back?

Afterward, we pile into cabs that race over the city's famed hills at enormously inappropriate speeds to Howard Street to dine at a restaurant called Town Hall—the perfect bookend with our earlier errand at city hall. Town Hall is housed in a much simpler structure, brick instead of marble, red awnings instead of a dome. The sun has dipped below the sweeping hillsides and the air has turned cold. Inside, the exposed brick and modern chandeliers are warm and welcoming. I'm offered a seat between Jeffrey and Franklin's mother.

"I'm sorry about the way we're dressed. I was supposed to pick up our suits from the dry cleaners before we left, but my dog, Lily, had to have emergency surgery. On her spine. We found her partially paralyzed, you see, and this will hopefully allow her to walk again, but it's too soon to tell if she actually will."

I have no idea how much English Franklin's mother speaks or if she's understanding any of this, so I grab the water glass in front of me and drink until it's empty. Eventually my sister's new mother-in-law nods and I take that as an invitation to continue.

"I'm really nervous. Scared, if I'm being honest. I'll never find another dog like her. She's so funny. The things she says sometimes, they just crack me up. She's really good with a joke." Franklin's mother blanches, and it's then that I wonder if she really understands more English than she lets on.

"Anyhow, tomorrow we can bring her home and I worry if I'm up to the task of her care." I look down and fold the napkin in my lap a few different ways until I can't stretch the assignment any longer.

Franklin's mother adds a quiet "woof" and offers me a warm smile. I think she understands my plight.

It's a funny thing to worry about at a wedding dinner. Being up to the task. For richer, for poorer. In sickness and in health. I've never taken these vows before, nor do I know if I ever will. But I have felt them in other ways. I feel this duty with Lily. To stand with her in sickness, until she is able to stand on her own four paws again.

After dinner, Meredith, Franklin, Jeffrey, and I retire to the Top of the Mark, a rooftop bar across California Street from our hotel. At night, the buildings around us twinkle like the night sky; in the distance the Golden Gate Bridge is dappled with tiny, shimmering headlights. Meredith pulls me aside to a quiet corner at the end of the bar.

"Are you happy?"

"For you?" I ask. "Of course!" I look across the room at Franklin, who is telling Jeffrey an animated tale.

"No. Are *you* happy?"

I'm not sure how to answer her truthfully. "Why do you ask?"

"I don't know. I've been watching you this weekend." Meredith takes the cocktail menu from my hand and sets it down on the bar.

"I keep dwelling on this text message. I can't get it out of my mind."

"From who?"

"From no one."

"No one sent you a text message?"

"No one sent *Jeffrey* a text message."

Meredith looks at me, frustrated. "This isn't the punchline to some *Family Circus* cartoon, is it?"

"I'll tell you some other time. I have to get through this thing with Lily first."

"Lily will be fine. It's you I'm worried about." Meredith puts a hand on my shoulder, but I don't say anything in response. "Don't use Lily as an excuse to ignore your own happiness."

"I'm not," I protest.

"Speak up for yourself."

"I do!"

"No, you don't. We were raised the same, remember. I know you better than you think I do."

"Oh, really," I say with a smirk. "Did you know I was about to do this?" I swiftly kick her in the shin. Payback. I hope no one sees and thinks she just married an abuser.

"*Ow!* Actually, yes." Meredith rubs her shin while looking up at me. "You have to communicate your needs to get them met. That's all I'm saying."

"Bartender!"

Meredith sneers. "Not what I meant."

"I know what you meant."

We bring champagne to Franklin and Jeffrey, and I offer a final toast. "Wishing you all good things in your life together." Short. Simple. To the point. I look at Meredith, relaxed in her ivory gown. My sister is all grown up. I'm grateful we did our growing up together.

When we get back to our room, this time it's me who changes our itinerary and books us two seats on the first morning flight out. There will be no lavish brunch with the newlyweds, only airport coffee and whatever they serve on the plane. If we're lucky there will be a very quick good-bye before we sneak off to the airport.

I crawl into bed and let the day wash over me. As exhausting as it has been, our San Francisco adventure in many ways has been a small oasis of calm. I think of myself floating on the barge that sails the Tonga Room, swaying to Dan Fogelberg or Sheena Easton or someone who in the parallel universe of the Hurricane Bar is still popular.

I turn out the light.

Darkness.

The hard work of healing begins.

Squeezed

S queeze," I say.

"I am squeezing," Jeffrey replies.

"Squeeze *harder*."

"I'm squeezing as hard as I dare."

"Well, you're not squeezing her right, then."

"Do you want to trade jobs? Because it's easy to just stand there and hold a flashlight."

"Not the way you keep moving."

Jeffrey gets annoyed and he lets go. He stands up and hits his head on the outcropped tree branch above him.

"Look out for that branch," I say, completely unhelpfully. I know this will enrage him, but I feel entitled to say what I want because I'm scared.

I hand Jeffrey the flashlight and crouch down next to Lily, who cowers on the gravel in the harsh puddle of light. I place my hands as the vet instructed, on either side of her under her abdomen, and I squeeze her soft bladder, in and back, in and back. Nothing. The light glints off the staples that run the length of her back. She's laced up like a football.

"Anything?" Jeffrey asks.

I tip her up and look underneath for any evidence that she has peed. "Nothing." I run through the steps again. "The doctor said it feels like a water balloon?"

"Yes. Like a water balloon. About the size of a small lemon."

Lily's abdomen does feel like a water balloon. Soft and squishy. Expressing her bladder was not something I had steeled myself for on the flight back from San Francisco. I thought I had prepared mentally as well as I could. I drank coffee instead of liquor. I stayed awake instead of sleeping. I made a shopping list for all the things we would need on the back of a napkin: a pen to keep her quarantined to a small area, blankets so she wouldn't slip on the hardwood floors, toys that would keep her mentally engaged without exciting her physically. Treats—healthy ones, so that she wouldn't gain weight during the inactivity of recovery. Carrying added pounds would just be additional stress on her spine.

Learning to express a dog's bladder, however, was not on that list, despite how obvious it seems to me now. The vet who discharged us laid down a weewee pad on the cold metal examining table and showed us just how it was done. She made it seem so effortless, I assumed I had understood the lesson. Turns out I was wrong. We haven't been able to get her to pee since we left the hospital.

"My poor girl. The indignity of it all." I hoist Lily in the football carry that was demonstrated for us, supporting her hindquarters, careful to avoid the tree branch above. "Let's go to bed." Frustrated, Jeffrey switches off the flashlight. I know this means she may release her bladder in her sleep, in our bed, but we'll just have to get up and change the sheets. There's no squeezing her any harder.

Inside, I set her down on a blanket and she stands upright. I'm amazed by this progress, even though she can't yet walk. She can stand, unsteady though she is, and that in itself is a huge accomplishment. For now, that's enough. I read the instructions again on Lily's red prescription bottles and select a Tramadol for pain and a Clavamox to ward off infection and seal them into a pill pocket. She gobbles up the treat.

"Monkey, look at you. You're standing."

"My name is Lily."

"I know it is." I rest my hand on the top of her head, and her eyes blink heavily. She is only seven, but for the first time she looks old. A strip of bare skin runs down her back where the staples are. She looks sad, disrobed of her mahogany fur.

"What happened to you?"

Lily seems to concentrate on remembering. "I don't know. I woke up and I couldn't walk."

"You scared me." I cup her head in my hands and she looks like a nun in a wimple.

She licks her chops for any remaining flavor from the pill pocket. "I know you put medicine in those things."

"I know you know." Then I add, "The medicine will help you heal."

Lily considers this. "Can I have my red ball?"

I gently lift her up and study her Frankenstein scar. It's like she's now assembled from two different dogs: the puppy who will always want to play, and the senior dog who must come to understand her limits. I make her a promise: "Soon."

I place Lily gently on a layer of towels in our bed, nestled safely between Jeffrey and me, and the pain pill and the toll of the day knock her out within minutes. Sleep comes fast for me, as well. It's almost impossible to believe that when I woke up this morning I was in San Francisco.

I dream of the beach where Lily would run off-season when she was a puppy. In my dream she runs and runs, not getting anywhere fast. There are other dogs, bigger dogs, and she wants to run near them but not with them; she's slightly intimidated by their size and the sand they kick up with their paws. Her whole body is a compression spring that launches her with each step into momentary levitation. Her floppy ears bound upward with each gallop, sometimes floating there in the wind as if someone has put them on pause. When she comes back to me I know they will be flipped backward, pinned to her head and the back of her neck. I spend half my life restoring that dog's ears to their factory setting.

THE! SAND! IS! SO! SQUISHY! UNDER! MY! PAWS! AND! LOOK! HOW! VAST! THE! OCEAN! WATCH! ME! RUN! WITH-OUT! MY! LEA—

Before she can say leash, a wave sweeps in and engulfs her delicate paws in a strand of slick seaweed and a look of terror washes over her face.

SERPENT! SERPENT! SERPENT!

She turns and hightails it to drier sand, closer to the dunes where the last of the tall grass waves. Immediately, her nose picks up the scent of a dead crab. She rips off a leg and runs with it in her mouth off into the distance until she is no more than a speck on the horizon.

In the morning, Jeffrey and I dress quickly and immediately take Lily outside. We set her on the grass and again she is able to stand. She even attempts an excited step or two, looking not unlike Bambi but with shorter legs, before I can calm her to keep her from overexerting herself. "Shhh. Shhh. Shhh."

Jeffrey looks to intervene but I shrug him off. This is my job. This is my moment. I will not be a coward, I will not be afraid. I will not be someone who can love only so much. I will not be someone who is not whole or fully present when things get tough. I will not let others do the heavy lifting for me. I will not be distracted by a text message. Wringing the piss out of this dog I love—this is my Everest. This is on me.

I tuck Lily's hind legs under her and settle her into her usual crouch, legs slightly splayed like a frog's. From behind her I reach under her abdomen and feel for the water balloon, for the soft squish the size of a lemon. When I find it, I take a deep breath, gird myself, and squeeze. *Up and to the back.*

I don't know what's different in the morning light—the fullness of her bladder, her willingness to do her part, my fearlessness brought on by the dawn of a new day, the dream of her running, the desire to see her run again. Whatever it is, when I squeeze up and to the back her tail rises to that familiar forty-five-degree angle that makes it look like a missile about to launch and slowly she starts to pee.

"She's doing it! You're doing it!" I'm so excited I almost let go. But I don't. I continue to squeeze.

Lily is startled by the sensation and overwhelmed with relief. Jeffrey pumps his fist and we both break out in smiles.

"At last," Jeffrey says, relieved.

"Ha-*ha!*" I am triumphant.

Lily attempts to stand and I realize I can stop squeezing. I gently guide her over the puddle of her making.

"You did it, Bean." Everything else fades away.

I'm the happiest I have ever been.

Suction

Monday

The octopus sits in his usual perch as Lily and I make our way to the veterinarian's office. We skirt the construction around LACMA because no one in Los Angeles knows how to merge. Lily sits as she always does when I drive, in my lap with her chin nestled in the crook of my left elbow—the arm I try in vain to steer with as I downshift with my right. She looks up at me, annoyed, whenever we actually have to make a turn. The octopus hasn't said anything this morning. He doesn't have to; the echo of his voice rings hauntingly in my brain. He's getting bigger by the hour.

The waiting room is small and dark and cramped, the brown linoleum floor is peeling in the corners, and any available breathing room is filled with shelves of dietary pet food and supplements with names like Rimadyl and Glycoflex. I'm not sure why I still go to this vet, other than that it's close to my house. This is a pattern in my life I need to rethink: Jenny the therapist, this dumpy veterinary office. I will say there are new doctors here who are better than the last rotation, who disappeared suddenly after some unflattering Yelp reviews.

I find a seat on an empty bench made of wood and wrought iron. It makes me feel like I'm waiting for a trolley. The shelves tower over us, which would be our doom in an earthquake, but also mercifully provide at least the illusion of privacy. Veterinary offices can be a grab bag of emotions. Cats are always frightened and in crates, their owners equally skittish. There are happy dogs here for simple things like checkups, excited to be out in the world and scenting the lingering promise of a biscuit. There are nervous dogs who hate the vet under any circumstance. There are sick and injured dogs with fretful owners who may bark and lunge and bite. There are owners leaving with no pets, having just received some kind of devastating news. And then there's us. People with dogs with octopuses on their heads. We, apparently, are the worst of the lot. Since we are too horrific and deformed to look at, others who pass through give us a wide berth.

After some time, we are led into an examining room to wait for the doctor. I set Lily down on the table and she flinches as her pads make contact with cold metal. I stroke her back to get her to stay calm. This room is also small. On the wall is a poster promoting pet dental care with photos of dog teeth in varying stages of decay. The wallpaper, somewhat ironically, is the color of gum disease.

The vet enters with a smile. He's the cutest of the newer staff and I've named him Doogie in my head because he looks too young to be a doctor, even an animal doctor, which may (or may not, who really knows?) require fewer years in school. His khakis have pleats and I wonder if I should mention something about how outdated they look, but maybe he wears them in an attempt to look older.

"What brings you in today?"

Flabbergasted, I stare at him square in the eye. If he was reading a chart, or looking at notes from Lily's patient file, that would be one thing. But he's looking right at my dog with that grin. This is probably where his inexperience cuts against him.

"Are you serious?" It's all I can stammer.

"How is Lily?" He pulls back her lips and stares at her teeth. What's he getting at? I know they are old. I know they're rotting. I know both her teeth and her gums are victims of my tight budget and neglect. But are they worse than what's on her head? Is that really what he's saying? What is the obsession in this place with teeth?!

"Well, for starters, she has an octopus on her head."

The vet lets go of her jaw, looks at Lily's head, and blanches. "Oh."

Yes, *oh*.

The vet crouches down to get a better view of the octopus.

"How long has that been there?"

"I first noticed him late last week."

He grabs Lily by the snout and angles her head around to get a good look at it from all sides. "And *an octopus*, you're calling it."

"What would you call it?" I begin to scan the room to see if there is a framed veterinary degree of some kind on the wall that might inspire confidence. I remember Internet-stalking Doogie after our last visit because I thought he was handsome. I think he went to school in Pennsylvania, but now I'm not so sure. The pants, his cluelessness. Maybe he just purchased a degree from a fake school in Guam. I won't be Internet-stalking him again.

Doogie doesn't break his study of the octopus. He touches it, taps it, and then reaches for a few gauze squares and tries to squeeze it. "*Octopus* is as good a word as any." His tone suggests that he's trying to keep me calm.

"Careful," I tell him. "You're going to make him angry."

He gets his hands fully around the octopus. "I'd say he's already pretty angry." Doogie stands up, steps on a lever to open the lid of a covered metal garbage can marked Medical Waste, and tosses the gauze away.

"Well, what are we going to do about it?"

"First, we need to know more. I'd like to take Lily into the back and see if I can't get a needle into it and extract some fluid. Then we can run some tests to see what we're dealing with."

Lily looks up at me, annoyed as I am. This makes me lose my patience.

"We're dealing with an octopus!" I'm red in the face and I can feel sweat forming on my back even though I don't want to be this worked up. So help me god, if he wants to look at the octopus's teeth.

"I know that. But the more we know about the octopus, the more we will know how to fight him."

This is the first reasonable thing he has said, so I crouch down to speak directly to Lily. "Go with the doctor. He's going to get a better look at the octopus. I'll be right out here."

Doogie collects a veterinary assistant and they whisk Lily away. Back in the waiting room, I flip through an old copy of *Dog Fancy* magazine. There are articles like "Five Mutts Who Rose to Fame" and "Spotlight on the English Springer Spaniel." These don't interest me. But "Dental Debate Erupts over Teeth Cleaning" does, at least enough to dog-ear the page and hopefully catch the attention of at least one rational thinker in this godforsaken place.

I pull out my phone and go to my photo archive to look at pictures of Lily before the octopus came. She and I on a cliff overlooking Santa Barbara that one time we took a drive up the

Pacific Coast Highway. Her asleep on her paw-print blanket, the sun from the window highlighting the red in her brown coat. Her in the bathtub, wet and annoyed. The two of us in a selfie, exchanging good night kisses in bed before sleep. Her on the sofa sitting like the Great Sphinx of Giza, because I liked the way her coat looked against the gray tweed upholstery. Another selfie—this time we're in the backyard and she's wearing a lei I got her on Maui. This one is only a few weeks old, a happier time already long ago.

Something in the picture catches my eye. I use two fingers to zoom in on the photo until I'm focused on her right temple, and there he is, in his usual perch just above her right eye—the octopus, but smaller, younger, less pronounced. How could I not have seen him then? Did he come back with me from Hawaii? Catch a ride in that lei? Did I somehow pick him up from the beach that day when I walked with Wende and Harlan and Jill collecting sea glass? Or when I was swimming in the ocean, my guard down, my cares floating away? Did I bring this upon us by needing to get away with my friends? Or did he crawl out of the Pacific at Santa Monica Beach while I was not there to stop him? Attach himself to my dog while I was on an island sipping rum thousands of miles away? I'm awash in horrible, stomach-churning feelings of guilt. It was just five nights in Hawaii—how could that come with so huge a cost?

"Excuse me, hon." The large woman who answers the phone is trying to retrieve a few cans of diabetic dog food from the shelf near my feet. I sit up in the chair and swing my legs in the other direction. She grunts as she bends down to get them.

I put my phone away and turn my attention back to *Dog Fancy*, but I don't even get into the debate over teeth cleaning before Doogie calls my name.

"Edward?"

When I get back to the examining room, Lily is there on the table waiting for me. She looks pained.

"How did it go?"

"We weren't able to get a needle as deeply into the octopus as I would have liked."

"He's a tough sonofabitch," I concede.

"We were able to extract a few cells, hopefully enough to tell us if the octopus is malignant. We'll have to send them out to our lab."

I show Doogie the picture of Lily in her lei, with the octopus in his infancy. I tell him about the octopus as I know him, about the seizure Lily had last night. He nods and listens and makes a few notes in his chart. Lily doesn't add anything, but that's not unusual. She often clams up at the vet.

"Once we get the report back from the lab we'll know more. We can try her on certain medications, an antiseizure medication for one, but you know, our best options for dealing with the . . ."

"Octopus." *Why is everyone so stupid?*

". . . *octopus* are probably surgical."

I look away, purposefully. It would help if there were a window to gaze out of; instead, I'm confronted with the dental care poster again. I think of the dog-eared copy of *Dog Fancy* in the waiting room and hope to god someone who works here finds it.

"How old is Lily again?" The vet flips through her chart for the answer.

"Twelve," I say. "And a half."

He puts the chart down. "That's older than optimal for invasive surgery. The anesthesia alone can be a risk for older dogs. But we can discuss our options in more detail midweek."

"When you hear back from the lab." I sound defeated. I feel defeated, especially when I'm asked to pay $285 for the privilege of being told to wait until Wednesday to be given options that aren't really options at all.

We get in the car and someone signals their blinker for my parking spot but I emphatically wave them away like they're after my soul and not just my parking spot and so we sit there for the twelve minutes until the meter runs out. Lily silently crawls from the passenger seat into my lap and curls up in a little ball. She lets out an enormous sigh.

"You okay, Bean?"

"They put a needle in my head."

"They put a needle in the octopus."

Lily looks at me as if they're one and the same and I wonder if she's already giving up hope. I feel like I've swallowed my own bag of wasabi peas as my throat starts to burn and then close. I try to focus on something, anything, and I choose the spelling of wasabi and how odd it is that I can't remember if it ends with an *ie* or just an *i*. I think it's just an *i*. Can that be right? Both ways I can see a squiggly red line underneath, like the word processor in my brain is telling me there's no correct way to spell it. Is wasabi a proper noun? Should it be capitalized? No, it's just a plant, isn't it? I want to run back inside the veterinary office and have them do for me what they did for Lily all those years ago: give me back my ability to breathe. And maybe confirm the spelling of wasabi. I can't remember the last time I've taken a breath, a long, deep, true breath, the kind they talk about in Lamaze classes and on yoga DVDs. Hawaii, I guess. Vacation. When I was free of work and deadlines and dating and the need for anything else but to just be. But the last time at home? Without mai tais easing my circulation? I can't say.

I feel a sudden need to forget the morning, to turn the day around. To vomit the wasabi peas.

To breathe again.

"You know what we need?" I ask. I don't even wait for her to guess. Lily perks up; she can tell by the tone of my voice I'm going to say something that she finds exciting. "Ice cream."

On the way home, we stop at the corner pet store near our house, the one the Korean family runs, and I select a peanut butter frozen yogurt made especially for dogs. I don't even wait for us to get home.

The octopus blinks and asks, "What you got there?" I don't think I'll ever get used to hearing him speak.

"Nothing," is my reply. I hold the Styrofoam dish for Lily right there in the car and she laps at it hungrily until the frozen treat is gone. Even then she licks the empty dish for another three minutes, her mood brightened.

The octopus eyes me hungrily the whole time, but I don't let him have any. I hope not to pay dearly for that later.

Tuesday

Lily and I have no standing plans on Tuesday nights, so when Trent calls and says we should go grab a drink by the beach, I agree. It's night, and I immediately have second thoughts—it feels like a hassle to go all the way to the beach this late when you can't even see the beach—but Trent is already down there for a business dinner that's just ending, and the beach always seems like a getaway, a respite, a destination. Even in darkness you can smell the saltwater, hear the crashing waves, feel the cool ocean breeze. These used to be of comfort; now, the ocean is mostly the swamp the octopus crawled out of. Trent wants to know what the vet said about Lily's prognosis, and since I don't have Jenny until Friday, it's probably a good idea for me to talk.

Trent is feeling nostalgic and suggests this gay bar we went to in the nineties that's right across the Pacific Coast Highway from Will Rogers Beach, specifically the gay section of Will Rogers Beach known affectionately as Ginger Rogers. Parking is usually a nightmare, but I luck out and find the perfect spot under a broken streetlamp, hidden from drivers in a pool of gloom. It's maddeningly too small, and after five minutes of trying to fit in the damn thing I have to concede defeat and move on to the next spot I find a good quarter mile away.

On my hike back to the bar I step in a puddle. It hasn't rained in weeks, so that's of some concern. I try to text Trent but my phone is frozen and I have to give it a hard reboot. When I finally make it to the bar, the exterior looks different. It has a nautical theme like I remember, but something is amiss. I guess the bar could look at my haggard face and say the same about me.

The place is dimly lit, but it's easy to spot Trent sitting at the bar; he's one of the few people here. I pull back the stool next to him, wave for the bartender, and take a seat.

"What made you think of this place?" I ask.

"Client dinner. The fog of work. Remembering simpler times."

The bartender comes over and he's good looking, but not the threatening kind of good looking that's usually a job requirement for bartenders in gay bars. I ask Trent what he's drinking and he says vodka tonic so I order the same.

"What did the vet say?" Trent asks. "What are the options?"

The bartender pushes the drink in my direction, at the last second adding a lime. I reach for my wallet before Trent stops me. "I opened a tab."

I take a sip of the drink and it's strong, which I like. "They can either make her comfortable with medications to stop any pain and seizures, or they can put her under, take a bigger sample of the octopus, and devise a more aggressive treatment plan."

"What are you going to choose?"

I shrug and take another sip of my drink. "I dunno. I have to talk it over with Lily."

"It's your decision, though."

"Is it?" I look around the deserted bar. "Where is everyone?"

Trent turns around and flinches, like it's the first time he's noticing the emptiness. "Don't know. I guess it's a later crowd."

The bartender must be eavesdropping because he chimes in. "It picks up after eleven."

I take out my phone to check the time, but it's not rebooting and I plunk it down on the bar. "Great. Fucking Tuesdays."

"What's wrong with Tuesdays?" Trent asks.

"Everything. Monday's always Monday, but at least it's the start of something new. Wednesday is hump day, Thursday's almost Friday, and Friday brings the weekend. But Tuesday? Nada."

Trent looks at me and shakes his head. "What difference does it make? You work at home."

"I work *from* home," I say, but I don't know why it makes a difference to me. "My phone is fried, my parking spot was too small, I stepped in"—I look down at my shoe—"urine. I don't know what to do about Lily. Should I go on?"

Trent puts his hand on my shoulder. "We need to get you laid." He surveys the room again, but the prospects are dim.

"Oh, I got laid."

"When?"

I reach for my phone to check today's date before remembering it's dead. "I don't remember. Recently." I guess there's life in me still.

"Recently?" He sounds skeptical.

"Yes. Recently." And then I'm forced to concede, "I think it was recently." Time runs together.

"Well, we need to get you laid again. At least some uncommitted lip." That's what he calls casual kissing.

"Maybe after eleven."

Why did I have such a distaste for Tuesdays, now that I freelance from home? Trent has a point. If I hated Tuesdays for their sameness when I was part of the world, a member of a more traditional workforce—their lack of anything to help them stand apart—wouldn't it make sense that I hate everything now? Every morning I rise at eight. It takes a little effort to wake Lily, but not much. I throw on some clothes, usually something that I can wear to the gym as a motivator to go. We head outside for the first of the day's walks. The morning sun feels just right, not too hot or oppressive. I know this in part because Lily only starts to pant when we round the corner in front of our house, and the panting goes away after she has just a few sips of water. I give Lily her breakfast and I have one (always one) cup of coffee sweetened with Stevia. I bring my laptop from my desk where it has charged overnight and sit in the kitchen in the spot where the glare from the window misses the screen. I write for an hour or maybe two and then have a bowl of Kashi covered with half of a sliced banana (the other half goes in the fridge). Then I allow myself the day's procrastination: I read the news, I argue with dumb people on websites, I stalk random crushes online. Sometimes I actually make it to the gym; lately not as often. In the afternoons I try to get out of the house, but even then the errands and the distractions have a sameness to them. Groceries for the night's meal, coffee on Larchmont, a movie at the Arclight I don't particularly want to see. I get in the car, I park the car, I get out of the car. The driving, the destination, I don't always remember. Lily and I take a second walk, an evening walk, where we enjoy the soft haze in the sky except at the height of summer when it is still quite bright, or the turn of the winter solstice when it is already dark. Lily gets dinner and a rawhide chew. I have a glass of wine and something to chew on myself, usually dried mango or apricot, but the unsulfured kind that doesn't give me headaches. I write for a spell. It's only the evening activities with Lily, game nights and movie nights and pizza, that provide a small respite from the monotony. At night I put my laptop back on my desk, and my phone back on its charger. Lily and I go out one last time. I never set an alarm before bed. I don't have to: my insides are as tuned in to the sameness as my everything else.

Someone has taken a seat on the barstool next to Trent and the two of them are talking. Trent gestures back at me. The guy leans in to see past Trent, looks at me, then holds his hand up as if to say "not interested." Trent turns back to me and shrugs.

"Who did you hook up with?" It's an obvious attempt to keep the conversation on my successes.

"Massage guy. The one who came to my house."

"Theodore," Trent says disapprovingly. He calls me Theodore instead of Edward when he wants to full-name me, because he knows it gets under my skin.

"Not my name."

"Isn't that like paying for it?"

"No," I say with four or five o's, partly in defense of my reputation and partly in defense of massage guy's. "I paid for a massage. Then we got to talking, I offered him a drink, we each had a few while we continued our conversation, he's a writer, too, a librettist . . ."

"Libidinous?"

"No. Well, that, too. A *librettist*, he writes the words for . . . The point is, we had a surprising amount in common, so we talked for a while—and *then* . . ." I let the sentence finish itself. "It was like a date. Except, you know, I was wearing a towel."

Trent laughs. "I should have seen that one coming."

"It took me by surprise." But maybe I should have seen it coming, too. At least an indication it might happen.

An omen.

My eyes are too often closed to these things. Should I have seen it coming? Should I have seen the octopus coming? An omen for that? Octo. Latin for eight. But who did I know who was Latin? Any number of people. This is Los Angeles, after all. Maybe the Latin origin is the wrong thing to focus on, maybe it's the eight itself. The bartender pours a beer. There are eight pints in a gallon. Eight crayons in a box of Crayolas. Eight nights of Hanukkah. Eight atoms of something in octane. Carbon? Compounds of carbon form the basis of all life, could that be it? A stop sign has eight sides; is the octopus a sign for me to stop? And if so, stop what?

But can't omens be good as well as bad? If there was an omen of the octopus coming and I missed it, shouldn't I be looking for an omen of recovery, an omen of the octopus leaving? Omen is also Latin. Back to that again.

My brain hurts.

"What time is it?" I ask.

Trent checks his phone. "Eleven fifteen."

As if on cue, the door opens and a few people enter, laughing. They're all wearing black pants and white shirts. I elbow Trent who just mouths "Weird," studies the late arrivals, and lands on one guy with a pen stuck behind his ear.

"What about that one?" He's still focused on my getting some uncommitted lip.

I flag down the bartender. "Another round?" he asks.

"Can I ask you a really stupid question?"

"Shoot," he says.

"Isn't this a gay bar?"

The bartender laughs. "Used to be. The owners sold it. Now it's mostly a hangout for local restaurant servers when their shifts end. That's why it picks up late."

I look at Trent, who just shrugs.

My head hits the bar and I speak into the crook of my arm. "We're really bad at this," I say. "I blame you. You've been happy too long."

"I blame you. You've been *unhappy* too long." Trent fixes his gaze on the blank space above me.

"What are you doing?"

"Looking for the black cloud over your head." He punches me playfully. I punch him back, a little less playfully.

"One more round," Trent says to the bartender, who places two fresh cocktail napkins on the bar before retreating to make our drinks.

Friday

"How was your week?"

It's Friday again, which means I'm back in Jenny's butter office having scant recollections of Wednesday or Thursday. There was another seizure, not as bad as the first but still scary. There was a call from the vet, but they were not able to extract enough cells from the octopus to find anything conclusive; Doogie wants to put her under general anesthesia to collect a larger sample. There was supposed to be another date with the hugging guy, but I canceled, since I was feeling gross and unattractive and unworthy of being loved. Ironically, this will probably help him clarify his feelings; men are hunters and tend to like other men who don't make it easy.

Mostly, this week I withdrew.

Withdrawing, however, is difficult in therapy—even therapy with Jenny. It's especially hard today, as Jenny sits forward on her chair with renewed zeal for her occupation. As if another patient weary of her obtuse observations has reported her to some board and she's trying to avoid additional complaints.

Or maybe she's finally cleared whatever hurdle of ambivalence was blocking her getting involved. In either case, great time to come alive, Jenny.

I don't want to answer her question, or maybe I don't know how. How was my week? The visit to the vet was . . . *irritating*? Not knowing the difference between a straight bar and a gay bar was . . . *humiliating*? My mouth is empty of adjectives and qualifying words, so I relent and swallow and sigh and tell her something else. "I might as well fill you in on our visitor."

"When you say *our* . . ." Jenny pauses. This is the kind of thing she never would have questioned in previous sessions. She would have figured it out contextually, or just not have been invested enough to care. This is an entirely new Jenny, and I don't like her.

"Lily and me. And my. And mine." The proper syntax eludes me.

"You and Lily. Okay. Proceed."

Proceed. Oh, goody, may I?

Jenny licks her upper lip, hungry for more of the story.

"Lily and I have an octopus." I pause for dramatic effect, but only get a confused stare. Then I launch into the whole ordeal, like I did for Trent, like I did for Doogie. It's already becoming like the package of stories I have preselected to recount on dates; I bore myself in the telling. Jenny nods as she listens and her eye contact is unwavering. I almost don't know who this woman is that I'm pouring my heart out to. Seriously, her scrutiny is unnerving.

"And when you say *octopus*, you mean . . ."

"Octopus. When I say *we*, I mean Lily and me, and when I say *octopus*, I mean octopus." Jenny still looks uncertain, so

I pull out my phone and show her the picture of Lily and me with the lei. "Look. Right here. Except now it's bigger and more prominent and angry."

Jenny studies the photo and uses her fingers to zoom in on the octopus. This in itself enrages me (even though I did the same thing), like she's saying I'm making mountains out of molehills, that I have now been living a week and a day on the edge of hysteria for nothing. Plus, I just *told* her it was bigger now. Meaner. When she looks up there's something akin to pity in her eyes. Something more than a sorrowful understanding, yet shy of commiseration. But I don't want her pity, or whatever is pity-adjacent. I don't need it. I am going to fix this. I am going to prevail over the octopus. I don't want this look.

Jenny hands me back my phone. "Have you been to the veterinarian?"

Duh. "On Monday."

"What did she say?" Jenny does this thing where she defaults to the feminine pronoun to make some sort of point about a male-dominated society, something she probably picked up in a women's studies class in the late nineties and that now feels woeful and stilted.

"He"—I emphasize the *he*—"couldn't say much of anything. He took a few cells to run some tests and the tests were inconclusive. Now they want to put Lily under anesthesia and take a larger sample."

"How do you feel about that?"

When I don't want to answer the question someone asks, I just give the answer to another, unasked question. I realize in this moment that I do this a lot. "I find myself leaving her alone for short periods. I don't want to be apart from her, but to be with her means I also have to be with him." I pause and Jenny nods. "Plus, the octopus came when I wasn't there, and there's a part of me that thinks I need to be gone for him to leave."

"Maybe the octopus isn't going to leave."

My answer to that is a glare.

"Maybe the octopus isn't going to leave, and what you're doing is emotionally detaching from Lily."

My stomach turns. "That's offensive. You're being offensive."

"I'm not meaning to be. It's a natural reaction to grief."

"Grief?" I say it with three question marks, as the word catches me by surprise. "What are you talking about? I'm not grieving."

Jenny raises an eyebrow as if to say, *Aren't you?*

"Grieving what? I'm fully focused on forcing the octopus to leave."

"Why can't you do both?" she asks.

Look who showed up to play.

Jenny continues. "Why can't you focus on getting the octopus to leave *and* prepare yourself for the possibility that he may not?"

"He will leave."

"I'll leave that for you and the vet to say. But Lily is older, and you've said yourself that she was the runt of her litter and her health has at times been tenuous. Unless something catastrophic happens to you in the near future, in all likelihood she is going to predecease you, and in the greater context of your life, relatively soon. If it's not the octopus that takes her, something else will eventually. A rhinoceros or a giraffe."

"A rhinoceros or a gir— How would a dog have a giraffe?" New Jenny has gone completely around the bend.

"It's natural, as our loved ones age, to start grieving their loss. Even before we lose them."

I run her words by my imaginary therapist, the one who I count on to take Jenny's bungled advice and turn it into something less botched. He's strangely silent for once; I'm afraid it means he finds nothing wrong with her diagnosis.

"What is *grief*, anyhow? What does it even mean?" I'm being obstinate.

"People describe it in different ways. I'd say it's a temporary derangement. Freud put it as something like a departure from the normal attitude toward life."

I stare Jenny square in the eyes so she can see my annoyance. "One, my questions were rhetorical. I know what grief is. Two, thank you for calling me deranged."

Jenny smiles as if to soften her insult. "Grief is a pathological condition. It's just that so many of us go through it in life that we never think to treat it as such. We just expect people to go through it, endure it, and come out the other side."

The sun pours through the window and lands in a puddle just beyond Jenny's feet. She kicks off her shoes and stretches her naked toes into the sunlight. It reminds me of Lily, who makes a catlike effort to find whatever sun she can to nap in. It's not uncommon for me to find her with just her hind legs resting in her bed, the rest of her body stretched across the sun-warmed linoleum.

I think of the Valium and Vicodin that have sometimes been my sunshine; my desire to crawl into their warming rays. "Fine. I'm grieving. Maybe you can write me a prescription."

Unfortunately, Jenny knows my fears about addiction (we've covered that topic exhaustively) and doesn't bite. "We'll see."

Maybe I, too, am suffering impairment from the presence of the octopus, seizures in reason. My thoughts of late have resembled those of a small child more than the thinking of a grown man: the magical rationalization of needing to be gone so the octopus can leave; my desire to be intimidating, bigger than I am, to have the hurricane in me; the need to express everything in a tantrum.

"What do you think of when you think of mourning?" Jenny asks. The question snaps me back to attention.

I answer without really thinking. "I guess 'Funeral Blues' by W. H. Auden. I think it was Auden. I suppose that's not very original."

"I don't know it."

"It's a poem."

"I gathered."

"I'm just clarifying. It's not a blues album."

Jenny ignores my swipe at her intelligence. "Does your response need to be original? Isn't that what poetry is for? For the poet to express something so personal that it ultimately is universal?"

I shrug. Who is Jenny, even New Jenny, to say what poetry is for? Who am I, for that matter?

"Why do you think of that poem in particular?"

"*'Stop all the clocks, cut off the telephone; Prevent the dog from barking with a juicy bone; Silence the pianos and with muffled drum; Bring out the coffin, let the mourners come.'*" I learned the poem in college and it stuck.

Jenny savors these words like she's testing a bottle of wine before saying, "Not inappropriate."

And this is where Old Jenny returns. This is where her observations are all wrong; this is where she's a nightmare as a therapist. It *is* inappropriate. It does not fit the situation or merit consideration in the context of our discussion, mostly for one glaring reason: *Prevent the dog from barking with a juicy bone.*

I can feel another tantrum rising inside me.

"It's inappropriate if it's the *dog* you are mourning!"

Sunday

The frozen turkey lands with a thud in the sink and it startles Lily awake. "Keep it down! Jeez." Lily hates to be interrupted from a good nap.

I hadn't intended to buy a frozen turkey, or a turkey at all, for that matter, but it's hard to find a fresh turkey in June and I was desperate to prove I'm not grieving. What better way to demonstrate I'm not suffering a pathological condition than to throw a celebration, in particular a celebration for everything we have to be thankful for? And nothing accompanies the giving of thanks better than turkey. And stuffing. And gravy. And mashed potatoes. And squash. It wasn't until checking out at the grocery store and the looks I got from the cashier that I realized that cooking a full Thanksgiving dinner in June was in fact its own form of derangement.

"Is that Tofurky?" Lily has risen from her bed and sits at my feet by the sink.

"Yes, it is. We're having Tofurky." Years ago I flirted with vegetarianism, and one year went so far as to make a Thanksgiving Tofurky. When Lily asked for turkey, I told her we didn't have any turkey but that we had Tofurky, and when I gave it to her she gobbled it up just the same. The gravy wasn't quite vegetarian, and her feelings pretty much fell in line with mine: smother anything in enough stuffing, potato, butter, and gravy and it's pretty damned good. Since then she's called all turkey Tofurky, and the way she says it is so unbearably cute I haven't had the heart to correct her.

"Tonight we are going to feast."

OH! BOY! TOFURKY! IS! MY! ABSOLUTE! FAVORITE! I! COULD! EAT! ALL! OF! THE! TOFURKYS! JUST! GOBBLE! THEM! UP!

Lily is now fully awake. She places a paw on my foot.

"If I can only figure out how to defrost this motherfucker." The turkey just about fills the sink.

Lily gives the microwave a sideways glance and I get as far as trying to shove the damned thing in before realizing there's no way an eighteen-pound turkey is going to fit in a standard convection microwave.

OR! WE! CAN! EAT! IT! FROZEN! LIKE! ICE! CREAM!

"Tofurky is not good frozen like ice cream." I look down at Lily, who looks up at me. She's anxious for me to fix this. "Warm water bath it is!" Lily starts to retreat. "For the Tofurky," I tell her. "Not for you."

She immediately comes back. *YES! DO! IT!*

I slide the drain cover under the turkey and fill the sink with warm water. I have a *Cook's Illustrated* magazine with an article entitled "Roasting the Big One" and I find it among a stack of never-read cookbooks. I don't know why I have saved this, but the title has been responsible for several fits of adolescent giggles.

While the turkey defrosts, Lily and I set the table. As a kid I was always enchanted by the holiday tables my mother would set. How she had special tablecloths for Thanksgiving and Christmas, and how there was white china rimmed with gold that would magically appear in November. The budding homosexual in me would study the plates, turning them over and drinking in words like *Wedgwood* and *bone* and *England*. One year my mother even provided glass finger bowls on their own saucers, and Meredith and I dipped our fingers in them after the meal and before the dessert course. It all seemed so elegant to me, I wondered if we didn't secretly descend from royalty on my mother's side. I tried to coax her with my eyes to share with me our closet lineage (I could be trusted to keep the secret safe if we were in fact in hiding from some evil czar or queen!), but she never did. I remember thinking this is how I was going to eat every night when I was grown up. Of course, even though I inherited my aunt's set of china after she passed away, this is rarely how I eat.

Our Thanksgivings usually consist of Lily sitting by my seat at the head of the table, anxiously licking her chops. Only when the humans have gorged themselves on seconds, and sometimes thirds, is she allowed her holiday meal, served in her supper dish on the kitchen floor. I always crouch beside her, holding her ears back and out of the way like a supportive college boyfriend holding back the hair of his vomiting sorority girl. It's my favorite part of the holidays, if not the entire year. It's almost like I can absorb the pure joy she radiates. This time, I pick her supper dish off the floor and set her a place at the table. The silverware and cloth napkin at her place setting will go untouched, but they bring symmetry to our table.

"Do you remember our first Thanksgiving together?" I ask Lily.

"Did we have Tofurky?" Lily asks.

"You, in fact, had a lot of Tofurky."

That year after dinner, while others did the dishes and after most of the leftover meat had been carved off the carcass, I double-bagged what was left of the turkey, placed it with the other trash by the back door, and reset the table for dessert. Later that night, I found both bags chewed through and the carcass picked clean. It only took following a short trail of greasy paw prints to find Lily under the kitchen table, engorged to nearly twice her normal size. She looked up at me, still licking her oily face. *PUNISH! ME! IF! YOU! MUST! BUT! IT! WAS! WORTH! IT!*

When I finish telling this story to Lily she laughs and says, "That was my favorite Thanksgiving."

"It was not your favorite day-after-Thanksgiving."

Lily thinks about this and delivers a flat, "Oh, yeah." Ever since then I've boiled the carcass for soup.

"Roasting the Big One" suggests cooking the bird breast side down for one hour at 425 degrees to crisp the skin and seal in the juices before lowering the temperature to 325 degrees and flipping the bird breast side up until the turkey registers 165 on a meat thermometer. Overall, this should make the cooking time between four and five hours.

The oven radiates a lot of heat on this already warm summer day, and Lily and I nap between bastings to escape from it. We don't have a lot of other Thanksgiving activities, so I play my DVD of *Home for the Holidays* starring Holly Hunter. Halfway through the movie, I have to start peeling vegetables. I let the movie run for Lily while I get on with preparing the meal.

Trent arrives around five.

"Wow. It smells great in here. Did you make pumpkin bread?"

"No," I reply, annoyed. What with the turkey, the stuffing, the potatoes, the squash, the gravy, and the green beans, I didn't have time to make pumpkin bread.

"It's not really Thanksgiving without pumpkin bread." Trent pouts.

"It's not really Thanksgiving at all."

Trent uncovers the pot containing the mashed potatoes and sticks his finger in. He scoops up a mouthful with his index finger and tells me they need more butter. "What else am I tasting?"

"In the potatoes?"

He nods.

"Nutmeg." It's my secret ingredient.

Trent goes to the fridge and grabs himself a beer. "Can I see the octopus?"

"Lily's in the living room. But, hey"—I grab Trent by the elbow—"let's not mention him again tonight."

I follow Trent because he's my best friend and I know his reaction will tell me everything I need to know. He will cut through the bullshit and give it to me straight. Lily is asleep, octopus-side up, giving us both a good view.

"Oh, god." His reaction confirms what I already know, that this is a big fucking deal and there's no messing around. "Have you made a decision about what you're going to do?"

"I've decided not to talk about it on Thanksgiving."

When it's time to sit down at the table, I produce three hats I purchased from a store that sells old movie costumes. Two tall pilgrim hats for Trent and myself, each with a smart buckle, and a pilgrim bonnet with chin straps for Lily. (What movie these were from, I have no idea.) Trent balks at wearing his hat but I say, without room for negotiation, "Put it on."

When I affix Lily's hat, the octopus, who has been eyeing the day's activities with suspicion, says, "What are you doing? I might like turkey. Or *Tofurky*." He rolls the one eye I can see.

"Unfortunately, you're not invited." I place the bonnet on Lily, covering the octopus completely. For once, she doesn't protest the idea of wearing something. I lift her up to her chair and set her on a pillow that boosts her up to proper table height.

"Let's begin by saying what we are thankful for while I carve the turkey."

TOFURKY! Lily corrects, incorrectly.

The turkey looks so beautiful that I almost don't want to carve it. It seems golden and crisp and juicy and delicious; whoever wrote "Roasting the Big One" knew what they were talking about. But once I make the first cut, to slice off a drumstick, the smell that fills the room produces such hunger pangs that I realize I haven't eaten all day. It's hard not to just tear into the thing with my teeth.

Trent starts. Despite the lack of pumpkin bread and his having to wear a hat, he's getting into the spirit of the whole thing.

"I'm thankful for Matt and for Weezie," he begins, listing his boyfriend and his bulldog. "I'm thankful for good friends, of course." He raises his glass to Lily and me. "And for good food, continued success, and togetherness. And the Dallas Cowboys."

I'm suddenly aware that the sounds of football and parades are missing from our makeshift holiday.

"Lily, how about you?"

I'M! THANKFUL! FOR! TOFURKY!

"What else?" I ask.

THAT'S! ALL! TOFURKY! ME! She licks her chops.

"Okay, I'll go." I slide a few slices of turkey into Lily's supper dish, and a few more onto Trent's plate and mine. "I, too, am thankful for friends and for Tofurky. And for leftover Tofurky sandwiches, and the adventure of Thanksgiving in June. I'm thankful for family. My sister, Meredith, called to say I am going to be an uncle again, and I love being an uncle."

"Congratulations!" Trent says. I hold up a finger to say I'm not done.

"But most of all, I am thankful for Lily, who, since she entered my life, has taught me everything I know about patience and kindness and meeting adversity with quiet dignity and grace. No one makes me laugh harder, or want to hug them tighter. You have truly lived up to the promise of man's best friend."

Trent throws his fork at me, because he doesn't like the idea of anyone but himself being called my best friend, but I toss the fork back, asking him to think in a larger context. Lily looks at me in annoyance, her shade made even cuter by her pilgrim bonnet; all this praise is just delaying our meal.

I finish plating (or bowling, in Lily's case) our meals and drizzle our food with gravy. Between Trent and Lily, it's hard to say who digs into the food more ferociously. I don't touch mine. Instead, I watch Lily consume every bite, observing the strange faces she makes as she drags her bonnet straps through the gravy and then desperately tries to lick them once there is no more food in her bowl.

Dammit, Jenny.

I am in mourning. That much is clear to me now. There is

a recognizable departure from the normal attitudes of life: An eighteen-pound turkey is an acceptable meal for three. A dog's supper dish can be on the people table. Pilgrim hats are appropriate haberdashery in June. An octopus may take my dog.

There may not be a November.

Monday

The day after our impromptu Thanksgiving, it's mid-afternoon before it occurs to me that it's not Black Friday. It's not even Friday at all—it's Monday—but I'm already at The Grove wandering the sidewalks of the outdoor shopping mall aimlessly in search of a good sale. I pass a number of stores that usually interest me, but my mind is somewhere else. With every good memory comes the memory of a mistake. A parallel memory. A darker recollection. The memory of Lily as a puppy transporting all my shoes to the top of the stairs calls up the terrifying incident of her falling down those stairs because I hadn't had the foresight to block them with a gate. The triumph of expressing her bladder after surgery ushers in another flashback, when I was frustrated that she wouldn't pee and I yanked her leash so hard she squealed in pain. The memories of our longest talks couple with those of our longest silences, either when we were mad or when we weren't, when maybe we just presumed the other was mad and we never bothered to ask if that was true.

If I remember all of the good things, isn't it my responsibility to also remember the bad? If I remember the consumption of happiness at Thanksgiving, shouldn't I also remember the downing of poison, the force-feeding of hydrogen peroxide? If I can feel her heartbeat through her chest as she sleeps nights snuggled next to me, shouldn't I also hear her gasping for breath when that same peroxide went down wrong?

The bookends of these memories join to create a vise. My head is stuck between the moveable jaws, which also act as giant conch shells to create the white noise of the ocean, as someone cranking the vise handle makes everything tighter and louder and more unbearable until I struggle to remember why I'm even here. A sale, yes, but a sale on what? What am I shopping for? I search vainly for my bearings in a place that is not that big, not that overwhelming, and not at all unfamiliar. A trolley of tourists passes by with its deafening clang, a sound simultaneously muffled and piercing. I think of the trolley bench in the veterinarian's waiting room; does the trolley make its last stop there? People exit shops like they're coming right at me. A man walks two dachshunds on leashes; they cut through the crowds, laser-focused.

Just as they pass me, I start to dry heave.

Everything is a blur, and the only thing that registers in my brain is that I've got to get out. My car is on the sixth level of a parking garage that I suddenly feel incapable of navigating. Escaping it would require a tight series of right turns down a central vertigo-inducing ramp that would be the end of whatever shreds of equilibrium I have left—never mind driving home. I stagger past two restaurants, both so unappealing and bland that even on my best days I wonder who dines in them.

I know these restaurants mark the exit from the mall, the way to the garage, but I can't bring myself to walk the narrow path between them. My brain fills with thoughts of the man who jumped off the roof of the parking garage and landed with a splat at the base of the escalator some months ago. Not thoughts about the man, exactly; I know nothing about the man except what they reported on the news. But of death.

Of bones crunching.

Of finality.

Of strangulation.

Of the octopus.

I stumble forward, knowing this commits me to another lap around the eastern end of the mall. Out of the corner of my eye a sign registers, announcing a J. Crew Men's store that is "coming soon." I think to myself that I would like that, if I ever get out of here alive. If I ever have the nerve to come back.

Somehow a table presents itself near the grassy area where they erect the skyscraperlike Christmas tree each November, the one that would be here now if it were actually Black Friday. I slump into a chair and put my head down. The tabletop is sticky, but I don't care. I don't even know who this table belongs to. I'm probably supposed to purchase a Häagen-Dazs ice cream or a Wetzel's soft pretzel to sit here. And maybe I will, but for now I just need the spinning to stop. I need thoughts that don't squeeze me. I need good feelings that don't bring bad ones; I need the deafening roar in the conch shells to subside.

I need to not be rankled by self-doubt.

My head continues pounding, and the air is thick, like trying to breathe custard. I've sweated through my shirt; it sticks to my back like Saran Wrap. I think of pills, little candies of pleasure and relief. I can't remember if I have any at home.

Goddamned Jenny, not prescribing me more. I try to imagine the calming whoosh of a Valium. The mounting clumsiness as the brain's messages are transmitted more slowly. The calming happiness. The warming embrace. Maybe I can will myself into a more placid state just with the idea, the memory, of pills.

A piece of fuzz lands near my feet. Then another. I wonder if it's snowing. Not actually snowing—it never snows in Los Angeles, except at The Grove at Christmastime when they launch fake snow from the roof of the movie theater with these cannonlike machines. Have two flakes coasted on a gentle breeze for six months, only now coming in for a landing? No. A mother chases a toddler blowing dandelion fluff. I should have known. Nothing floats effortlessly in limbo—not for six months.

From underneath my armpit I can see the dachshunds pass by again. I can just see their little feet, their short legs, eight of them in total, like the octopus's, but they move at such speeds they look like more, like million-legged millipedes out for an afternoon stroll. Seeing how they deftly maneuver around huge obstacles and through loud noises, coupled with the idea of pills, slowly brings me some calm.

Lily would never tolerate The Grove. Not anymore. Not in old age. She would not have the wherewithal to navigate such a crowd. She would cower, with her head down, until I found a safe place for us to sit. She would be like me now: helpless, spinning, afraid.

As Lily aged and her reactions slowed and her eyesight became less crisp, Doogie's predecessor warned me that she might develop something he called Enclosed World Syndrome. I told him I hadn't heard of Enclosed World Syndrome, only New World Syndrome (the introduction of a modern, sedentary lifestyle to indigenous peoples, along with obesity, diabetes, and heart disease—you're welcome, Native Americans). I don't know if Enclosed World Syndrome is an official syndrome or something this vet made up, or who is even in charge of anointing syndromes officially. But Lily did rather quickly come to find comfort only in smaller and smaller concentric circles with our house at the center and, coincidentally, so did I. Or maybe Lily's aging coincided with the end of my relationship with Jeffrey and the stalling of my writing career. "How's Jeffrey?" "How's the writing going?" These were questions that had irritated me to my core. Not because of their illegitimacy, but because I had no response. How was Jeffrey? *We can't go two days without fighting.* How was the writing? *I haven't written anything in months.* It became easier to avoid people than to have to explain that I was struggling. My Enclosed World Syndrome got a little better, partly out of necessity, when I became single again. Lily's never did.

Since the arrival of the octopus, I find myself spinning a familiar cocoon. It's impossible to talk about what I can't bring myself to say. If I were to join friends at a noisy bar or in a crowded restaurant and anyone were to ask, "How's Lily?" what on Earth would I say?

"Well, there's an octopus on her head."

"There's an *ostrich in her bed*?"

Any conversation would only unravel from there.

Slowly I lift my head and take in my surroundings. There's a shirtless model outside of Abercrombie & Fitch. Nordstrom is undergoing some sort of storefront remodel. Crate & Barrel is pushing patio umbrellas in bold, striped fabrics. Someone who may or may not be Mark Ruffalo is making a beeline toward Kiehl's. Slowly, the pounding in my head stops. Slowly, my body temperature lowers, my normal heartbeat returns.

I wish there was a way I could see from my phone if the octopus was gone. Some sort of app connected to a series of nanny cams to spy on every room in my house. Something that would allow me to look at Lily asleep in her bed, her head unencumbered by that beast, her mind deep in the sweetest dream. Or maybe I'm glad that there's not. Maybe it would just be one more thing on my phone for me to check obsessively, taking me out of the moment, taking me away from life. Maybe I would use it as permission to stay clear of Lily in my magical thinking that that's when the octopus will leave, even though I know deep down it's going to take a lot more than a trip to the mall for him to go.

When I get home the octopus is still there. My heart sinks, despite my brain telling it not to. I saddle Lily in her harness and grab her leash and we head out on a walk. Our old walk, the one up the quieter street with the hill. The one we used to take daily before our syndrome made us hermits and our outdoor excursions became limited to the shorter route that looped us quickly back home.

As we walk two blocks and round the corner and climb the hill that gives us a distant view of the Hollywood sign, Lily catches the scent of something on the grass between the sidewalk and the street. I let her sniff. There will be no yanking her by the neck. She can have all the time in the world. And I will forgive myself for the mistakes I've made. For the times I got so angry. For the times I've acted hatefully.

The afternoon air is cool, the haze is soft. The last few petals of the jacaranda trees color the sidewalk. The streets are empty. People are not yet home from work to walk their dogs. We don't get any strange looks or sideways glances. No one stops to ask why there's an octopus hitching a ride on my dog.

In the distance, soft mountains and rolling hills mark the edge of the Los Angeles basin. There's the slightest hint of salt in the air—you'd have to really want to smell it, but it's there.

"Oh, look! The Hollywood sign." It's the octopus. Lily has finished sniffing and has turned to look back at me.

I roll my eyes.

"It's smaller than I imagined."

"You're smaller than I imagined." It's not much of a come-back and I'm not even sure what I mean by it, but it's all I have. Smaller as in petty, I guess.

For the briefest of moments, I think maybe the octopus just wants to see some sights. The Hollywood sign. Grauman's Chinese Theatre. Venice Beach. The building where they filmed *Die Hard*. That maybe he mistook Lily for a small, four-legged tour bus, and he's riding up top on a double-decker waiting for the next photo op.

But I know this isn't true.

Still, it's important for us to get out more, I think, while looking out at the expanse. Not so the octopus can leave, but because maybe the octopus is here to stay.

Wednesday Night

I wake to find the bed shaking and immediately think it's an earthquake. We haven't had one, a memorable one, for years, and in the back of my mind I've been preparing.

Expecting.

Waiting.

I prop myself up on my elbows and stare into the darkness. Something's different; something's not right. There's not the usual rolling sensation of surfing tectonic waves. My stomach isn't sinking in the way it does when you reach the top of a roller coaster, in the split seconds before the first drop. There isn't the usual calmness that overtakes me, the antithesis of how you think you'd react in an earthquake—the ability to think where flashlight batteries are, to count the ounces of bottled drinking water in the house, to remember how a transistor radio works, to wonder if you're wearing something acceptably dignified for when your body is found.

I place my hand on Lily and the source of this seismic activity becomes clear—she is in the throes of another seizure. I roll onto my side and pull her tightly to my chest. My lips are right behind her ear, behind the octopus, and I whisper angrily, "Let go of her. Let go of her. Let go!" And then to Lily, "I've got you. I'm here. Shhh."

My mind drifts and I think of us in a tented war hospital, somewhere not far from the battlefield. The air is hot and thick, and Lily, the wounded veteran, is shaking in a morphine haze, deep in jarring flashbacks of the horrific events of war. I am the loving nurse trying to calm the soldier, telling her to ignore the blasts of distant shells, ignore the moans of her fellow wounded, ignore the stench of charred flesh and destroyed lives, ignore the cawing of spiteful magpies singing gleefully of impending death, all while calmly wiping her forehead.

Lily continues to convulse with her eyes rolled back and my terror metastasizes into helplessness, paralysis, as I wait for the convulsions to stop. I hold my hand under her chin to keep her from thrashing her neck. It occurs to me that she may bite, involuntarily or out of fear, but I don't care. Let her bite me. I would welcome the pain. I would rather something awake me from my utter uselessness. My tears start as I begin to feel like the octopus is squeezing my own head, his eight arms suctioned to my skin, compressing like the vise of my panic attacks. I almost remove my hand from under Lily's jaw to see if the octopus has not in fact jumped from her head to mine. Almost. Because I know he hasn't. I can see him still, his tentacles gripped firmly around her.

As the shaking slows, I'm aware of a growing warmness underneath me. A wetness that spreads like a drop of food coloring in water. The warmth quickly cools. Lily has wet the bed and her urine seeps across the sheets. I don't try to remove either of us from the puddle until the seizure fully subsides, and even then, we lie there unwavering as my alarm clock ticks off several more minutes.

I think of all the nights when Lily failed to pee on our bedtime walks. How much stress this would cause me. How difficult it was on those nights to fall asleep, to stay asleep, frustrated that I might have to take her to the yard in the darkness of predawn. So many arguments this caused between us. I always thought I knew better when it came to her needing to pee, but until this night she had never once actually wet the bed. And now that she has, we just lie there in the accident and the minutes on the clock keep changing and the love I have for her keeps growing and we both keep drawing breath.

What was so horrible about it?

Why had I always been so angry?

What was with my need to be right? To win every argument with her? To outstubborn a dog?

And just like that, all of the anger is gone. Released, like the emptying of a bladder, into soft cotton sheets as we lie in the wetness.

Lily tries to regulate her breathing, but it quickly turns to panting.

"Do you want water? You can drink mine." I indicate the glass of water I always keep on the nightstand.

Lily shakes her head no.

"I'm so sorry," I say. "For all those other nights."

"Wh-y-y-y-y?" The panting continues.

And this makes me cry even harder. All those nights she had no idea that I went to bed angry at her. Or if she had known, she has forgotten. Because dogs live in the present. Because dogs don't hold grudges. Because dogs let go of all of their anger daily, hourly, and never let it fester. They absolve and forgive with each passing minute. Every turn of a corner is the opportunity for a clean slate. Every bounce of a ball brings joy and the promise of a fresh chase.

She wants to know why I'm sorry. I don't want to tell her about my anger. I don't want to tarnish my image in her eyes. Not now. Not with the octopus listening.

So when I respond, I lie.

"Because I'm going to have to give you a bath."

A Complete List of Lily's Nicknames

Silly
Little
Lil
Monkey
Bunny
Bunny Rabbit
Mouse
Tiny Mouse
Goose
Silly Goose
Mongoose
Monster
Monster Dot Com
Peanut
Penuche
Pinochle
Sweet Pea
Walnut

Walnut Brain
Copperbottom
Crazy
Baby
Puppy
Guppy
Old Lady
Crank
Cranky
Crankypants
Squeaky
Squeaky Fromme
Tiger
Dingbat
Mush
Mushyface
Hipster
Slinkster
Slinky
Bean
Dog

Saturday

The sun rises with a surprising intensity, a sign that June gloom has cleared the runway and July is on approach. We're both tired, and it would've been easy to return to the bed after our morning walk, read from a book maybe, drift lazily in and out of sleep. But the sun beckons with a blazingly confrontational message: There is darkness, but there is also light. To stay in bed would be to embrace the darkness, the seizures, the octopus. To go outside is to embrace the light.

"How about we go somewhere?" I suggest this as we eat breakfast. Kibble for her, Kashi—per usual—for me.

Lily doesn't answer until she finishes her meal and sniffs around the kitchen floor to make sure no additional kibble has escaped the confines of her bowl. "I'm fine staying in."

"I know you're fine with staying in. But I think we should take a ride and see the ocean."

Lily thinks about this, and I wonder how much she remembers the ocean. If she misses it. We used to go there a lot. My hope is the octopus misses it and will take one look at his home and crawl back into the sea.

The car is warm from the morning sun, and I open the sunroof. Lily lasts about thirty seconds in the passenger seat before she climbs into her customary perch on my lap. She turns around three times and I wait at a stop sign until she settles because it's hard to drive when your dog is stepping on sensitive bits that she shouldn't. As always, she quiets herself with her chin in the crook of my left elbow, and we turn down the street heading west.

We hit the Pacific Coast Highway in no time. Where is everyone? It's almost like an entire city has been so lulled by the gloom and the haze that they've all given up their identity as early risers. Their loss, our gain. The sun is even shining as we emerge off the 10 and through the tunnel that gives us our first glimpse of the Pacific. This is a hard one to explain to visitors, the weather differential between most of Los Angeles and the ocean. The beach is often the last part of the city to see sun. But not today. Today, the sun sparkles majestically off the water.

I stream some music from my phone and crank it loud, but this seems to bother Lily—she has the look of someone with a crippling hangover, the thumping bass going right through her—so I turn the volume down until you can just make out the music over the sound of the air that whooshes over and past the open sunroof. We pass a string of familiar landmarks: the restaurant where Jeffrey and I had our first date; Paradise Cove, where I had lunch with my father the last time he visited; Trancas Market, where in my twenties I used to buy bottled water and snacks before hitting a Malibu beach. I see a younger version of myself at each and it's all I can do not to wave; I wonder what my younger selves would think of me now, if they would recognize me or even care to wave back.

We stop at El Matador, ten miles or so north of Malibu, a

beach that's always brought solace and a certain clearheaded-ness. There were days after I first moved to the city when I would grab a friend or two and a towel and sunscreen, and we'd go to this beach and you'd have to drag me away under protest at sunset. Now, it always seems there's too much to do to indulge in whole days of such leisure, but that's probably just an excuse. What is there to do, really?

Despite the early hour, there are only three open spots in the tiny parking lot and I grab one of them. The rest are taken by surfers, no doubt—their internal clocks align with the tides. The lot sits maybe 150 feet up on a cliff above the beach, and the views from the parking lot alone are spectacular. You can easily see the other pocket beaches, El Pescador (the fisher-man) and La Piedra (the rock). I've wondered why El Matador is thusly named. The bullfighter. Perhaps it's the craggy stone formations that emerge from the sea. But they are less like bulls to me than sea monsters. Like the octopus. El Pulpo, as a name, is probably less inviting.

Lily and I get out of the car and stroll a bit to the cliff's edge. I pick her up and we survey the horizon together.

"So, do you remember the beach?"

"Is this the beach?" she asks.

"Yes, yes—down below, it is."

Lily looks down. "I remember." Then, tentatively, "Are we going down there?"

"Not today. Dogs aren't allowed on this beach." There's a sign that says as much, but I think about breaking the rules. What is anyone going to do? Call a park ranger? The police? But Lily looks content, and there's a picnic table that's not being used, so I decide not to ruffle any feathers. "I thought we could just sit here for a while."

Lily agrees, and we sit on the table and listen to the ocean, to the sound of the pounding surf that, because it is so far below, sounds farther away than it is. The muffled cackle of people laughing in the water and the distant cries of soaring gulls add layers to the symphony.

"We have some decisions to make, Monkey."

Lily mulls the weight of this for a moment before asking, "Why do you call me that?"

"Why do I call you what?"

"Monkey."

"Why do I call you Monkey?"

"And all those other names."

"Those are terms of endearment."

"I don't understand." Lily squints as she stares out into the sun.

"Terms of endearment are names or phrases that you use to address someone that you feel great affection for."

The wind picks up and we sit quietly for a moment.

"You have a lot of them for me," she observes.

"That's because I have a lot of affection for you." And then, almost as an afterthought, "Do you have any terms of endearment for me?"

Lily thinks about this. "Mostly, I think of you as That Guy."

I could let that bother me, but I don't. Terms of endearment are probably a human thing. They're certainly not a dog creation. They have other things—tail wagging, for instance—instead. To her, I am That Guy. The guy.

Her guy.

In the water, a pod of dolphins breaks the surface and we watch them as they dive up and down over the forming waves. Part of me wishes we were not high on a cliff; part of me wishes

I could swim out to the dolphins and enlist their help in prying the octopus from Lily with their bottle noses and returning him to the ocean depths.

"Can the octopus hear us now?" I ask.

"No."

"You can tell?"

"Sometimes. He gets bored with us a lot and tunes out."

"If he's so bored, then he should leave." I scratch the back of Lily's neck while trying to choke down my offense. Bored with *us*? Really? He's not exactly a master of witticisms and repartee. Who the hell does he think he is?

Lily does this thing where she lifts her snout in the air, and I can tell that the backrub feels good, so I continue. I'm more comfortable snuggling with her when I know the octopus isn't going to interfere. "We have some decisions to make, Goose. Hard ones. About how to get rid of . . ." Instead of saying *the octopus*, I point at it. I don't want his curiosity piqued by his mention. "And to be blunt about it, all of the options suck."

I continue stroking Lily's back. I'm not sure how much of this she grasps. Sucks for the octopus? Sucks for her? Sucks for us. I think of what Doogie has told me, as well as what I've read in my own research, although my own research is limited—if you Google "octopus on dogs," most results you get are about making an octopus out of a hot dog by cutting the bottom two-thirds the long way into eight sections to look like arms and leaving the head of the hot dog intact. Apparently the Japanese add these to bento-type lunch boxes for children. This makes me think less of the Japanese.

"There's surgery, where they'll try to cut him off. That's perhaps the most obvious thing to do. But the doctors won't know if they can get all of him until they put you under and see what kind of grip he holds." Lily looks confused, so I remind her, "You had surgery once on your spine."

Lily recoils and I feel her tremble. "I don't like surgery."

"I don't think anyone does." Maybe only surgeons.

"What else?"

Her reaction confirms what I already know, but surgery in many ways would be the most satisfying. The idea of stabbing a scalpel into the octopus and starting to cut is so appealing, I almost want to do it myself. To bring about his demise at the violent end of a knife. But there's no way for even the most decorated surgeon to do this without also stabbing a knife into Lily. Neither of us can abide by this, if it's even a worthwhile option at all.

"There's chemotherapy and radiation."

"What do those things do?"

"They would try to shrink the octo—him, I suppose." It's a funny visual, like a cartoon. The octopus getting smaller and smaller in front of our eyes until he has only a high squeaky voice and croaks something along the lines of "I'm mellllt-t-t-ting," like the Wicked Witch of the West.

"Do those hurt like surgery?"

I try to imagine putting Lily through either. What they would both do to her already subdued spirit. Her voice would be lost. I can't imagine ever hearing her exclaim *I! JUST! CAME! BACK! FROM! CHEMOTHERAPY! AND! IT! WAS! SO! MUCH! FUN! LET'S! ALL! STICK! PEANUT! BUTTER! TO! THE! ROOFS! OF! OUR! MOUTHS! AND! LICK! FRANTICALLY! UNTIL! IT'S! GONE!*

I can't imagine ever hearing her exclaim anything again.

"Neither is pleasant," I say.

"Next," she says dismissively.

"They can put you on steroids to try to reduce the octopus that way—reduce the swelling he's causing on your brain—and start you on anticonvulsants to lessen the frequency of seizures. But those do a lot of damage to your kidneys."

Lily has already had several courses of steroids on occasions when swelling returned to her spine. I used to find the idea of her on steroids funny—that I might come home and find a dachshund-shaped hole in the wall and half the cars on the block overturned in a Hulk-like rage. But only funny because I was so scared. I needed to think of the steroids as superhuman, supercanine. There could be no surgery for her again on her spine. The steroids had to be powerful. They had to work.

"Harrumph," Lily scoffs, summing up her feelings on all the choices.

She's not going to help me make this decision. She's a dog and has other concerns, and what about any of this can she really understand? Or maybe she's made her decision, and what I need to do is listen. Maybe she knows what the vet says, what may seem obvious to anyone who thinks about it. That there is no true cure for canine octopus. Not any that has been discovered yet.

Lily stands on my lap and raises one of her front paws in her best guard-dog stance.

LOOK! THE! DOLPHINS! ARE! BACK! AND! THEY'RE! JUMPING! I! WANT! TO! JUMP! IN! THE! WAVES! LIKE! THAT!

I look up and the pod has returned, and sure enough, they are jumping and twisting and flipping and flopping playfully in the rising tide.

And yet even more enchanting is Lily's voice. The one I can't bear to dim or silence. It's older, and her exclamations are fewer and farther between. Her puppyish enthusiasm is gone. But it is still her voice. It is still her.

"You don't like to get wet," I say.

"Oh, yeah," Lily says. She settles back down in my lap.

"It's a fun idea, though, Mouse. Splashing in the waves."

After a pause Lily looks up at me. "Sometimes I think of you as Dad."

My heart rises in my throat.

That's the only term of endearment I need.

Ink

I.

It's late, past the time I usually go searching for Lily to bring her to bed, except tonight I don't have to search for her because she's creating such a ruckus in the hallway, barking and growling and carrying on. When I catch up to her, she's staring into the corner between the bedroom and bathroom doors, in her offensive low crouch, hackles raised, clearly startled and upset.

"Goose? Goose! Mongoose! What is it?"

She doesn't miss a beat or move to back down or acknowledge my presence in any way. She just barks at the damned corner like it's an advancing battalion. I'm already leaning down to grab her when she stops me cold in my tracks.

THIS! LLAMA! BEACHBALL! SEVEN! PARLIAMENT! CASSEROLE! ANTARCTICA! PAJAMAS!

What the . . .

We both stare at each other, frozen. It's like being in a horror film when someone starts speaking in tongues and the whole room falls silent. I'm almost waiting for Lily's head to rotate like an owl's and for her to start vomiting pea soup. But I know for a fact she's not possessed by demons—just one demon, a squishy, eight-tentacled prick. I scoop her up and squeeze her tight to soothe her, but she wriggles left, then right, then nearly out of my grip altogether. It takes a moment pressed against my chest for her to snap out of whatever trance she's in, and when she does she begins to shake uncontrollably in my arms.

"Guppy, what was that?"

Lily turns from me to the light, then from the light to the dining room, then from the dining room to the bedroom.

"I can't see," she says.

This startles me. "Can't see what?" I turn on the light, hoping it will help.

There's a long silence. "Anything."

I look at the octopus. "What have you done?"

The octopus looks annoyed. "Have you noticed there's an emerging pattern in this household? I'm always the first to be blamed."

"What have you done!"

"To her?"

I've resisted doing this previously, but since Lily is in a state anyway, I swat the octopus. Hard. I immediately regret it, but Lily remains oblivious.

"Ow!" One of his arms reaches up to soothe the spot where I hit him. "I released my ink sac. Satisfied?"

"She can't see!"

"That's really the whole point of releasing an ink sac." The octopus's ability to stay calm in the face of my rage is one of the things I hate most about him.

"And you wonder why you get blamed."

"Oh, hey, look at that. Yeah, I guess this one is on me." I loathe his epiphanies.

I wish there was a way to punch him, really deck him square in the jaw, but there isn't. Not without also risking further harm to Lily. So instead I kiss her on the neck, on the far side, away from the octopus.

"Get a room," the octopus says.

I imagine grabbing that arm of his and wrapping it around his neck and choking the life right out of him, much as Princess Leia did to Jabba the Hutt, until his obnoxious tongue hangs limply in death. But I don't. I set Lily down on the ground and continue to stroke her back in a way that calms both of us. After a moment or two she gathers some initiative and takes three steps forward straight into the wall.

"Whoa. Take it easy, Monkey."

Lily backs up, adjusts her course, and takes another few steps, again into the wall, but this time a little closer to the kitchen door.

"Where's my water?" Lily asks.

I grab her around the middle and gently guide her through the doorway into the kitchen toward the water. Before I can stop her, she walks into the side of her bowl and water sloshes over the edge and onto her feet.

"Found it," she says, lifting her paws away from the puddle, then thirstily lapping at the remaining water in her bowl.

"Aren't you supposed to leave now, octopus?"

"I don't think so," he says as Lily continues to drink. "Why?"

"Releasing your ink sac is what you do so that you can make your escape. It's what you do to cloud the water to evade a predator."

The octopus shakes his head, which throws Lily slightly off balance, but she recovers easily enough. "Oh, so suddenly between the two of us *you're* the octopus expert?"

"Don't kid yourself into thinking that the instant you fall asleep I'm not reading everything I can about your kind so I can find a way to kill you." I probably shouldn't have said that, played that hand in so obvious a fashion, but since Lily's usually in my lap when I'm doing my research, I figure on some level he already knows.

Lily finishes drinking and takes a few steps toward her bed and I almost yell at the octopus *don't you walk away when I'm talking to you* before remembering he's only a passenger, and I want Lily to move around to help her orient herself. She knows where her bed is in relation to the water bowl, and she makes it there without incident.

"Well, I wouldn't exactly call this thing a predator," the octopus answers. He shakes his head in pity as Lily turns her usual three times before lying down.

"Why don't you crawl down off her head and see how long you last against *that thing*." This may be the only moment that I'm not horrified by Lily's hunting instincts, her skill in eviscerating plush prey, her innate Germanity. If only she could grab the octopus by his squishy flesh and shake until his insides decorate his outsides.

"That's okay. I'm fine where I am." He smiles a crooked smile. Lily settles her chin over the side of the bed. It's probably the best thing for her to do, sleep. But part of me wishes she was not giving in to the blinding. Part of me wishes she was charging, head down, at the walls of the kitchen full speed, that she would ram the octopus into submission, making him choke on his hubris.

"So if she's not a predator, and you're not scuttling away, why release your ink?"

The octopus rolls his eyes. "I thought you were the octopus expert."

We glare at each other and I know neither of us is going to back down, just as he knows it, so I answer my own question. "Because sometimes you get bored."

The octopus looks surprised, maybe even a little impressed, but he tries to mask that quickly. "Very good."

"How long will the ink last? When will she be able to see?"

The octopus shrugs. I don't know how he manages it, because an octopus doesn't have shoulders, but that's exactly what he does—he shrugs. "I don't know." He sounds genuinely baffled.

"Why not? Why don't you know? How long does it usually last?"

"I don't know because I'm usually long gone by the time it clears."

"But you're still here!" I'm on the verge of pulling my hair out in clumps.

"You know, I take it back. You really are becoming quite the expert."

I turn away from him and place my hand over my mouth to muffle my agonizing scream.

"Also, I don't know because I've never released my ink sac directly into someone's brain." He blows air through his lips, causing them to vibrate, to intonate that it's anyone's best guess.

And just like that, I understand that Lily's eyesight is not coming back. The octopus took it simply because he was bored and he could. She has seen my face, the world, her world, for the last time. She's a blind dog now.

My quiver is emptying of arrows, but I mentally draw one of the few I have left and carefully take aim. "The octopus does have predators, you know."

The octopus laughs. "Ha-ha. Yeah. Sharks!" He looks around the kitchen. "I don't see any sharks here!"

This time I don't say what I'm thinking. This time I hold my cards close to the vest. This time I don't spill what my late nights of worry and reading have taught me. This time I'm one step ahead of him.

That's right, sharks. And it's true, there are no sharks here. But I also have reason to feel emboldened.

For octopuses have two natural predators:

Sharks.

And humans.

2.

The sun is hot and it's burning my eyes, and the tighter I close them the more they itch with heat and sweat. I scrunch my eyelids, then loosen them; a kaleidoscope of colors and patterns floats in front of me. TV static, paisley, comets trailing fiery tails, sunbursts, tornados, violence, calm—all happening in the darkness behind my closed eyes. I wonder if this is what Lily sees, blinded as she is, if she can sense light, if her blindness is rich with colors and patterns. Or is it just darkness, her eyes painted in the total blackness of octopus ink?

I prop myself up on my elbows and slowly open my eyes to see the blue waters of Trent's swimming pool. I look over at my friend. He's lying on his stomach with his sunglasses hanging crooked on his face. I can't tell if he's awake or asleep. I reach for the plastic tumbler under the chair in the only shade to be found, but produce a bottle of sunscreen instead. When I find my glass it's empty.

"Shall I make us more drinks?" Trent's voice is groggy and thin and disappears into the ambient sound of the afternoon.

I turn to Trent, who still hasn't stirred. "I'll do it. In a minute." My body is cemented to the lounge chair. There is no graceful way to get up, and it feels good in the sun. I'm almost relaxed, the most I've been in weeks. Lily would like this, the warm afternoon, the soft grass, a quiet backyard filled with smells. But since the octopus took her sight, I can't trust her around water. A casual stroll across the yard could result in an unexpected dip in the pool.

Home life has been an adjustment, but we've managed. She has the layout of the house down from memory, but she can sometimes miss a doorway by a few inches or so. Our efforts remind me of the old Helen Keller joke: How do you punish Helen Keller? *Rearrange the furniture.*

Doogie was not surprised to hear of Lily's blinding, although there wasn't anything he or his staff could do to bring her eyesight back; our options are as bleak as ever. Instead, he said to pick a spot in the house to call "home base." When Lily gets disoriented I'm to place her there, always facing the same direction, and say out loud, "Home base!" It's like pressing a reset button to instantly orient her again. I always feel stupid doing this (*Marco! Polo!*), but it seems to work and Lily responds with appreciation. Slowly, we're figuring this out.

How did Helen Keller meet her husband? *On a blind date.* Why was Helen Keller's leg wet? *Her dog was blind, too.*

Over in the grass near the deep end, Weezie slaps around an inflatable beach ball. She's easy to spot in her orange life vest made specifically for dogs. You don't usually associate English bulldogs with swimming, and she looks a bit out of place—like Winston Churchill at the beach. I turn my head just in time to see her swat the beach ball into the pool. She watches with dismay as it slowly floats out of reach. Her tongue falls limp and she pants, anxiously begging for the ball to float back her way. It doesn't, and just as well. If she had been able to get her teeth into it, that would have been the end of the ball.

"Where do you get your pool toys?"

Trent groans. He turns his head away from me, knocking the sunglasses completely off his face.

"Your pool toys. Where do you get them?"

"This place on Ventura." He rolls over onto his back. "I thought you were making more drinks."

"Do you think they have sharks?"

"Sharks?"

"Inflatable sharks."

Trent thinks for a minute. "They have . . . dolphins."

I mull this over before deciding dolphins won't do. The octopus won't fall for dolphins. "I need them to be menacing. I need them to be sharks."

"Paint teeth on them."

"It's not just the teeth, it's the blowholes."

"What do you need them for?"

"For the octopus."

Trent props himself up on his elbows, fishes for his sunglasses, and puts them back on his face. He looks at me. "You're buying that thing presents now?"

"Not presents. Impediments. Octopuses are afraid of sharks."

"Are they." Trent shakes his head and swats his arms wildly at nothing in the air. He's fearful of bees and swats at the air a lot, even when I don't see any bees.

"Never mind. I'll go make us more drinks."

I grab his glass and mine and head for the kitchen. The pool deck is hot and I have to move quickly to avoid burning my feet. Before stepping inside, I catch my reflection in the sliding glass door and it stops me cold. I can feel the concrete burning my soles and I don't care. My vision, compromised from the sun and the afternoon drinking, registers a reflection that is foggy and hazed. Despite the soft image of my mirrored self, I make out a clear harshness to my face, a disheveled quality to my appearance. I squint and take a step back. There's almost a double reflection now. Instead of two arms and two legs I have four arms and four legs. *Eight.*

I am becoming someone I don't recognize.

I am becoming harder, meaner, wilder.

I am becoming the octopus.

3.

I reach into the paper bag containing six cookies and three napkins, pull out an M&M cookie, and take a bite. It's warm from the bakery's oven, or from sitting on my dashboard on the car ride over here, or who really cares. All I know is if I have to spend another Friday afternoon in this soft, buttery hell, I am going to eat cookies, and lots of them.

I do not offer one to Jenny.

"What are those?" I eyeball the stack of oversized cards in Jenny's hands skeptically.

"I thought we'd try something different today."

"I don't like different." Not right now—certainly not with Jenny.

Jenny nods, but plows forward anyway. The size and shape of the cards reminds me of the sewing cards I used to do with Meredith when we were kids. I liked a lot of Meredith's toys more than my own, especially her stuffed animals and anything to do with crafting. One Christmas she received a kit to make animal finger puppets and she just handed it over to me. I wish

I had one of those finger puppets now, as I have a particular finger in mind for Jenny.

"Are you familiar with the Rorschach test?"

"Isn't everyone?"

"Is that a yes?"

Dammit, Jenny. I take another bite of cookie and speak with my mouth full. "Inkblots."

"Have you ever taken this test?"

"No. And I don't know why I'm about to now."

"It can help me learn about your emotional functioning, thinking processes, internal conflicts, if you're experiencing any kind of underlying thought disorder . . ."

"Like thinking there's an octopus on my dog's head? That kind of thought disorder?"

"That's not what I said."

"That's what you meant."

"That's not what I meant."

"Because I showed you a picture!"

Jenny leans forward in her chair and attempts to sweep aside my concern with an innocent gesture, but she loses her balance and does something that comes close to genuflection. "I thought it would be fun."

I fully realize I'm saying this as someone with his own form of Enclosed World Syndrome, and I realize I'm saying it to someone who knows this, but I can't stop myself from saying it anyway. "You really should get out more."

Jenny smiles and bangs the cards on the table with a certain flair, the way a croupier in a James Bond movie might before cutting the deck. But Jenny doesn't cut the deck, she just hands me the one on top. "Why don't we just get started?"

I hold the last of the cookie between my teeth, shake the

crumbs off my hands, and take the card, turning it first left, then right. I haven't quite figured out if I'm dealing with Old Jenny or New Jenny today, so I decide to just go along. I can practically see my imaginary better therapist encouraging me to participate.

What do you have to lose? he says.

What do I have to gain? I ask in return.

I study the card. Mostly it looks like an inkblot, but when I turn the card upside down I finally see it. "It's the octopus," I say with cookie still between my teeth, crumbs falling down my front. I'm reminded of something a friend who works at the White House once told me about the journalist Candy Crowley always having crumbs on her bosom from eating. I don't know why I think of this other than that I feel like a reporter under rapid fire, doing my best to report what I see.

Jenny turns the card back around so that she can see it, too. "Most people say *bat*, or *butterfly*."

I take the cookie out of my mouth. "Most people would be wrong, then. That's the octopus. I mean, it's sort of a view from above. What he looks like when you're looking down on him, which is what I'm doing most of the time, because he's on top of a dachshund, and dachshunds have short legs."

Jenny looks at me skeptically to see if I'm putting her on. I can see that she wants to ask if I'm taking this exercise seriously. I think I need to put us both at ease.

"Did you know that Hermann Rorschach was hot?"

"Excuse me?" she asks.

"The inventor of this test." My intent is to catch her off guard. Maybe turn the tables a bit.

Jenny sets the first card down on the table between us and sinks back into her chair. "No, I know who Hermann Rorschach is."

"Oh. Well, he was hot. Like crazy next-level Brad Pitt kind of hot. I had to research him once for this writing project I was doing. Turns out he died at the age of thirty-seven. Of peritonitis."

Jenny looks at me and jots down a few notes on her pad. Maybe my knowing this is more telling than what I saw in card number one. Maybe she's writing down the word *peritonitis* to remind herself to look it up later. I mean, she probably knows what it means, but this is the problem when you have a name like Jenny. People like me tend to assume that you're dumb.

"Anyway. You should Google him." I reach into my bag for another cookie. Cinnamon sugar this time. Normally they're not my favorite, but I'm in the mood for one today.

"Let's just continue with the second card." Jenny hands me a card similar to the first one, but with the addition of four red splotches. "What do you see?"

This time I don't have to study it. I see it right away. "That's the octopus. Four of his arms dripping in blood."

Jenny purses her lips. "Where is the blood coming from?"

I refuse to answer this. Instead, I just shrug and brush excess cinnamon off my cookie and it gets on my shirt and I have a sudden sympathy for Candy Crowley. I can see peripherally that Jenny is scratching more notes on her pad. Maybe she's deciding whether to press me for more. If she does, she won't get anything.

"Try this one." She hands me a third card; this one also has splotches of red.

"Cockroach."

"Not octopus?"

"You can't ask me leading questions like that. That's tester projection."

"I'm just making sure," Jenny says.

"What I see is a cockroach." I pause for a bite of cookie before adding, "Known in some circles as the octopus of the land."

Jenny tosses her pad down in frustration and leans forward in her chair. She rests her chin in her hands and her pen makes a small blue mark on her cheek. "What circles would those be?"

"Some circles." I really don't know the answer. "Among entomologists, perhaps."

Jenny sighs.

"Look. Let me save you some time." I pick up the stack of remaining cards. "This is the octopus hang gliding. This is the octopus after I pry it free from Lily and sizzle its brains with an electric cattle prod. This is two Tinker Bells kissing." I pause for a moment and pull the card close to my face, but sure enough, that's what I see. This time it's me who makes a mental note. That's of some concern. The rest of the cards are in color. "That's the octopus in the ocean pouncing on some unlucky prey, that's the coral reef where I imagine the octopus lives, and that's two seahorses holding up the Eiffel Tower." I toss the cards down onto the table. "I may have missed one."

Jenny doesn't like it when I'm such a smartass, so I open my bag and hold it out for her. "Cookie?"

She glares at me for a moment, and then I see her face soften and she reaches into the bag and pulls out a chocolate chocolate chip. "What the hell."

"C'mon, Jenny. You know as well as I do that this is pseudoscience."

Jenny takes a bite of her cookie, then rests it in her lap. "These are good." She reaches for the discarded stack of cards and puts them back in order. "Rorschach testing has been widely criticized for certain purposes, but it's still a pretty good indicator of anxiety." She looks me straight in the eyes. "And hostility."

"He blinded her." I just blurt it out. What I want to say is, *Of course I'm anxious, of course I'm hostile,* but when I open my mouth, that's what comes out instead.

"Lily? Who did?"

I tap my finger pointedly on the first card, which is sitting on the top of the stack. "I have to act, and I have to act now, and I have no viable options, medically at least, and every hour that passes I hate myself more and more for being so incapable, so helpless, so trapped in a cocoon of the octopus's spinning."

"Do you have nonmedical options?"

I shrug. I know I set myself up for that question, but I don't like any of the possible answers. Love? Scented oils? Prayer?

"Analytically speaking," Jenny continues, "cocoons aren't necessarily about entrapment. They can be symbols of growth, of transformation, of metamorphosis."

I think of my double reflection, the one I saw outside in Trent's backyard. I reach into my bag of cookies for another but withdraw empty-handed, and instead I crumple the bag, smashing the remaining cookies to crumbs in my fist, and throw the whole mess on the floor.

To Jenny's credit, she remains unfazed. "Why don't we run through these cards again. This time you can give me real answers, and we can maybe determine something about your emotional functioning and response tendencies."

She reaches for the deck without breaking eye contact. We stare at each other resolutely.

I will give Jenny the answers she wants; I don't have any more time to waste arguing with her. I'm really using this hour for something else. I'm using all my hours for another purpose. For letting the anger take root in my cocoon.

It's perhaps the oldest trope there is, but in this moment there's no denying its core truth:

To defeat my enemy, I must become him.

I look at the bag of cookies, burst and spilling crumbs on the rug.

A sea change is coming.

4.

I visit four different pool stores before I find inflatable sharks that will suffice. I purchase six of them even though they're not exactly as I pictured. They have two handles on either side of the dorsal fin—I guess to make it easier for children to ride them. Also, their mouth openings are painted red where gnashing teeth should be, which should suggest they're hungry for blood but instead make them look like they're wearing lipstick (if sharks even have lips in the first place). They are the right size, though, and should fulfill their intended purpose nicely.

Lily is asleep when I get home, so I decide to inflate the sharks in the backyard. Blowing them up takes some effort in the heat, and after inflating one, and half of another, I feel light-headed and unsure of my plan and need to sit down. I look at the sharks, one at full attention, the other slumped at half-mast, as if it were suffering from some sort of palsy, and it occurs to me that Lily would have enjoyed these in her youth. Enjoyed destroying them, as she destroyed all of her toys except red ball. When she was a puppy, my dad's wife had given her a stuffed monkey toy with these oversized orange arms. One day I noticed one of those arms was missing. I searched the house high and low, but it was nowhere to be found. It wasn't until the next day while walking her with a friend that the arm made a dramatic return.

"Oh my god, what's wrong with your dog?"

I turned to find Lily crouched as she does, an orange monkey hand, then arm, making its way out of her like some sort of hernia exam in reverse.

"Oh. That happens," I said, lying, crouching with a plastic bag to pull the rest of it out of her, a magician doing the most disgusting magic handkerchief trick.

In the little storage space under the house I find an old bicycle pump that belongs to my landlord, and after a few false starts I use that to inflate the remaining sharks. Finished, I sit in a semicircle with my new menacing friends like we're at the oddest tea party this side of Wonderland. "No room! No room!" cries one of the sharks, playing both the Hatter and the March Hare. Of course, he's wrong. There's plenty of room, as we're sitting in the empty yard.

"We're a team, you and I," I tell the sharks. "Normally we have only each other as enemies, but today we are hunting octopus. Together."

"Octopus?" another of the sharks exclaims, before they all start talking over one another, making it difficult to hear.

"Guys, guys, guys! Only one of you talk." I look around the circle to see who they will elect to speak. It's the one sitting next to me on my right.

"Sure. We could eat some octopus."

"Here's the thing. Now, this is important, so listen up." I look around the circle to see if any of the sharks have ears, which they don't, at least not that I can see. "Do you guys have ears?"

"We have endolymphatic pores." It's the shark across from me now. "They are like ears."

"Where?"

The sharks kind of bow down. "Here," one says. "On top of our heads." It makes me feel powerful to have all these sharks bowing in front of me. I can just make out these so-called pores near where the plastic handles are attached.

"Good. Now, listen up. The octopus is stuck to a small dog."

"Dog?" they exclaim, and start talking over each other again. "Canine." "Mongrel?" "Pooch!"

"Guys!"

The shark next to me remembers his role as elected speaker. "Sure, we could eat some pooch." Murmurs of agreement and consensus.

"*Do not eat the pooch!*" I clap my hands together loudly and repeatedly to grab their attention. One of them covers his hearing pores, or whatever, with his fins. I wait until I have their attention again. "Do not eat the dog. That is what I'm saying. You may eat the octopus. But I am trusting you to *not* eat the dog. Does everyone understand?"

I survey the circle and the sharks nod their agreement.

I repeat. "*Does everyone understand?*"

"Yeah!"

"Yeah!"

"Sure!"

"Yeah!"

"Octopus!"

"Dog."

"*No dog!*"

"No dog."

"Good!"

I wonder what I've gotten myself into.

I tiptoe inside, carrying the sharks two at a time, and I place them around Lily's bed so they'll be the first thing the octopus sees when he wakes up. It's a horrific sight. Imagine waking up to a shiver of red-lipped sharks grinning from ear to . . . well, not ear. Endolymph . . . whatever . . . pores. Never mind, that's a bad example, but you get the picture. I hope it literally scares the octopus to death.

When everything is set up, I call for Lily with a quick whistle. She lifts her head and shakes her ears and when she stops she stares through the sharks, unfazed. She can't see them. The octopus, however, screams.

"*Aaaaauuuuugggghhhhh!*"

He covers his eyes with two of his arms.

I bite my lip with anticipation. Will he have a heart attack? Will he just die of shock? Will his eyes turn to Xs like in a cartoon while his mouth goes slack?

"Just kidding, governor," the octopus says, dropping his arms back down to their resting place on Lily's head. "Nice pool toys."

"Those aren't pool toys, they're sharks. Real sharks! Right, guys?"

Instead of murmuring their agreement, this time they all lie silent. In fact, one tips over on its side. Not very menacing. The jig, sadly, is up. "How did you know?"

The octopus shakes his head. He can't believe how pathetic I am. "They smell like condoms."

"How do you know what condoms smell like?"

"Oh. Lily and I got in your goodie drawer. I tried a few on." I look down at Lily, wondering how she could be such an unwitting accomplice. How she could possibly ever team up with this monster. But she's blind and trusting and sweet, and he may be steering her in ways beyond her control. As if to underscore this new reality, Lily stares blankly into the void. "By the way, there were only nine left in the box and I used eight, so . . ."

"And you smelled them?" I'm incredulous.

"Our smell sensors are at the ends of our arms. Kind of hard not to."

I look down at the sharks lying limply at my feet. "I, too, can command the sharks, sir!" I wonder if Cate Blanchett ever said that. To the sharks I yell, "Get him!" I point at the octopus, but nothing. I'm so enraged that I pick up one of the sharks by the dorsal handles and throw it right at the octopus. I yell again. "*Get him!*"

The shark bops Lily in the nose, and she mistakes the command as being for her. She springs to life, running in circles, bumping into inflatable sharks at every turn. She wrangles one by the caudal fin and swings it around like a wrestler slamming a mismatched opponent. The other sharks make a safety bumper for her mania, and she can run every which way in her hunt to bring the one unlucky shark to its demise and I don't have to worry about her running headfirst into the stove. This is a first since the octopus blinded her, her having this much fun and my allowing her to have it without constantly interfering to redirect her away from injury.

Finally her teeth puncture the luckless fish, and it slowly starts to deflate. Lily lies in wait until just enough air has been expelled from its tail, then pounces. She lands between the dorsal handles and her weight slowly presses the air out of her prey, the shark's creepy red smile melting into a grimace. It occurs to me that to Lily, the inflatable sharks do not smell like condoms. They smell like red ball did when it was new. They smell like adventure. They smell like fun.

The octopus laughs, and I'm still angry. But I also can't help but feel joy at watching Lily prance and play. There is still vitality inside of her. There is still grace and jubilation and puppyness and wonder.

I take a seat in order to fully appreciate her frivolity, her silliness. This may be the last time I see it in her. The last time I appreciate it myself.

We are both transforming.

5.

Lily yawns and stretches awake from her afternoon snooze and struggles to get down from my lap. I place her gently on the floor by my feet; she looks bothered by something, and I'm about to carry her to home base ("Home base!") to re-orient her when she scrambles up my leg and starts humping. This hasn't really happened before—maybe once or twice in the manic hysteria of puppyhood, but that seemed less sexual and more a function of uncontainable joie de vivre. This, how-ever, is uncomfortable in its single-mindedness of reproductive purpose.

"Lily, stop that."

I'M! HUMPING! YOUR! LEG!

She grabs my leg tighter with her front paws, doubling down on her thrusting.

"Lily. No! You're female!" Meredith would murder me for bringing gender into this. Why can't girls—dammit—*women* be sexual thrusters? I have to shake my sister's voice from my head as I pry Lily off my leg. It's hard at this angle to pull her free, but I get my hands around her chest and yank. Finally Lily's front paws release like Velcro and I lift her back up in my lap.

"What was that about?" I ask.

Lily shakes her head and her ears flap and she licks her chops. "What was *what* about?" She is as bewildered as I am.

The octopus opens an eye and says, "That was embarrassing."

"No one is talking to you." I say it as dismissively as possible, hoping he'll go dormant again.

Lily turns three times and then plunks down in my lap with a sigh.

Puppies sighing.

"She can't help herself anymore. It's Freudian."

"Freudian?"

"Sigmund Freud? He was known as the founding father of . . ."

"I know who Sigmund Freud is!" I realize now how obnoxious I sounded when I tried to explain to Jenny who Hermann Rorschach was. "We share the same birthday." I don't know why I say that last part, why I engage the octopus in further conversation, but it's true and I just blurt it out.

"Tauruses," the octopus says with a shrug.

My phone rings. I can hear it but I can't see it. "Why do *you* know who he is, is a better question."

I spot my phone peeking out from under an accent pillow on the couch and I answer it just as the octopus says, "It's true that most octopuses are Jungians."

I can't take it anymore. "*You're so full of shit!*" And then, into the phone, "Hello?"

"Did I catch you at a bad time?" It's my mother.

"No."

"Who were you talking to?"

"You wouldn't believe me if I told you."

I can tell my mother is not satisfied with my response and my evasiveness will obstruct any real conversation.

"Religious people at my door. Jehovah's Witnesses." This seems more satisfying, although I probably would never have the courage to tell a Jehovah's Witness they were full of shit. I heard a rumor that Prince, a known member of the religion, has been spotted going door-to-door in my neighborhood to discuss the faith. I can't chance yelling at Prince.

"You should live in the country. They never come out this far."

Lily looks up at me expectantly, so I place red ball on the floor by her feet. "Why are you calling?" I realize how rude it sounds as soon as it's out of my mouth.

My mother sighs. "I haven't heard from you in a while. I was wondering if you were okay."

"I'm fine, Mom. Just busy." That much is not a lie.

"Did you hear Meredith's news?"

"Pregnant?"

"Isn't it wonderful?"

"She's a good mother," I say. Red ball glides under the couch and I get down on my knees to retrieve it. Lily, tail wagging, is facing the opposite wall.

"What does that mean? *Meredith* is a good mother." I can tell by her tone she thinks maybe I'm implying that she was not.

"What does it mean? It means she's a good mother. That's all. She's a good mother, you're a good mother. Everyone is a good mother."

"Well, not everyone." It sits uncomfortably in the air as we both know her own mother was not. I wonder how often she was chasing her own mother's affection while I was chasing hers. I picture us both running on a circular track with no beginning and no end. "You used to call me on your dog walks. About this time of day. And then you stopped."

I watch Lily sniff around for red ball, even though I placed it right in front of her face. "We don't go on as many walks anymore."

"Why?"

The octopus looks up at me, grinning. "Yeah. Why?" he repeats.

I clench my fist and take a step forward, drawing back for the punch. "You stay out of this."

"Excuse me?" my mother says.

"Not you. Not you," I assure her. I want to kill the octopus, now more than ever.

"Ted, is there someone else there?"

"Lily went blind, Mom."

"What?"

"She lost her eyesight." The explanation sounds dumb to me, like maybe she just misplaced it.

"How?"

I glare at the octopus. How much of this do I want to get into? "It's just, she's getting old."

The octopus looks up at me and rolls his eyes. "Pussy."

I swat at a stack of magazines on the coffee table, and a *Travel + Leisure* and *Entertainment Weekly* sail onto the floor. "She's getting older and I don't really like to talk about it. But we don't go for as many walks anymore."

"I think you should come home."

"No. Mom. It's fine."

"Not because of . . ." My mother trails off and I finish her sentence silently with *Lily*. "Meredith is coming up with the family next month; it's been a long time since we've seen you. You should think about coming home."

I tell her I will think about it without making any promises, and when I hang up the phone I wonder how long it has been since I have been home. Jeffrey and I used to travel to Maine every summer. We would go to the beach and eat lobster and fried clams and I would kayak with my mother while he would read on the riverbank, and then we would all sit on the deck of my mother's house and drink rosé. It all seems like someone else's life now.

But when was the last time my mother came to visit me here? I remember a trip she made, soon after Jeffrey and I broke up. She came for the weekend, almost spontaneously. Very unlike her. I don't know if I've actively pushed this visit from my memory, or it just got lost in the fog of that time. But my mother's last words on the phone just now ring familiar: "I know you think I don't worry about you, but I do."

I glance over at Lily and the octopus is laughing at me. He's still amused by Lily humping my leg. "*Jungian*. You're such an asshole," I gripe.

"We were just conversing."

"We are never just conversing. You converse, I plot your death."

The octopus chuckles. "How's that going?"

"*Give me back my dog!*"

Red ball rolls into the dining room and Lily ambles after it, taking the octopus with her. I think about what the octopus was getting at, float through Freudian ideas like free association, transference, and libido, until I land on Oedipal complex.

But why does he think Lily suddenly suffers from a desire to sexually possess an opposite-sex parent, at least strongly enough to hump my leg? And what of the call from my own mother—whose love I pursue—right in the middle of the discussion? Coincidence? I sink back onto the couch. It has to be because Lily is blind. Oedipus blinded himself; the octopus blinded Lily. But am I blind to something, too? What is it I cannot see?

I need to accelerate my transformation.

6.

The guy in line in front of me has the hottest tattoos I've ever seen on a man. There's a half sleeve of Japanese water imagery in the style of Hokusai that I imagine extends over his shoulder, as well as the most beautiful tiger on his opposite forearm that's almost serpentine in the graceful way it drips from his elbow to his wrist. It's hard to describe; you'd really have to see it to get the full effect.

"Can I ask you a question?"

The man turns around with a smile. If there was ever anyone's word I was going to take on a tattoo artist, it would be this guy's. Even though he's just some guy in front of me at the supermarket buying Soyrizo, mangoes, lighter fluid, and craft beer.

"I'm going to grill the mangoes," he says, his smile turning wry.

"No, no, no," I stammer. "Who does your ink?" I wonder if calling it *ink* makes me sound cool or ridiculously stupid.

"Are you thinking of getting marked up? You've got to see Kal. He has a real philosophical approach."

Philosophical approach to what? That would be a natural follow-up question, but instead I just say, "Thanks, man," when he gives me the name of Kal's parlor, and we go about our grocery transactions in silence while I try to imagine him shirtless.

I'm still not sure what a philosophical approach means in this context—philosophical approach to the whole thing? The artistic process? Pain management? I really have no idea. I don't know why it's appealing, or even why I would want this. But I do. So I take the mango griller's recommendation and call and make an appointment, and now here I am, parked on the street in front of a window with imposing designs, afraid to get out of the car.

What I'm doing at a tattoo parlor is a little unclear even to me, even to someone determined enough to ask for a recommendation from a stranger. Since the octopus blinded Lily with ink, I've harbored a growing obsession with getting marked by ink myself, creating a concord between us. Call it sympathy, unanimity, or the desire to mastermind a fraternity with only Lily and me as members, denying the octopus the opportunity to pledge. I've flirted with the idea of a tattoo before, but felt I lacked the occasion. This time is different. I feel much more like a soldier getting tattooed in wartime, with an almost ritualistic desire for body modification to mark solidarity to outfit and country. It feels like the rite of passage I need, except I'm not fighting for country and I have no outfit—only one comrade—in this war. I thought of getting Lily's birth date as my tattoo, perhaps coupled with the day we met—the day I fell in love—but a run of numbers on my arm seemed too evocative of another kind of war tattoo—the markings of war prisoners. One day it could become something to wear with pride, the hallmark of a survivor, but this war is too far from over to take that chance. Still, as I wait here for my appointment, my sitting with the artist named Kal with a philosophical approach, I'm almost giddy to enter this fraternity with Lily, even excited for the pain of the needle.

Excited to wear the mark of a real man.

With a few deep breaths, I gather the nerve to get out of my car and enter Kal's shop. The lobby is painted a stormy ocean green, and it's decorated with worn black leather furniture that still gives off an intoxicating animal smell. On the walls are photos of tattoos, I suppose ones with their origins here. There's no wall of suggested designs. It makes me feel like I've found the right place, like I'm not going to be modified in some cookie-cutter way that makes my attempt to stand apart backfire, making me even more identifiable as a part of the proletariat. A receptionist who looks like a younger, less angry Janeane Garofalo directs me to another room behind a velvet curtain. I have an appointment with the wizard. I hope he doesn't think me greedy when I ask for brains *and* heart *and* courage. I hope he is more than a fortune-teller scamming me and this tiny emerald city.

Kal is perhaps more tattooed than not and I find it immediately disarming, the amount of ink his body is able to absorb and, instead of looking marked, radiate empowerment back. He's handsome and slightly older and gray at the temples. Native American, maybe? But more like Native Canadian. Inuit or Eskimo. He cuts through my awkward attempt at a handshake with an encompassing hug.

"There is no real word for hello in Inuktitut," he says, "So we shake hands or hug."

"Hugging is good." At least it is when it's explained to me what the hug means.

Kal motions for me to sit on a stool. It's a slow day, and we talk for a while about life, about nature, about relationships—the ones that are fleeting and the ones that are not. I ask him about the tattoos of his that I find most interesting and he tells me the stories behind them. He can tell that I'm stalling, but he doesn't seem to mind.

"What's your favorite thing about tattoos?" It's such an amateur question, something a third-grader might ask while interviewing him for some school project, although I don't know what school would assign a project on tattoo artists. Maybe a charter school, or a Montessori.

"Their permanence," Kal says.

"But now there's laser removal."

Kal shrugs. "It still leaves a scar. Like a ghost." He looks deeper into me than anyone has in a long time.

"But eventually we die, and the flesh rots away."

Kal smiles at me with unwavering eye contact. It's unnerving, or at least I am unnerved.

"Let me guess, people leave ghosts, too."

"You're scared. That's normal for first-timers."

I don't recall mentioning that this is my first time, and I'm fully clothed, and so he can't possibly see that I am unmarked, but he knows. "I'm scared. But not about the needles or the pain or regret."

"About what, then?"

"About memorializing someone who isn't gone. That I'm giving up the battle. That I'm surrendering in war." I can hear Jenny tell me to say what I really mean. I carry my thesis further. "Afraid of death, I guess. And, maybe for the first time, of my own mortality."

"Death is a unique opponent, in that death always wins."

Kal offers a small hiccup of a shrug, as if this is of little significance. "There's no shame in surrender when it's time to stop fighting."

"Comforting." I say it sarcastically, but I'm not sure sarcasm is a language Kal speaks.

"Isn't it?" Kal asks. I don't think he's without a sense of humor, but he's completely serious here. I laugh, but in that nervous way you do when you can't think of something to say. Kal opens a drawer and pulls out a Polaroid and hands it to me.

"What's this?"

"The last tattoo I did. I don't like to do quotes. Not much challenge in them for me as an artist. But I like this one, and we were able to do it in an interesting way."

I look at the photograph. Across a guy's rib cage are scrawled the words "To die would be an awfully big adventure."

I recognize it immediately. "Peter Pan."

"J. M. Barrie," Kal corrects. "Peter Pan isn't real."

"Isn't he? I always thought Peter Pan was death. An angel of death who came to collect children."

Kal raises an eyebrow. "You're darker than I thought."

"I didn't used to be." I am transforming.

"What is death? Is it the end of photosynthesis, chemosynthesis, homeostasis?" Kal has the rhythm of a poet. "The last heartbeat? The last cell generation? The last breath of air?"

"Maybe all those things."

He has a real philosophical approach.

"We don't know, do we? It could be the tipping point, the point in life when extinction is assured."

"If that's the case, isn't death the moment of birth?"

"Or conception, even."

"Your favorite thing about tattoos doesn't really exist." I look down at my feet. I'm almost embarrassed to have to point this out.

"Permanence?"

"Not really. Not if we're all past the tipping point."

"Permanence is a relative idea."

I smile. "What, really, is permanence anyway?"

Kal smiles, too. He gets that I'm being cheeky. "Let's not go too far down that rabbit hole."

"It's hard not to." But he's right, we could be here all day and all night. I look at Kal. Not that that would be so bad.

"If you spend your entire life trying to cheat death, there's no time left over to embrace life." He puts his hand on my shoulder and it is warm. "Don't be afraid. That's all I'm saying."

Kal's right. I'm done being afraid. Having ink, like the octopus, is the final step in my metamorphosis.

"Besides," Kal says. "I have a better idea."

"What's that?"

Kal opens a drawer, pulls out a sketch pad and charcoal, and sets them down on a drafting table. "Let's draw."

I smile the way I did as a child when receiving a fresh box of sixty-four Crayola crayons—unabashedly, showing all my teeth. I remember how much I used to love to draw, and I wonder why I don't do it anymore. I write, I guess. I draw with words. But when I see Kal's pad and charcoal, I'm overwhelmed with the feeling that it's not the same.

I use my words, my artist's charcoal, to describe to Kal what I'm thinking. He draws with an imperfect fluidity, pausing only occasionally to shade the drawing with his thumb, or brush the paper with the back of his hand.

He listens and nods and doesn't interrupt, and when I'm done speaking he looks at the drawing and his eyes get really big. Slowly he turns his pad around for me to see.

My heart stops. And then starts.

"Yes," I say.

It's perfect, alive with added detail and beautiful Inuit soulfulness I couldn't have even imagined sitting outside in my car. My fear is gone. There's a tingling in my skin, like I can feel the thousand needle pricks to come.

I am alive.

Kal picks up an ink gun and raises it to eye level. He's as excited as I am. His eyes sparkle, then squint as he prepares to do what he does. "Shall we begin?"

7.

My fingers hovered over the call button for so long I can't remember pushing the damned thing, and now that the phone is ringing, I'm having second thoughts about dialing. *Dial.* Why do we still say that? When was the last time anyone used a phone with a dial? It's midnight and I'm exhausted, and maybe a little delirious, I don't know. Dial. I associate that word more with soap than with telephones. Or maybe something more sinister. *Die-all.* And yet the phone is ringing, and the ring itself is mildly comforting. There should be some sort of number that you can call late at night just to hear a phone ring. No one would ever answer, but there would be the promise that someone was out there who would listen to you and all you had to say. *Ring.* Now, even that word is weird. How can it mean both the circles in a tree stump and the noise a telephone makes? *Dial, ring. Dial, ring. Dial, ring.* Just as I hear "Hello?" I hang up.

Well, damn. Now I've probably woken him up for the pleasure of having someone unceremoniously hang up on him, so I feel committed to calling him back. He answers on the first ring.

"Hey." It's Trent.

"Hey."

Long silence.

"What time is it?" He was asleep. He's trying to orient himself.

I think about how to phrase what I want to say. "Am I crazy?"

"Huh? Hold on."

I can hear him get out of bed, probably so as not to wake Matt. Lily is nuzzled into my armpit as I lie on top of the covers in my own bed. She's radiating heat like the sun, but as long as she's comfortable I'm not going to move. My sweat is cementing us together. I find the idea of adhesive, the idea of her being tethered to me, comforting. Trent shuffles into the other room. I can hear the squeak of a bedroom door closing behind him.

"Okay."

"I want to know if I'm crazy. I don't mean crazy as in silly, or even offbeat. I want to know if you think I'm certifiably insane."

Long pause.

"I don't think that. Do you think that?"

This time it's me who pauses.

"Sometimes."

"Well, I don't think that you are."

"There really is an octopus, you know."

Pause. "I know."

"He's taking her."

Trent sighs or yawns. "I know that, too."

We sit quietly for a moment. Trent is the only person I can be on the phone with and not feel pressured to speak. But I suddenly feel terrible for dragging him out of bed—his own bed, with his boyfriend and his healthy dog—to talk to me, in my bed, with an octopus and my sick dog, feeling so very alone.

It brings back this memory of when Lily and I had been together for maybe only a year and a half. It was November. The Leonid meteor shower was going to be spectacular that year; it wouldn't be that spectacular again until sometime like 2098, or 2131—a year when Lily and I were certain to be stardust ourselves. So I woke us up in the middle of the night, grabbed our pillows and a blanket, and spread them out on the back lawn. I snuggled her in close to me and we lay there looking up at the fire raining across the sky, though she never really understood why we would leave the warmth of our comfortable bed for this weak recreation on the cold, hard ground. I don't think she got the magic of meteors.

Trent speaks again, since I can't. "I don't know what I would do if I ever lost Weezie. The thought to me is . . . unfathomable."

But you will *lose Weezie,* I almost say. I no longer live in a world of ifs.

I think of Kal and the tipping point, the point where death is inevitable. Was he right? Is that tipping point actually birth, the beginning of life itself? We will lose everything that matters, or everything that matters will lose us. It is predestined, the nature of life. But I don't tell this to Trent. I don't see the point in dragging my friend out of bed to depress him.

"I used to think that way about Lily."

"And now?"

"Loss is no longer just an idea."

"Did you see that guy about the thing?"

"Kal. His name was Kal."

"Did you like him?"

"I did."

"Was he handsome?"

"Very."

"And?"

"You'll see. I'll show you."

Lily burrows her head deeper into my armpit, but in that way she does when she's using me to scratch her nose. In doing this, she raises the octopus toward me—only just the slightest little bit, but I flinch. I hate that I still flinch in his presence.

"I can't imagine losing Weezie."

"Don't think about that now." I'll be there for him when he does.

"You called wanting to know if I think you're crazy?"

"Yeah." That, and to escape debilitating loneliness.

"I think you need to do something big. I think you need to grab life and shake things up. Turn the whole world on its head. Stop playing the octopus's game." It's the Ferris Bueller in him talking. Over the years Ferris has become somewhat muted; I like when he bubbles to the surface. "You want to know what I think? I think maybe you're not crazy enough."

When we hang up I stare at the phone for a while, in that strange way you do when you stop taking technology for granted and suddenly you can't imagine how there was just a voice in there, talking to you, even if that voice couldn't fully understand you and what's happening in your world. I feel perhaps even more alone than before I called. Although I'm not alone. Not anymore. I can see the anger gestating inside me, growing exponentially, as surely as if I were holding a sonogram printout. It's about to erupt in unimaginable ways.

I lift Lily gently from her sleep and grab a blanket from the linen cabinet and we head outside. I lay the blanket out for us on the grass as best I can with one hand. There is no meteor shower to see tonight, so I turn on the strings of antique lightbulbs that hang decoratively over the yard, the ones I usually only turn on for barbecues and parties, the ones that make my backyard look like a festive catalogue page where plastic people live carefree lives. We lie on the blanket and look up at them.

"What are we doing?" Lily yawns and nuzzles into me again. The night air is warm and still.

"We're creating a memory."

"Why?"

I don't tell her why. The answer is I need it. I need this memory to hold on to if my plan fails and she is no longer there.

"Because sometimes it's nice to have memories. Don't you have any favorite memories?"

Lily thinks about this. "All of my memories are my favorite memories."

I'm amazed by this. "Even the bad ones?"

"Dogs don't remember bad memories." Envious, I scratch her on the velvet part of her chest. What an incredible way to live.

"We did this once when you were a puppy. We got out of bed and brought our blanket outside and we lay on the grass looking at stars."

"Are those stars?" Lily looks up at the shimmering lightbulbs, and even though she can't see, I wonder if she can make out just enough light to imagine them.

"Yes," I lie. "Those are stars. Their light has traveled for billions of years. Aren't they magnificent?"

Lily agrees, because she is small and she's a dog and to her even little things, even things she can't see, seem magnificent.

"We can go back inside in a bit."

Lily thinks about this. "No, this is nice."

"I'm glad you like the stars; we're going to be spending a lot more time underneath them." I pause before telling her my plan, or at least that the time for my plan has come. Trent has confirmed it for me. "We're leaving here soon, and I don't know if we're coming back."

"We're leaving here soon? Where are we going?"

I squeeze her tight in the way I do when I'm asking her to trust me, to follow me as we leave the only home she probably ever remembers.

Maybe you're not crazy enough.

"We're going on an awfully big adventure."

Death. Death is the awfully big adventure. But not this time. Not this adventure. The greatest adventure, our adventure, is the fight to live.

I place my hand over the clear plastic bandage that covers my tattoo. I was only supposed to wear it for a few hours, but I figured a few hours more wouldn't hurt. I peek underneath and see the tips of eight arms dangling to breathe.

I am done waiting. I am done being walked all over by a spineless intruder. I'm tired of fighting the fight on his terms. Trent was right. I haven't been crazy enough.

Haven't. Been.

That all stops now. I can feel the change surging inside me—in my nerves, in my organs, in my veins.

My transformation is almost complete.

8.

I'm able to navigate the streets of Chinatown with relative ease, relying on memory, even though I haven't been here since they closed the Empress Pavilion, a place I used to frequent for dim sum and celebrity sightings. I cruise the streets, trying to distinguish the fish markets from the groceries. I creep along slowly in the outside lane, but no one honks. There are a number of mom-and-pop stores along both Broadway and North Spring, but since the awnings are in Chinese (except for one, which may be a bodega), it's hard to tell which is what, so I nab a metered spot on Spring to continue my investigative errand on foot.

The Chinatown in Los Angeles is not nearly as chaotic (nor as Chinese) as the Chinatowns in New York and San Francisco. On a weekday afternoon it's easy to stroll in and out of stores, taking in their exotic contents. The fish market I come to first has nothing more exotic than Maine lobster and Dungeness crab. I think of asking if they have hidden inventory in back, but I'm afraid that they might sell some sort of illegal catch, like endangered sea urchin or poisonous puffer fish, and I don't want anything like that. I'm not *that* crazy.

The second place I try on Broadway is more to my liking. It feels less touristy, more authentically Chinese. I don't immediately see what I'm looking for laid out on crushed ice, but I have no problem asking the fishmonger. He has a kind and wizened face.

"I'm looking for octopus."

A kind and wizened face that looks back at me confused. I try to explain so that he doesn't inadvertently sell me some sort of Chinese goblin, a Mogwai, like in the movie *Gremlins*—something that will ultimately do more harm than good. But I don't know the Chinese word for octopus, so I hold up eight fingers, then invert my hands and wiggle them.

"Ahhh. *Zhāng yú.*"

He walks me to the end of the case and I see them lying motionless on the ice, a half dozen or so. They're far less menacing when they're dead.

"Hmmm." I make a show of studying them as if I'm looking for something very specific. "Do you have anything, I don't know, bigger?" I hold my hands farther apart for emphasis.

The fishmonger holds up his index finger for me to wait while he disappears into a walk-in cooler. The air-conditioning is working overtime, and the whole place is alive with an electric hum. The windows are yellowed with cellophane, giving everything a doleful pall. A few flies buzz near the doorway, but they steer clear of the fish. I wonder if they don't like the ice. An elderly Chinese woman looks at oyster sauces. We make eye contact and I offer a smile. She is nonplussed.

The man returns with a larger specimen, one that I think will do nicely. I nod and he smiles and wraps it up in waxy paper.

When he hands it to me I say, "There's one more thing I need."

The fishmonger looks expectantly at me. I nod to what I see behind him. He gestures at some prawns. I shake my head no. "That."

He turns around confused, until he sees what I'm pointing to: I want to buy his cleaver. Now he shakes his head. Not with disgust, but almost. Certainly profound disapproval. This is just like *Gremlins*. I can hear him say, "You do with Mogwai what your society has done with all of nature's gifts. You do not understand!" But instead of *Mogwai* I hear *octopus*. I doubt the octopus is a gift; if it is, it's a gift I'm hell-bent on returning.

I point again, insistently, and pull a small wad of twenties from my pocket. He looks at the money. After some hesitation, he pries the cleaver free.

When I return from my errand, Lily is sitting in her bed, awake, staring off in the direction of the stove. She doesn't hear me, but the octopus does. The paper package under my arm rustles as I enter the kitchen and my keys land on the table with a jingling clang. I place the package on the large cutting board by the sink, then pick up the cutting board and the package together and bring them to the table where the octopus can see. I cast a sideways glance back at Lily to make sure he's watching.

He is.

I fumble for a moment with the string that ties the package. While I often have difficulty with knots, this fumbling is mostly for dramatic effect, mostly so I can produce my new cleaver and bring it down with a thud on the string at the flatter end of the package. I can feel it sink into the cutting board. While I don't particularly want to sacrifice my good cutting board, the overall effect is without equal, so I can't help but not care.

We're leaving here soon anyway.

"What's in the package?" It's the octopus talking. Success. I have piqued his interest.

"Oh, you'll see."

I carefully undo the bundle and the paper makes an awful, rumpling sound. The smell hits me before I even have the last of it folded open. It hits Lily only a nanosecond afterward, and she rouses from her trance and her sniffer hits the air and she makes her way over to where I am, stopping only when she bumps into my shins. She plays her part perfectly, a stretch limousine to deliver this party's guest of honor.

"Seriously," the octopus says. "What's in the package?"

"You want to know?" I gnash my teeth into the most evil grin. "THIS."

I unfold the final flap of paper and hoist the dead octopus by its head. Juices drip from its flaccid arms onto the floor.

"Whoa," the octopus exclaims, and uses one of his arms to shield his eyes. "Is that what I think it is?"

"Yup."

"That's barbaric!" The octopus has no sense of irony.

"Yup," I say again.

"Oh, god, the smell. Who is that, even?"

I don't know its name; I never thought to ask the fishmonger if it ever had one. I look at the dead octopus, limp and gray. It has only a faded purple hue, like a dying violet. The color is the only thing about it, really, that even suggests there once was life in it.

"Iris," I answer. I look down at Lily, who is hungrily lapping up octopus drippings from the floor. I always did like naming things after flowers.

"Aw, man. I have an aunt Iris."

This causes me to cackle wickedly, like one of Shakespeare's witches. "Probably not anymore!"

When the hurlyburly's done. When the battle is lost and won.

I push the paper aside and slap the dead octopus down onto the cutting board. It lands with a moist and meaty splat. I pry my cleaver loose and bring it down hard on one of the arms, cutting off a good three inches.

The octopus screams.

Fair is foul and foul is fair: hover through the fog and the filthy air.

I toss the arm piece to Lily and it lands on the floor with a wet slap. Lily finds it almost instantly and gobbles it up with one bite.

"Stop! Stop! Stop! Are you crazy?"

I think about my new mantra. "Not crazy enough!" I pry the cleaver free of the cutting board and bring it down again, trimming a few inches off another arm.

"EGAD!" the octopus gargles with horror. I toss more of the dead octopus to Lily, who seems to be enjoying this as much as I am.

"I'm sorry, is this bothering you?" I ask the octopus, faking concern.

"Of course it's bothering me! Oh, gah! I can actually taste it through her skull." The octopus is turning green. "I think I'm going to throw up."

I shrug. "Be glad it's only your aunt."

Cleaver. CHOP. Toss a bite to Lily.

"What do you mean?"

I grab the cleaver and crouch low to look the octopus in the eye. Lily continues to cooperate by licking the floor where the octopus bits have landed. With her head bowed, the octopus and

I are face-to-face, eye-to-eye. *Mano a mano*. I hold the cleaver an inch from his face.

"Make no mistake, octopus. You leave tonight. You leave tonight or I will rent a boat and I swear to god, I will trawl the oceans with a fucking net until I catch everyone you love." The octopus looks up at me like I wouldn't dare. "And then I will come back here and I will chop them up and I will feed them to my dog and you can taste their stinking flesh."

To drive my point home, I stand up and firm my grip around the cleaver.

WHOMP!

"Your mother!" I toss a piece of octopus to Lily and she catches it before it hits the ground.

WHOMP!

Another piece. "Your father!" This one hits the floor with a splat and Lily is on it in seconds.

WHOMP!

"Your brother!"

"I don't have a brother!"

I snarl.

WHOMP!

"Your sister!"

"Stop it!"

"You got a wife? I've got all day! How about it, Lily—do you like this game?"

YES! CHEWY! HAPPINESS! MORE! SALTY! MEAT! FOR! LILY! PLEASE!

"Okay, okay, okay! You've made your point."

"You'll leave?" I wave the cleaver ominously in front of him.

"You said I have until tonight." The octopus remains sly to the very end.

194

Did I say that? I don't remember what I said. I'll have to find out if blinding rage—murderous rage—is a natural part of grief. Is it normal for me in this stage to want to make my enemies suffer, or have I gone irreparably too far?

I lock eyes with the octopus and tug at my shirtsleeve.

"What?" he asks.

I roll up the sleeve to slowly reveal my tattoo. Eight octopus arms hang from my bicep, and I can feel the octopus's eyes growing bigger. I pull up my shirt even farther, revealing Kal's work from the bottom up in dramatic fashion. Finally my shirtsleeve is up near my shoulder and my entire tattoo is revealed: a dachshund standing triumphantly on the head of an octopus.

"This is good-bye, you sonofabitch."

I flex, making sure the octopus drinks it in before striking the cleaver down on the cutting board with such force it shatters the board in two.

"*I AM THE OCTOPUS NOW!*"

The Pelagic Zone

The Law for the Wolves (continued)

When Pack meets with Pack in the Jungle,
and neither will go from the trail,
Lie down till the leaders have spoken;
it may be fair words shall prevail.
When ye fight with a Wolf of the Pack,
ye must fight him alone and afar,
Lest others take part in the quarrel,
and the Pack be diminished by war.

—Rudyard Kipling

Fishful Thinking

I have been preparing and packing for days, meticulously checking off items and tasks on a half dozen carefully constructed lists. Lily is still asleep when I zip the last of our bags closed; they lie stacked in a pile by the bedroom door, dwarfing Lily and maybe even me, waiting to be carried, first to the car and then onto our waiting ship. The supplies are daunting; there's no telling how long we'll be gone, how dangerous our voyage will be. Trent (despite his suggestion that I need to stop playing the octopus's game) has warned me that I am running from an obvious fate, and I understand his concern for us: This is a dangerous undertaking. I, on the other hand, feel like I'm in control for the very first time since this whole ordeal began.

I drink in the sight of my sweet gosling resting peacefully in the feathered nest of our bed's duvet. It's almost enough to make me want to crawl back under the covers with her. It has been two days since the octopus left. Without fanfare or good-byes, he just fled in the night. Disappeared, just as he promised he would when I fed Lily her gruesome meal. Without our unwanted visitor, it feels like we are in the calm eye of a storm. The waters are still and the winds have subsided and there's great beauty in the fragile peace, despite the promise of the storm soon to rage again.

Asleep like this, whiskered cheeks puffing with each gentle breath, Lily reminds me of her puppy self. The puppy who dreamed of badgers and beaches, of warm laps and wrestling and sunshine and hunting. I don't know if I've scared the octopus into permanent retreat, or where he has even gone. It almost doesn't matter.

Almost.

Neither Lily nor I can sit idly by hoping he doesn't return, perhaps this time with reinforcements. There's only one option that lies ahead for us. I place one hand on Lily's chest and, startled, she jerks awake. "Shhhhh. Shhhhh. Shhhhh," I say.

She looks up at me and yawns, her jaw squeaking like a hinge and her legs stretching horizontally for ground that isn't there. It takes her a moment to notice the stack of weathered oilcloth duffel bags creating a mountainous sculpture in the corner. With the octopus gone, she can once again see.

"What in the world?" Lily asks. I remember again her climbing into my suitcase as a puppy when I would haul it out of the closet to pack for a trip. A pile of bags such as this one must be confusing. Which one should she jump into?

"Those are our supplies."

"Those are our supplies for *what*?" She slowly sits upright on the mattress and shakes the sleep out of her head, ears flapping madly like wings.

"For our adventure." I scratch her on top of her head where the octopus used to sit. My touch is gentle, in case it's sore. It's good to feel her soft fur there again. "Remember? I told you. We're going on an awfully big adventure."

Lily turns and licks herself in an awkward place before asking, "Yes, but an awfully big adventure *where*?"

I look her square in the eyes. I want to protect her, at the very least not to startle her. But there's no benefit in soft-pedaling if she is to be my cocaptain on this voyage. "We're going on an octopus hunt."

It's still dark when Lily drags the last duffel bag down the few steps from the house to the curb with her teeth. I load them carefully into the car. Inside are clothes for me, to protect against the elements (including a cabled sweater I wear during Christmases back east because it makes me look like a fisherman); blankets for Lily, as well as a lifejacket, like Weezie's, sized just for her; canned goods and kibble; rawhide chews; a few books on sailing and the sea including works by Hemingway, Melville, and several by Patrick O'Brian; fishing nets and a harpoon; a compass; jugs of drinking water; matches; a deck of cards; Lily's red ball; three bottles of Glenlivet, aged eighteen years; and a harmonica—which I don't know how to play. The car full, we say good-bye to the house. It's hard; I didn't really think about this part in formulating my plan. Neither of us can say with certainty when (or if) we'll see our home again.

We drive the thirty or so miles to Long Beach. Despite the early hour the route is surprisingly populated with cars, but not enough to cause a delay. The drive is mostly silent, except for quiet wet sounds as Lily continues to lick herself. I wonder if in the course of this whole ordeal I've forgotten to give her her flea medicine. Nothing I can do about it now. On the plus side, there probably aren't many fleas at sea. The sun is just cracking the skyline when we reach the marina and I pull into the only available spot and stop the car. It sits underneath a sign that says No Overnight Parking and I can only imagine the stack of tickets that will greet us if we ever return.

Through some tough negotiating via telephone over the past two days, I've secured us the use of a trawler named *Fishful Thinking*. She presents herself at the end of the docks just as the morning fog is lifting, and I get my first real glimpse of her. The boat is not fancy and needs a fresh coat of paint, but she's sturdy, romantic even in her slight weariness, and she has logged time at sea. *Fishful Thinking* has a forward deckhouse, two masts—main and secondary—an aft working deck, and outriggers on either side that extend beyond the gunwales. Our lease is open-ended.

"Are you Ted?" The man who owns her is salty and gray; he wears a sweater like the one I've packed, but his is full of holes. Instead of a pipe, he smokes (or *vapes*, I guess) an e-cigarette, which surprises me, and I find the whole thing distasteful and inauthentic. I don't know why his poor lung health would be essential for a successful launch, but somehow in my head it is.

"I am. And this is she?" I ask, tapping my hand on the roof of the deckhouse.

"This be her." He helps me load our supplies belowdecks as Lily mostly sits back on the wharf and watches. She shifts her feet when the dock rocks underfoot as we carry the heavy bags. I let her sit and enjoy a quiet moment getting used to her surroundings. She will need to gain four sea legs, while I will only need two.

"Sure aren't packing light," the man says, his voice full of gravel and booze.

"No, sir. We aim to be prepared."

"What are you preparing for?"

I think about this. I've never been on an octopus hunt before, and since it's impossible to foresee all the potential dangers ahead, I choose my reply carefully. "For anything."

"There's only one of you, and the little one can't require much." He nods at Lily.

"We may be gone some time." The truth.

"Where you headed? Can I get that much out of you?"

I throw down a heavy duffel and it kicks up dust and we both cough. The man inhales deeply on his cigarette and his vapor cloud mixes with the dust before the air settles and I answer, "Out where the octopuses live."

The man looks startled and nearly drops the bag he's carrying, but he catches it at the last second and sets it down. I can hear the clink of glass bottles; it must be the bag with the scotch. His face takes on an apprehensive expression and he stands and twists, cracking the bones in his spine, his old sweater hanging loose and tattered off his frame. "The waters neither close to the bottom, nor near to the top, nor within reach of any shore."

"The pelagic zone." I've done my reading. "That's where our destiny lies."

The man nods. "What the Greeks would call the open sea."

I don't give a damn about the Greeks, but I smile anyway. I only care about one thing. "Will *Fishful Thinking* make it?"

The man takes another drag on his blue-tipped cigarette and sizes me up and down. He blows vapor into our tight quarters, our shared breathing space. "It's not the boat I'm worried about."

I look past the man just in time to see Lily appear on the steps that lead below the deck to where we are. She sits quietly and listens. I wonder if she overheard his concern.

"You don't need to worry about us," I say. "We're adventurers, she and I. This is nothing new. We may not look like much, but we are stout of heart. And we have a mission. The open seas don't frighten us." At least not as much as doing nothing, sitting home and waiting for the octopus, or worse, to return. I suppose we had a deal, a truce of sorts, but I'm confident he won't keep his end of the bargain, so why should I keep mine?

"The sea is full of things not seen, things that don't care how stout you've been." There's menace in the rhyme.

"It's exactly one of those things we are seeking." And oh, what I'll do to him when I find him.

The boat rocks gently in the harbor. Not far away, angry gulls are fighting over a scrap of food.

"Suit yourself," the man says. He can see that there's no changing our minds.

"We'll have her back safe," I say, rapping the walls of the boat with my knuckles. Made of solid bones, she echoes a sturdy reply.

The man takes another puff of vapor. "Either way. I have your deposit," he says, and cackles a smoker's laugh, full of phlegm and wheeze. He turns and heads for the deck before stopping. "How many tickles does it take to make an octopus laugh?"

Is he serious? In my experience, octopuses are foul creatures incapable of the lightness of laughter. Not knowing what else to say, I answer, "Does it matter?"

"Ten—tickles." The man guffaws until he almost chokes. He bends forward, almost in half, and braces himself on the rail. I tense up, worried I may have to perform CPR—I don't want to put my mouth anywhere near that old goat. Slowly, he gets himself under control and waves us off. "That's an old joke."

On his way up the stairs he pats Lily on the head, and repeats himself to her. "An old joke, that one."

The whole time Lily doesn't break wary eye contact with me.

When the man is gone, I do my best to deflect her concern. "Don't worry," I tell her. "I remembered to pack red ball."

She looks at me like I'd better have.

The Old Lady and the Sea

No matter which direction you look from our perch inside the deckhouse, there's nothing to see but sea. There's blue and there's gray and there's green, plus every combination those colors can make, and it's hard to spot the horizon. I can no longer tell what is water and what is the great expanse of cloudy sky. We're seventeen days into our journey and I wonder if we're still alive. The pelagic zone is unyielding.

Lily and I were game at first, keen for the adventure that lay ahead. But around day eight we succumbed to the lethargic nature of life at sea, to the monotony of it all. The deckhouse was closing in on us and could, in the extended days, roast as hot as an oven, the air fouled by our own perspiration and cooking flesh. (The one thing I forgot to pack was sunscreen, and we burned for days until we tanned.) Everything on the boat seemed coated with grime and salt. We took turns with the chores—scrubbing the deck, cleaning up after meals, steering, keeping watch for the octopus. I did most of the food preparation, mostly because Lily has no ability to stop herself from eating whatever rations she can get her paws on before it's even cooked. At night we traded the watch, sleeping in shifts so we always had two eyes on the water. That lasted three nights before exhaustion settled in and we curled up together, she in the nook behind my knees, the way we would always sleep at home. It was comforting for us both. I kept a logbook of our progress, detailed accounts of the days and how the time ticked by. At least I did at the outset of our journey. The last entry reads simply: *Daylight. Head W by S, distance 65 nautical miles. Winds light.*

On day six we saw lightning, and the swell rose with an advancing storm. We rode out the worst of it belowdecks playing Crazy Eights, but the game reminded me too much of the octopus and I quickly soured on it. I let Lily win two hands, and while shuffling the discard pile a second time I suggested we play War.

On day nine I took to carving some driftwood we picked out of the sea. I'd read in one of the books on sailing that whalers used to carve ivory and bone (and sometimes coconuts and tortoise shells) in an art they called scrimshaw. My knife would never have carved ivory or bone, and I don't know if I'd call what I did art, but I managed a pretty good likeness of a dachshund out of the driftwood. I told Lily it was her mother, Witchie-Poo, who would look out for us and keep us safe.

"My mother's name is Witchie-Poo?" she asked.

"Yes," I replied. "You know that."

Before two weeks were even out I was unrecognizable as my former self. I was desperate for a shower. My beard had grown out rough and scraggly, filled with salt, both in color and from the ocean air. My skin had burned and peeled and leathered. I caught a glimpse of my reflection in the deckhouse window and thought I was someone else. I don't think Lily would have recognized me, either, were she not here to witness my slow mutation.

"Your coat is mahogany," Lily told me. "Like mine." We both now have gray hairs under our chins.

On day fifteen I swallowed my fear and jumped off the bow and into the ocean. The water was shocking, then invigorating. I thought of the monsters below, of the octopus attaching itself to my leg and pulling me down to great depths, of my head exploding from the density of water, of drowning. But only for the briefest of moments. I felt too alive to die. It took a great deal of encouraging, but at sunset I talked Lily into a swim. I held her tight with two hands and close to my body, using my legs to kick and keep us afloat, and she paddled with her paws but mostly out of panic.

"I've got you, Monkey. And I'm never letting go."

Together we drifted, looking at the orange sky, clouds tinged with lava from an unseen volcano. I put my head back in the water, submerging my ears, and for the first time in days everything fell quiet. I kept one eye on *Fishful Thinking* so we wouldn't drift too far, but I let all of our other cares wash away. It felt like a baptism of sorts. Once we had been submerged in the ocean, we were protected by it. We were now pure.

It's now day seventeen. We've stopped putting tuna fish on bread or a plate and just eat it out of the can. It's easier that way, and there's less to clean up. I glance at Lily, who finishes her can first. She gazes stoically ahead. The light accentuates the gray on her neck and around her whiskers, and the little bit between her eyes. She is no longer young; she is no longer my girl.

"I think it's funny you packed canned tuna for an adventure at sea," she says, with only a modicum of judgment.

I look around at the nets and the trawlers and all the

gear that decorates *Fishful Thinking*. "Funny ha-ha? Or funny strange?"

She doesn't answer. I finish my meal and I gather the empty tins. We'll run out of canned tuna eventually and have to fish for our meals from the sea. But I don't tell her this. There's no need to play on her fears.

"How will we know when we find the octopus?" she asks again, studying the ever-changing ripples surrounding the hull.

I have only the answer I have given her each time she has asked this question before. I scratch her under the chin and the tags on her collar shake. "We'll know."

For the past two and a half weeks, despite the boredom, despite the monotony, I have thought of little else but the octopus. He will not allow us this deep into his waters and resist the urge to announce himself. He'll take our presence in his home as a personal affront, much the way I resented his presence in ours.

At night, when I have trouble sleeping, I steel myself for a great battle at sea. I picture this monster wrapping his muscular arms around our vessel, trying to pierce the hull with his beak while Lily and I try desperately to outmaneuver, fight back, and harpoon. It's nothing I haven't dreamed of doing to him in other ways. With surgery and radiation and pills. It's two to one, this fight, but I'm still not sure we're evenly matched. He has the advantage of the sea.

"And why are we hunting him again?" Lily asks.

I check the ship's compass and correct our course five degrees southwest. "It's the best chance we have of staying together."

Lily stands, turns around three times, then sits again. She does this when she's bored.

"Do you want to sing a song?" I ask.

"Not really," she replies.

"I could try my hand at the harmonica again."

Lily cringes, but remains polite. "No, thank you."

"We'll find him," I assure her. "It's just that the ocean is so vast."

"So is Los Angeles." To a dachshund, that probably seems equivalent.

"Not this vast."

I study our charts. If I'm reading them correctly, we're over a particularly deep trench. Something in me tells me the octopus is near.

Lily looks over the side of the boat and says, "It's a wonder he ever left all this to come and live with us."

I'd never given much thought to the octopus's motivations; the why of it all seemed irrelevant. But Lily's right. It is a wonder. "I hope the octopus has the same thought about us, right before we harpoon him through his fleshy head."

Lily blanches in a way that makes me question for the first time whether she's come to feel some sympathy for that parasite. Stockholm syndrome. Capture bonding. Whatever they call it. I hope she doesn't. I don't want that to be true. I don't want her to hesitate when it comes time for the kill.

The sun fades. We've made a habit of watching it sink below the horizon, and tonight is no different. We sit out on *Fishful Thinking*'s bow, me Indian style and her perched in the gap in my legs, and as the sun dips out of sight I say, "Going, going, going . . . gone." And then usually we make some kind of wish. It's my favorite moment of the day.

"What's the first thing you want to do when we get back home?"

Lily considers this. "I'm not sure I've thought about it."

Does she know something I don't? Or is this just part of her canine ability to live entirely in the present? Part of me doesn't want to know. "Well, I don't know about you, but I want to take a hot shower and sleep a good long sleep in our own bed. And have a slice of Village Pizzeria pizza with roasted red peppers and black olives and a cold Sam Adams beer."

The idea of it, of going home, piques Lily's interest. Even if she's not confident of it happening, even if it's only a game. "I'd like to have peanut butter in my Kong, I want to sniff around the backyard, and fall asleep in your lap when it's still." The rocking of the boat has been getting the better of us both.

"Good choices!" I say enthusiastically. A cool breeze sweeps across the deck of the boat, causing an eerie, almost haunted whistle.

"And I'd like a large bowl of chicken and rice, even though I'm not sick."

"Seasick, maybe," I say.

"Sick of the sea," she replies.

I nod. She means the chicken and rice I always make for her when her stomach is upset. I don't know why I don't make the effort more often, since she clearly loves it. I can't really make it for her here. We don't have any chicken.

Suddenly the stars appear, brilliant and sparkling, in all their majestic glory.

"Can I tell you something else?"

"Always," she says.

Immediately I say, "Never mind."

"No. What?"

I should never have said anything. I think about how what I was going to say would sound to Lily, about how it suggests a future without her, at the very least a future where it is no longer just the two of us. But I've opened my stupid mouth and I can't think of a plausible lie, so I feel compelled to finish my thought. "I'd like to fall in love again."

In the silence that follows, all you can hear is the rhythmic hum of *Fishful Thinking*'s engine. We're so far from shore there's not even the caw of a passing gull. I know this makes Lily jealous. The idea of my falling in love. She doesn't like to share my affection with anyone. I never explicitly told her that dogs don't live as long as people. I wonder, from her time with the octopus, how much she knows. I wonder if in the last few weeks she's contemplated mortality like I have.

"You will," she says. Then, almost as an afterthought, "I promise."

A shooting star zips through the sky and I point and yell, "Look!" but Lily doesn't turn fast enough to see it.

Scar Light, Scar Bright, First Scar I See Tonight

The light of a full moon streams through the opening at the top of the stairs, casting a bluish pall belowdecks. Maybe *pall* is too strong a word. Maybe it's the scotch and not the moon coloring my mood. Even so, I pour myself another two fingers. I should ration it more carefully, but right now it's a smoky salve I crave.

I undress Lily for bed, which means unsnapping the life jacket I've insisted she wear at all times since I first sensed the octopus nearby. She looks up at me as I do this, with an inquisitive expression.

"What?" I ask her.

"There's a patch, just under your chin, where your beard doesn't grow."

I feel under my chin. The coarse hairs are getting almost unruly and I separate them with my fingers, finding just the spot Lily mentions. I can feel smooth skin.

"Oh, that. That's a scar."

Lily is only momentarily satisfied with my answer. "What's a scar?"

"It's the spot that's left behind after the healing of a cut or a burn or a wound."

Lily considers this. "How did you get it?"

"When I was five I pushed my sister, Meredith, into the coffee table and she split open her chin. It was mean and careless and a dumb thing for me to do. I don't even remember why I did it, except I used to do a lot of things to Meredith because she was close to me in age, and often simply there. One time, I shoved a pink crayon up her nose and snapped it off. A doctor had to remove it with tiny forceps. Another time, I convinced her to rub an entire jar of Vaseline through her hair. She had to have a drastic haircut after that."

"None of that explains really how you got the scar on your chin."

I think about the point I am trying to make. "The best answer I can give you is that karma can be a bitch."

"What's karma?" Lily wants to know.

"Karma is the belief that a person's actions in the present decide their fate in the future. A week after I pushed Meredith into the coffee table, I fell in the bathtub and split my own chin open. And that's how I got this scar."

Lily mulls this over before saying, "I have a sister named Meredith."

"No," I correct. "I have a sister named Meredith. You have sisters named Kelly and Rita."

"And my mother's name is Witchie-Poo!"

"That's right." I take the Witchie-Poo talisman out of my pocket and place it over our bed. Lily hops up on the mattress and sniffs it.

"I have a scar," Lily says, turning around on the bed so that I can see the length of her back. She looks back at me with doleful eyes.

"Yes, you do. From surgery when you ruptured two discs in your back. You gave me quite a scare." I often wonder how much she remembers the experience, or if she's blocked most of it from her mind. I guess if she's aware of the scar on her back, the events have left her scarred in other, less obvious places.

I take off my pants, fold them, and put them aside. I've been wearing the same underwear for three days without taking the time to wash them. "See these here?" I place my bare leg up on the bunk. "These scars in my leg are from my own surgery when a doctor opened my leg to pull out several veins."

Lily makes a sour face. "Why did he do that?"

"Their valves had collapsed and they had no way to return blood to my heart. The doctor yanked them out like a bird pulling worms from the ground."

Lily blinks and lowers her head. "What about this mark over my eye?"

I grab her snout and lower her head even more. "That? That's nothing. A pleasure scar. You were chasing your red ball so diligently you ran headfirst into the stove."

Lily laughs as if even she thinks that's a dumb thing for her to have done. And then, as if by instinct, she scurries across the room and finds her red ball under the little table where we sometimes eat when we tire of looking at the sea. She hops up onto our bunk and drops the ball safely at her feet.

I hold out the index finger on my left hand as scotch laps against the sides of my glass like the ocean against our hull. There's a mark just above the knuckle that joins the finger to the hand. "This here I got battling you."

"Battling *me?*"

"That's right. I was putting groceries away and you snatched a chorizo sausage right out of my hands, chomping down on my finger in the process."

"I did?"

"You wanted that sausage so badly you wouldn't let up on my finger."

"What did you do?"

"I punched you in the snot locker and laid you among the bok choy. Just so I could have my finger back."

Lily shrugs. "I'm a sausage dog."

"I know you are."

Lily twists again. "What about this thing poking out the side of me here?"

I press on the side of her abdomen and feel her floating rib. "Oh, that. When you were a puppy you fell down a flight of stairs. The doctor thinks you broke a rib. I didn't know it at the time, but it must have healed funny. You scared me a lot when you were a puppy." I raise my glass and toast. "I'll drink to your floating rib."

Lily hops off the bed and over to her water dish on the floor. "And I'll drink to yours." She laps thirstily at the water. I don't bother explaining that I don't have a floating rib. I get where she's coming from.

Lily jumps back onto the bunk and asks, "Do you have any more scars?"

"Just on my heart. But only the figurative kind."

Lily looks like she's trying to figure that one out. Over the years, I've tried to explain about Jeffrey—about how he was there for six years and then suddenly he was not. How the yelling and the sadness and the quiet and the deceit were not how love was supposed to be. Even now, I'm not sure she entirely understands.

I sit down next to her on the bed and scratch behind her ears. "Did the octopus come to me because of karma?" she asks.

I'm taken aback by the question, and when I finally understand what she is asking, the whole thing is like a meaty punch to the gut. "No. No, of course not."

"But you said a person's actions in the present—"

I cut her off. "That's just it. *A person's*. Dogs, on the other hand . . . dogs have pure souls. Look at me." I grab her chin and look straight into her eyes. "Dogs are always good and full of selfless love. They are undiluted vessels of joy who never, ever deserve anything bad that happens to them. Especially you. Since the day I met you, you have done nothing but make my life better in every possible way. Do you understand?" Lily nods. "So, no. The octopus did not find you because of karma."

She nods again and I let go of her chin. I throw back the last of the scotch and set the empty glass down on the floor with a clunk.

"Shall we?" I climb into the bunk with her. Something is catching me not right under my back and I reach under the blanket and produce red ball. I set it on the floor next to the empty glass. I tap on the Witchie-Poo charm for luck and I blow out the candle in our lantern. Lily gives me a gentle kiss on my nose and I kiss her back in the groove between her eyes.

I don't tell her what I've wondered myself in the darker moments since our ordeal began: if the octopus, in fact, did come to her because of karma.

But not karma for her actions.

Karma, perhaps, for mine.

Midnight

I'm straddling Lily, punching her repeatedly in the snout and yelling, *"Die! Die! Die!"* Tears are falling from my face and my knuckles are searing with pain and the air is fire and my lungs and my heart and my everything burns. I don't remember anything but betrayal. The sharp realization that Lily is the octopus. That she has been deceiving me all along. I no longer know anything. I don't know where the boat ends or the water begins, where the water ends or where the sky begins, where the sky ends or near space begins, where near space ends or where the darkness begins.

Or where the darkness ends.

I don't know if the boat has capsized. I don't know if the bed has crashed to the ceiling, if the windows will burst and water will rush in, if we will drown. I don't know if the whole world is upside down, or just mine. I don't know anything except the pain of betrayal as I pummel my sweet dog in the face.

And that's when I wake up gasping for air.

I turn immediately to Lily, who is sound asleep. Her face is perfect, unmolested by violence. She is not the octopus. She could never betray me. It's not possible, it's not in her to do so. And yet the dream was so real, as if it were foreshadowing gloom. She looks so beautiful, so calm. I force myself to shake the feeling, but not before whispering, "Please don't ever die."

Which is an impossible request of any living thing.

There's a wetness by my side and I'm immediately afraid that the octopus is back, but the culprit this time is me, or more accurately the now empty scotch bottle I find by my side. I reach to wipe my eyes awake but miss and hit my nose.

That's when I realize I'm drunk.

Wash daily from nose-tip to tail-tip;
drink deeply, but never too deep.
And remember the night is for hunting,
and forget not the day is for sleep.

I don't know the rhyme or why that's in my head, or who said it or where it's from. Kipling? It doesn't matter. I just have the overwhelming feeling I'm breaking rules. Laws. Edicts. Things meant to be followed. Things not meant to be broken. Forces not meant to be tested.

Complete darkness falls over our quarters as the moon passes behind a cloud. As are we. Behind a cloud. We've lost sight of the journey, our purpose in being here. We are hunters, and the night is for hunting. And here we are drunk and asleep. If the octopus were to strike now, we would be easy prey. Pathetic. Ripe for the killing. How did this happen? How did I allow it to be?

I look at my sleeping love and silently beg her forgiveness. What have I gotten us into? She doesn't need this. She doesn't want this. She doesn't understand revenge. And while I prefer to think of our voyage as an offensive maneuver, there's no denying that's partly what this is. Revenge. *You weighed anchor in our waters, now we sail deeply in yours.*

I stumble out of bed in the way drunk people do, clumsily and with great kerfuffle. I stand up too tall and bang my head on the ceiling. I trip over the empty scotch bottle and it sends red ball scooting across the floor with a clang. Quickly I pick up the bottle to silence it. I look at Lily. If anything will wake her, it's the sound of red ball roaring alive to play and bouncing against the clapboard. Yet she sleeps soundly through it, a sign of our thorough depletion.

I climb the few steps up to the deck and let the night breeze wash over me. I inhale it deeply. The stars I can see number in the thousands; thousands more hang behind the clouds. The boat sways and I nearly lose my balance, so I lie flat on the deck and look up. I am so very small. Physically small, but also petty. Why am I driven more by revenge than by forgiveness?

I think about all the people I need to forgive.

Jeffrey? We loved each other, and yet love alone was not enough. Did he throw it all away with his indiscretions? Or was I never available enough in the relationship to keep his eye from wandering. In the end we were probably equally neglectful of what we had. So why was there so much anger when it was time to walk away?

My mother for not saying she loves me? We're too often guilty of thinking that our parents arrived on this planet as fully functioning adults on the day that we were born. That they don't have pasts of their own prior to our birth. That the father is not also a son, that the mother is not also a child. My mother had a tough beginning, enduring things I know little about. And yet I more often discount her pain and overvalue mine. This is suddenly funny to me, ridiculously selfish, and I laugh and the outburst is startling. I lie still as the sound launches skyward like a rocket, reaches the stratosphere, then quietly falls back to earth in the form of a quote I once read: *Yours is by far the harder lot, but mine is happening to me.* In this moment, I miss my mother.

The octopus? Does he merit my forgiveness? Was he just doing what octopuses do? Would I blame the lioness for taking down the gazelle? Or should I blame the ecosystem—the creation of a world where flesh is food?

The worst of my scorn and derision has always been reserved for me. But what did I do to deserve it, really? Allowed a relationship to fail? Permitted the octopus to come? Tolerated depression without fighting back? Dragged Lily and myself out to sea?

And suddenly I want to turn the boat around. I ache for home; grieve for it as if it were gone. But it's not gone, it's just far away. Waiting for us. What are we doing? We're adrift in the middle of nowhere, and it's only a matter of time before we run out of food. Why? All I have to do is turn the boat around. Point the compass east instead of west. There are tears in my eyes. It's what I want. For me. For us.

But I don't.

Some things are unforgivable. My problem is the opposite of mankind's: not having gone into battle often enough, not having waged enough war. I've always shied from confrontation, more often than not backing down from a fight. Quarreling has always felt silly, bordering on the ridiculous. War, after all, was something that happened to faraway people in faraway places. Not something that is sparked by an eight-armed invasion of your own front lines.

But this, with the octopus, this *is* war. Guerrilla war. I can't feel self-conscious about it. I can't be chastened before the battle begins. We are soldiers now, like it or not. As such, we need to be alert, awake, and on guard. And we need to continue plowing west.

All of this is sobering. I rise again to confront the night—this time my feet are steady, and I remember to sway into the pitch of the boat.

Remember the night is for hunting.

I walk to the deckhouse and flip on the echo sounder. It whirrs to life, transmitting its sound pulses on cue. I chuckle. Three weeks ago I didn't know how to do any of this and now it's second nature. I wait for any hydroacoustic data that might signal the presence of our prey, but the pulses return little more than the depth of the trench below.

I know the octopus is out there. I move to the ship's edge and grab the boat by the stern. *"You hear me? I know you're out there!"* I yell. My voice is swallowed by the murky night; the only echo is in my head.

I check the data one more time before turning off the sounder. Nothing. Instead, I find a pen and some paper in the deckhouse and scrawl my ominous warning. I KNOW YOU'RE OUT THERE. I cram the message into the empty scotch bottle and screw the lid back on tightly. With all my might I hurl it into the darkness.

I do not hear it land.

The Squall

Three days later when the storm begins, it comes without mercy or warning or forgiveness. I have just enough time to secure Lily's harness over her life jacket and anchor her to *Fishful Thinking*'s wheel before we take the brunt of it. It is a fight to keep the bow of the boat heading into the gale. Lily vomits twice outside the deckhouse and asks for chicken and rice. I barely have time to explain how impossible a request that is while I scramble to weigh down our charts and maps and do my best to secure the trawls. The sky blackens so completely I forget that it isn't night; the falling rain hits like ice picks, every drop a skin-piercing sting. The boat takes on water until the engine sputters and quits. The waves crash hard over the sides of the boat, and Lily fights to keep her nose above the sudden onboard surf. I try bailing with a tackle bucket, but all of my efforts seem futile. The storm is going to rage.

There's nothing to do except pitch into the surf; at least with my hands free of the wheel I can focus my attention on bailing and keeping Lily afloat. In the back of my mind I think we might capsize, yet I have no choice but to banish those thoughts. Survival dictates absolute focus.

Lily shivers on her tether, and I crawl to lift her out of the water and onto a low shelf in the deckhouse. I don't want to put her atop her usual perch on the stool; the center of gravity is too high and I worry about her falling.

"Stay here!" She can barely hear me over the wind.

She nods her understanding and I return to bailing.

As if on cue the hail begins, hitting the deck with rhythmic applause. I thought nothing would hurt like the driving rain, but I was wrong—I can actually feel my body bruising. A forty-knot wind gust drives the hail and the rain every which way and visibility drops to nothing. I scramble for the cover of the deckhouse to be by Lily's side.

I! DO! NOT! LIKE! THIS! STORM! I'M! SCARED!

I huddle close to her for warmth. The wind shrieks across *Fishful Thinking*'s deck like a coven of angry witches. The gusts actually seem to flatten the seas, and the rocking calms just enough to keep me from vomiting, too. The water washing aboard over the sides seems to slow, and we drift, taking the wind and the seas a few degrees abaft the bow.

"I don't like being wet." Lily shakes as best she can in my grip and a wriggle moves through her whole body like a wave until it has been released from the very tip of her tail.

"I know you don't." I tell her a story to calm her. "When you were a puppy you wouldn't even go out in the rain at all. I bought you a little raincoat and everything, but you would have none of it. One night it rained very hard, and I was determined to get you to pee. I didn't want to crawl into a warm, dry bed only to have to take you outside again in the middle of the rainy night. You were being stubborn in not peeing, and I was being stubborn in not going back inside until you did, and we were each trying to outstubborn the other."

"How did we resolve that?"

"I found a small overhang with some dry gravel underneath and eventually you relented." I remember the satisfaction of victory, and how short-lived it would be in our relationship. "It was the first and last time you ever really gave in to me."

Lily seems to enjoy the story, and for a brief moment as we focus on each other the storm melts away. But it is in this sudden calm that I fear the octopus may strike, and once again I am shivering and clambering for direction. I spent so long thinking of the octopus as my only enemy, I hadn't dreamed of him double-teaming me with as mighty a foe as the sea. I realize how foolish it all sounds, how naïve, underestimating the ocean. This could be the end of us both.

Then Lily points with her nose off the bow where a shadow emerges from the darkness and fog.

LOOK! LOOK! LOOK!

The shadow becomes a shape and the shape becomes a ship and hope washes over me in a way I would have thought impossible just minutes before. Is it possible we are not alone out here after all? I sound *Fishful Thinking*'s horn to announce our presence. Foremost in my mind is avoiding a collision. I sound the horn again, and again every ten seconds until we're answered by the quiet bellowing of the other ship, which is closer than the horn's blast would suggest, most of her yell swallowed by the wind.

The other ship is a deep-sea yacht, and by the way it approaches, steadily and with purpose, it seems it still has the use of both its engines. I step out of the deckhouse and wave my arms furiously, signaling our inability to steer. The yacht approaches slowly, skillfully, eventually pulling up beside us before she cuts her engines.

After a beat, a man appears holding a coil of rope.

"Ahoy!" he yells.

"Ahoy there!" I reply. Water belches between us, wetting me with spray, but I don't care—I'm just so overwhelmed and relieved that out of nowhere help has arrived.

The man tosses the rope and it lands with a thud at my feet. I grab the end and pull us together, tying the lariat to a large cleat on the deck with a poor man's imitation of a sailor's knot, keeping us as close to the yacht as the side trawl will allow.

"Some storm." The man looks drier and more put together than I must, but he is weathered and scraggly, too. He's bald, with a round head, his skin almost bluish from the cold. Judging by our distance from shore, he has been at sea awhile.

"She was a rager," I say. And then, almost as an afterthought, "You think that was the worst of it?" I brace myself for the answer. If it's not, I don't know what will become of us.

The man smiles. A dog's bark pierces the wind and I look back at Lily, but she shivers in silence. A golden retriever emerges from the yacht's cabin, tail wagging. "Lost your engines, eh? Why don't you come aboard. We'll have what the whalers used to call a gam."

I remember gams from reading *Moby-Dick*. When two ships would meet at sea, they would drop anchor and whaleboats would ferry the crews of each to the other ship to exchange gossip and news. I look toward Lily. She seems unnerved, and I wonder why. It's not like her to be so still in the presence of another dog.

"Sounds good to me. May I bring my first mate?" I indicate Lily.

"Goldie here insists." The man pats his dog on the head, and I lift Lily and hold her close so that she feels safe. I grab the last bottle of scotch from the deckhouse, thinking it rude to come aboard empty-handed. There's only a swig or two left, but it will more than do.

The seas are instantly calmer aboard the sturdier boat. The yacht is named *Owe Too*, and is newer than *Fishful Thinking*. The cabin is warm and inviting, and while not overwhelmingly large, it seems absolutely palatial when compared to our deckhouse. The man pulls some towels out of a closet and tosses them to me. I undo Lily from her life preserver and gently rub her dry. She noses up to Goldie while I dry myself. Goldie sniffs her hindquarters in return and Lily relaxes in the dryness of *Owe Too*'s shelter. The overwhelming relief of seeing another person, and another dog, brings the feeling of tears to my eyes even though none appear. I'm too dehydrated and too shocked to actually cry.

"Goldie, why don't you take your friend to your special place in the hull." The man whistles and snaps and Goldie motions to Lily to follow, and they disappear through a small door together. "Wasted space under there, so I hollowed it out for Goldie. The enclosed nature gives her a safe place in the vast expanse of sea. I thought us captains could speak while I fix us something to eat."

I raise what's left of the scotch as an offering. The man smiles and pushes two glasses toward me.

He heats a stew for us, and chicken and rice for the dogs. Lily is going to be ecstatic. As he works I tell him our story. I tell him about the octopus's arrival, the vet's diagnosis, and all we've been through—the octopus's sudden disappearance, chartering *Fishful Thinking*, the details of our hunt. He listens intently, interrupting only twice to ask me to clarify a point. When I finish we are both quiet for a moment.

"Do you think you'll be able to kill this octopus?"

I answer truthfully. "I think I will enjoy it."

My response hangs awkwardly in the air.

"You know, yacht derives from the Dutch word *jacht*. Translated literally it means *the hunt*."

I nod as if this isn't new information, but it is. Even after three weeks at sea, my knowledge of boating is limited. The man serves us two bowls of hot stew and it is, in this moment, the best thing I have ever tasted. Salted fish and tomatoes and parsnips and other root vegetables. He puts the chicken and rice in two bowls on the floor and whistles for the dogs, who come running.

CHICKEN! AND! RICE! LOOK! I! GOT! CHICKEN! AND! RICE!

For Lily, it's Christmas morning. She is just as excited as I am. Her initial hesitance to come aboard has now fully abated. She wastes no time marveling to Goldie about how chicken and rice is her favorite, choosing to show her instead by sticking her whole face in the bowl of warm mush.

"This far out at sea. No one else around. Would it be correct to say, then, that you are on a hunt of your own?" I ask.

The man hesitates before saying, "Perhaps."

"And what are you hunting, if you don't mind me asking?" The man looks at me as if perhaps I've overstepped my bounds, and I look back at him without blinking. The silence becomes too much. "If we're just talking. Captain to captain."

"We're just talking," he confirms, before answering. "What is anyone hunting for? Peace. Solace. Meaning." Then, after a pause, "Spoils."

"Spoils?" The word strikes me as odd. Like the spoils of war? The man shrugs.

We eat our stew and the *Owe Too* rises and falls over a big wave and we both brace ourselves against the table, afraid that the squall has turned back in our direction. After a moment of relative stillness, it seems the wave was an aberration.

"You know, I may have seen your octopus," the man says.

I drop my fork and the tines strike my bowl with a clang. "You have?"

"Not three days ago. Goldie and I were enjoying the sunset when off the starboard side there was a slick reflection that sparkled differently off the water than the last of the sun. I looked more closely and I swear I could see an eye watching us. The eye blinked once before Goldie caught a whiff of him and started barking. The thing swam closer, eyeing Goldie, and I grabbed her collar and held her close. The whole experience was over in a matter of seconds, but it was unnerving. As it approached our ship it sank beneath the surface and I never saw it come up again."

The hairs stand up on the back of my neck and we both reach for our tipple. My gut was correct.

We are close.

I notice the man has a Magic 8 Ball on the shelf beside the table. The kind I had as a kid. I reach for it.

"Do you mind?"

The man nods his permission. I cup the black ball with two hands and ask my question aloud. "Will I ever catch up with the octopus?" I give the ball a good shake before turning it over.

Signs point to yes.

"There you have it," the man says as he smiles a crooked smile. "The 8 Ball never lies." He clears his dish and reaches for mine. "More?"

Before I can say yes, Lily starts to growl. I look up, afraid that her love of chicken and rice has emboldened Lily to challenge Goldie for the bigger dog's share. But their dishes are empty, and Goldie is nowhere to be seen.

Lily is growling at the man.

"Lily! That's not nice. He made you chicken and rice! Where's Goldie? Say thank you to our hosts."

GOLDIE! IS! A! FISH!

"What? What are you talking about? Goldie is a dog, like you."

Her growling continues, low and guttural. It's a noise I've only heard her make once before, when we were on a walk back home in Los Angeles one night and a coyote ambled across our path.

I'm becoming increasingly alarmed.

"Don't worry," the man says. "The storm has her on high alert. That's a good dog you have there." He sets the dishes near the sink. "Would be a shame if anything happened to her."

His every word exacerbates the situation, and things escalate quickly. Lily is gnashing what teeth she has left in her old age, and she crouches low, ready to attack.

"Lily?" This time I don't scold. This time I know better. This time I trust my dog.

I turn to the man. "How did you come to name the *Owe Too*?"

He answers without hesitation. "I owe too much on the title."

Owe Too.

Lily's barking is now out of control. Goldie is a fish? I look around for the retriever, but there is no sign of her. I can barely gather my thoughts over the racket, but I force myself to think fast.

Owe Too.

What do you see, Lily, that I do not?

Owe too.

Oh, to . . . *Oh to what?*

Oh two. It doesn't mean anything!

O2?

Oxygen.

I can barely breathe and my heart beats fast. Think, god-dammit. I can hardly hear my own thoughts over the yelp of Lily's barking. I look down at my feet for bearings. Oxygen. Breath. Life.

And then it hits.

The atomic number of oxygen is eight. Oxygen is the eighth element on the periodic table of elements.

Eight.

The Magic 8 Ball.

I lift my head slowly and look up at our rescuer with growing scorn. His eyes are fixed on Lily.

"She has a hurricane inside of her." The man winks at me slowly, deliberately. "Doesn't she."

Bile rises in my throat. Only three people know about the hurricane.

Myself.

Lily.

And the octopus.

The Hunt

I pivot quickly, positioning myself between Lily and the octopus. Reflexively, I grab the empty scotch bottle and whack it against the table. It doesn't break. I whack it again—nothing. Why is it so easy to make a jagged weapon in movies and I can't get this scotch bottle to so much as crack? The octopus stands between us and the exit and Goldie is still nowhere to be seen.

"It's you, isn't it."

"Who?"

"The one we hunt." There's another bottle, a second bottle, on the counter. I grab this one instead and bring it down on the table with all my might and this bottle breaks and out comes my scribbled warning: I KNOW YOU'RE OUT THERE. He found the bottle. My bottle.

The octopus wipes a string of drool from his human mouth. "I wondered when you would recognize me."

"Your ugly, fleshy head should have been a dead giveaway." I'm mad at myself for being so easily seduced by the idea of companionship and food. I should have known. He wasn't blue from the cold, he was purple from being a cephalopod. Twenty-four days at sea have weakened me, and I have failed at protecting Lily.

I lunge at the octopus with the jagged scotch bottle, but he grabs a single-flue harpoon that's leaning in the corner. We're both armed, him with a longer reach and with seven more limbs to take up arms should he decide to take octopus form again.

I grab a kerosene lantern hanging off the wall. "I swear I will burn this boat to the ground."

"To the ocean," he corrects. "Do it. Of the three of us, who is the strongest swimmer?" I'm keenly aware of Lily's life jacket crumpled uselessly in the corner. He's right, of course, as always. It's the most maddening thing about him.

"Monkey," I say calmly to Lily without breaking eye contact with the octopus. Out of the corner of my eye, I see her ears perk up. *"Run!"*

Lily bolts through his legs as he brings down the spear. I cringe, but my baby is fast and clears the sharp tip with hundredths of a second to spare. The harpoon buries itself in the cabin floor, and as he lunges to free it, I strike. I sink the toothy bottle in his shoulder with every one of my two hundred pounds. Immediately there is blood and I twist the bottle to extract even more.

"Go ahead and take my arm. I've got seven more."

Yes, but where? I don't understand how he looks like a man. I don't understand the depths of his dishonesty. He punches me in the nose, and as I fly backward he rips the bottle from his flesh and smashes it into pieces on the ground.

I stumble, but I don't fall. I can feel blood spill from my nose and the pain in my face is indescribable. I lower my center of gravity and go for the tackle. I've never been in a fight. Not like this. Not with a single-minded determination to cause catastrophic harm. To end life. To kill. Before I even know it's happening, I'm charging at him with maximum speed.

We crash into a wall of shelving and both slump to the

ground. One of the upright beams cracks, sending books and dust and nautical maps raining down upon us. I get in one good punch and I poke at his eyes with my thumbs, hoping to crush them. To blind him like he blinded Lily. Suddenly, I notice the whoosh of flames behind me. The lantern! I dropped it when I careened backward, and now the curtains are on fire. A small fishbowl falls from the shelf and lands on the octopus's arm, spilling water and a single goldfish onto the floorboards. I look at the fish flopping helplessly, gasping. It immediately flops toward the safe space in the bow.

A flash of recognition. Lily warned me. *Goldie is a fish.*

"Goldie?" The golden retriever was a lure, a trick. One of the octopus's fish companions taking dog form to lull Lily and me into a false sense of security. Everyone trusts a man with a dog. The octopus stomps his boot down on the goldfish, smearing its guts on the floor. I grimace. His first kill tonight.

Hopefully his last.

The octopus's good arm, the one in the puddle of fishbowl water, starts to twitch and twinge and transform. Before I can even get off him, it's the arm of an octopus, slimy and purple and long. It curls around me like a python, choking me, its suction cups sticking to my skin. Part man, part octopus, he squeezes so tightly it's unbearable, and the cabin begins to darken. I claw and thrash at the sludgy, toadlike arm, but I can't loosen his powerful grip, and as my vision starts to narrow and fade all I can think of is failure.

Lily appears through the smoke, charging forth with a rope in her mouth. At the end of it is tied a noose. Whether she has tied it, or it was waiting to hang us, I do not know. She shoves the rope in my hand, and as the octopus-man lifts his head, I reach behind me and slip it around his neck. Lily grabs the rope and pulls. She's low to the ground, her back haunches raised slightly, her teeth exposed. I've seen her in this pose dozens of times as we've played with her rope chew. I know how strong she can be.

With one last great effort, I swing completely around and jam my foot under the octopus's chin, pushing his jaw in the direction opposite Lily's pulling. The noose tightens further and his grip on my neck becomes tenuous.

"We've got to get out of here!" I yell to Lily, wrestling the octopus arm from around my neck.

The noose now tight, Lily lets go of the rope long enough to chomp down on the wound from the bottle. She gets a mouthful of flesh and shakes her head violently until it tears. I've seen her do this, too, with stuffed toys—grip their bodies, shaking them savagely to snap their necks. It's always a little unnerving, the instinct bred within her to kill. But now I cheer. The octopus lets go of me and swats her away and she flies across the room with a chunk of his still-human arm. I lunge for the rope and pull tightly again, and his face turns a deeper shade of purple. Both arms flail and strike at whatever they can, as the flames in the back of the cabin encroach.

Lily slides to a stop under the table, two of its legs already on fire. "Lily, look out!" Lily turns to see the flames and scrambles out from underneath the table just as it collapses on one end. Sparks fly, igniting some cushions. The cabin is choking us rapidly with smoke.

I pull the octopus by the rope around his neck. There are three steps up to the deck. He pulls at the rope with his octopus arm, slithering the tip underneath to give himself just enough slack to breathe. Lily chomps down on his Achilles tendon and he writhes with pain. I yank the rope hard up the stairs, me dragging the octopus-man, the octopus-man dragging Lily.

"Say good-bye to this world, you sonofabitch."

"GLRZHKZZZT," gargles the octopus, struggling for air.

There's an ax strapped just underneath the gunwale, and before I can process the decision to free it I'm already wielding it in my hand. I wrap the noose around my left hand and bring the ax down with all my might, grunting a murderous yowl. The octopus rolls on his side and I bury the blade deep into the deck.

"Lily!" I need both hands to free the ax, so Lily takes up the slack. She pulls at the rope, wrapping it around a cleat bolted to the deck. I pull at the ax, wiggling it free of its vise. Lily runs back around the octopus and pulls at his pant leg, again tightening the noose. I raise the ax again, taking aim at his one octopus arm. This time the blade connects, severing the arm with a deafening squish.

The octopus screams in pain.

He kicks Lily, who sails into the bulwark. There is just enough slack in the rope for him to scramble to his feet as I struggle to free the ax from the deck. Lily, stunned, shakes herself upright. The octopus limps starboard and turns back to look at us one last time.

"Be seeing you, governor," he says. Just as I free the ax, he calmly tosses himself off the side.

Lily barks and we both rush to the edge, expecting to see him hanging from his broken neck. Instead, he gasps and spits and chokes, hanging from the rope, his legs submerged in water below the knee. The ocean bubbles around him as he thrashes, and he's engulfed in a cloud of purple smoke. We can just make out his two legs becoming four, then five, then six. His upper body loosens as he fully retakes octopus form, and the last thing we see is his look of spite and hatred as he again becomes an invertebrate, slipping out of his noose.

Drowning

Fuck!" I spin around, grasping for a plan. One of us will regroup first, and I'd rather it be us than him. C'mon, focus. *Focus!* We cannot be so close to victory just to stagger backward into defeat. But the octopus has the home field advantage. We need a miracle. I look at the spot that held the ax and something bright catches my eye. Farther down the ship's side wall is an orange case. I race for it and pry it free. My knuckles are cold and achy. My fingers tremble in fear and anticipation. I struggle to open the case, but when I do we are rewarded. Inside are two flare guns.

Lily barks portside. The sea erupts and an octopus arm emerges over the side, jerking the boat counterclockwise. I'm alarmed at the sheer size of it, at this monster's ability to grow. Lily charges fearlessly at the arm, retreating only when a second arm emerges to pierce the windows of the cabin and send flames shooting over the deck. I grab the guns and charge the octopus as he rips a hole in the side of the yacht and we start taking on water.

We have only one chance—to make it back to our boat, where

we at least have the advantage of the trawls. *Fishful Thinking* floats calmly a good thirty feet away, safely out of reach of the fire. We can't jump. We can't traverse a plank. The only way to get to her is to swim. We have to enter the water, and to do so we must distract the octopus.

I whistle for Lily and slap my hand against my thigh. She immediately comes running and I crouch, catching her as she leaps into my arms; she hasn't moved this nimbly in years. I set the gun case down just long enough to untether *Fishful Thinking* from the sinking, burning yacht. Then I grasp Lily tight, grab one of the guns, and shout in the most pathetic and terrified voice I can muster. "Hey, octopus! I give up. You want her? You can have her. I don't want to drown!"

The octopus has spent enough time with us now to wonder if, when truly pressed, I'm not just this selfish. He raises his eye into view to see if my offer is true. Instead of seeing Lily outstretched in offering, he's staring down the barrel of my flare gun.

"Fuck you, you piece of shit." I pull the trigger.

The octopus is already retreating into the water as the flare strikes him like a lightning bolt on the top of his head. He makes a sound like a pile of hissing, screaming snakes as he sinks below the surface. Flames shatter another window in the cabin and broken glass explodes against the deck.

"We have to go. *Now!*" I drop the gun and hug Lily tight and we dive off the starboard side toward *Fishful Thinking*. I kick hard and try to cover as much of the distance underwater as I can. When we surface, I paddle furiously with one arm as Lily kicks with her short little legs. We have maybe ten feet to go. Behind us there's an explosion aboard the *Owe Too*, the flames having finally reached the engines.

The rope the octopus had tossed earlier inviting us aboard hangs off the side of our fishing boat. I give it a good tug. It's still secured tightly to the cleat. I grab on and lift us as high as I can out of the water before boosting Lily the rest of the way. She scrambles over our boat's wall just as the octopus wraps a tentacle around my neck.

"Li—lheeee," I manage before he cuts off my airway. It's enough for Lily to recognize her name and she ducks just out of the octopus's reach as a second arm strikes *Fishful Thinking*'s deck.

Just as my fingers turn white and I can no longer hold on to the boat, Lily reappears brandishing the jagged filleting knife from our set in the deckhouse. She stabs it into the tentacle around my neck, severing just through to my skin; I can feel the knife's craggy point at my jaw. The octopus lets go, giving me enough time to clamber aboard.

I run straight for the deckhouse to flip the trawler winches, and mercifully the squall has not robbed them of power. The side trawler whirs to life and I lower the net on the port side. The boom swings wide, and I worry about hitting Lily. I yell for her to stay low and close and she sidles up beside me. Instinctively, I turn on the echo sounder and watch breathlessly for any sign of life. After about thirty seconds, the octopus moves.

Blip.

"There!"

I turn over the engine.

Blip. Blip.

"C'mon, c'mon, c'mon . . ."

The engine sputters and coughs.

"Come on!"

Blip. Blip. Blip.

The octopus is upon us.

I pound my fists on the engine control panel and suddenly the engine wheezes to life. I pull the wheel hard to the left and *Fishful Thinking* starts her tight turn.

Blip. Blip.

We pass over the octopus, but the net sensors give no sign of a catch. Lily grabs the strap of our harpoon gun in her teeth and heads for the stern. She sets it down and stands with her hind legs on the transom.

Blip.

The octopus is getting farther away.

Silence.

Fishful Thinking completes her turn and we head into the surf. I scan the ocean in front of us, wiping the windows with my sleeve to clear the deckhouse of steam. The silence is thick and eerie.

I race for the stern and fasten the harpoon gun to the mount so it takes aim at the waters behind us. Lily can swivel the gun with her nose, and I show her how to do so. I tell her the few secrets I know about firing a gun—to put the butt square in her shoulder and weld her cheek to the stock—and how to hit a moving target, tips I've learned from my mother's husband, who is himself an impressive shot. She listens and nods with determination.

Blip. Blip.

The echo sounder picks up something off the stern. I run back to the deckhouse and call to Lily. "He's behind us! Headed right for you!" I see her place one paw on the harpoon gun's trigger. The octopus is forty feet away. Thirty. Twenty. "Steady! Steady! Get ready to fire on my command!"

Lily takes careful aim.

"Remember what I told you!"

I turn back to the echo sounder. Ten feet.

Lily makes one final adjustment, nosing the harpoon gun down just a hair.

NOT! WHERE! THE! OCTOPUS! IS! WHERE! THE! OCTO-PUS! IS! GOING! TO! BE!

"Fire!"

She pulls the trigger.

The harpoon catches and I pump my fist with excitement. Lily knocks the gun from the mount as the rope pulls taut and the gun rides up the side of the boat, anchoring just under the lip of the gunwale. I pull the wheel sharp, to the right this time, causing the net to drag toward the stern.

"Lily! Switch!"

Lily scampers to take the wheel as I charge to the back of the boat. I pry the gun loose, reeling in the rope attached to the harpoon. I give it one final yank as I see the net open wide and I drag the stunned octopus in.

"Raise the winch!"

Lily jumps with all her might and noses the winch switch upward. The net snatches closed as the jib starts to rise. The net emerges from the water slowly, the weight of its monstrous catch holding it down. The octopus rises from the ocean, beak first, his seven remaining arms pinned backward behind his head.

"Hello, octopus," I say coldly. "It's good to see you again." And like this, helpless, hanging in his prison of woven rope, for the first time I can say this is true.

Lily trots up beside me and sits.

"Let me out of this thing!" the octopus bellows. His breathing is shallow, his arms pinioned to his body by the net. I can see they are tightly covering his gills.

"You try to kill me, we have business. You try to kill my dog, you die."

Lily noses me in the calf as if to ask if this is really necessary. I look down at her in that way that I do when I ask for her trust—when we get in the car and we're not going to the vet and I want her to know we're about to have fun; when we try a new walk and she balks at the unfamiliar route; when I place her in a cool bath on the hottest of summer days, knowing this will end her discomfort. The way I did when I told her we were going on this awfully big adventure.

"You can't kill me! You'll never kill me!" The octopus starts to rock and the net begins to swing. The boat sways and the jib creaks and moans. Then the octopus crashes into the side of *Fishful Thinking* and the rope holding the net jumps off the pulley. The net plummets into the ocean and rope rapidly unspools off the crank. At the last second, Lily grabs the rope with her teeth and hunkers down with everything she's got. She's barely able to keep the rope from disappearing as her claws plow deeply into the deck.

"Hold on!" I sprint for the deckhouse, straighten the wheel, and give the engine full throttle. The boat lurches forward. I dive toward Lily and grab the rope. The octopus gives such a tug at the other end that it splinters painfully in my fingers. Together, Lily and I are able to maintain our tight grip as the boat gains speed, the rope sliding around to the stern. I know with his arms pinned back flush against his gills he can no longer breathe underwater, and with his beak exposed we only have to plow forward and force enough water down his throat to drown him.

If we can just hold on.

The more the octopus fights, the more we dig in our heels. I don't care if I lose all my fingers to splinters. I brace my feet against the bulwark as *Fishful Thinking* rams full speed ahead. I can feel the octopus flailing.

"If we can just grasp on for ten more seconds!" Lily nods and bites down harder.

I count backward from ten.

"Ten. Nine. Eight."

I loop the rope tightly around my left hand and pull.

"Seven. Six. Five."

There is a great final tug from beneath the surface of the water and I can hear one of my fingers break with a deafening snap.

I scream in agony.

Lily steels herself and takes up my count, gargled, though, with her mouth full of rope.

FOUR! THREE! TWO!

I look over at Lily and we lock eyes. Together we say, *"ONE!"*

It's only after the count hits zero and I keep a stranglehold on the rope for even another good thirty seconds that I realize the octopus stopped fighting when our count reached three.

I look to Lily. "It's done." My shoulders droop with relief and I loosen my grip on the rope. "He won't bother us again."

Lily lets go with her teeth and tackles me back onto the deck. She climbs my torso and stands with her feet on either side of my sternum and starts madly licking my face. It may take ten tickles to make an octopus laugh, but it only takes a few licks from a dog to get me going. We shower each other with kisses, laughing until we can't breathe.

Happiness.

When we regain our composure, I look down at my broken finger and the rope still clutched in my hand.

Solemnly we reattach the rope to the winch and I set my broken finger with some electrical tape. I turn *Fishful Thinking* again so that for the first time in weeks we are heading toward home, in the direction the sun rises. In the direction of new beginnings. Lily and I take our berths in the deckhouse, silently looking east, toward California, as we tow the dead octopus in our wake.

Infinity (∞)

8 A.M.

The night is restless and it's hours before we fall asleep, and when we finally do I wake again with a start to find the bed completely soiled and Lily's breathing labored, and I know almost immediately that this is our last day. I look down at Lily and the octopus is back and he looks even bigger than I remember and his stranglehold seems more menacing than ever, poised to asphyxiate us both. The room spins, or my head spins; something is spinning in a way that makes everything unclear. Nowhere in the room do I see bags in any state of unpacking, nowhere on my face do I feel the scraggle of a beard, nowhere on my skin do I see color or evidence of weeks spent under the harsh sun aboard *Fishful Thinking*, nowhere on my hands do I bear the calluses and scars and broken bones of a hard-fought battle at sea. It's so real to me, so rich in detail—my heart is still soaring from the triumph of our victory over the octopus, the violence of his death, the quiet sweetness of our journey home, the two of us in command of a vessel on the open waters of the Pacific. And yet, there is the octopus.

My stomach drops at the sharp vicissitude of our fortunes. I feel like I'm going to be sick, but I can't remember the last thing I ate, or what food is, or what hunger is, or what is real and what is not. I don't know if dogs can cocaptain fishing trawlers, or shoot harpoon guns, or if octopuses can shape-shift into men and back again. I don't know if we're alive or dead, or why the heaven of our complete thrashing of the octopus has turned into the fresh hell of our defeat, of having him back in our bed. I realize I just don't know anything anymore, and that's when the octopus says, "Good morning."

"Please go away, please go away, please go away," I plead. It's the first time I've thrown myself on the mercy of the octopus. Maybe I can appeal to something inside of him, some sense of justice or fairness. Convince him of Lily's sweetness, her innocence, convince him he has the wrong dog. But the octopus just cackles.

"WHY! WOULD! I! GO! I! HAVE! EVERYTHING! I! NEED! RIGHT! HERE!"

That's when I know he has absorbed Lily entirely. That the body drawing shallow breath beside me is only the shell of my beloved dog. That in almost all respects, she is already gone.

I scoop up Lily and hold her in my arms. She doesn't even have the strength to lift her head. After a few whispered *I love yous*, I place her on the floor in the hopes that she can stand and summon the strength to fight again. Her legs buckle and she tips straight onto her side with a thump, staring off into the near distance of the corner.

She begins to pant.

The decision is already made. I won't give the octopus any more of the satisfaction of my begging.

9 A.M.

A third of the way through my file cabinet drawer, under D for dog, I find the file I keep that has all of Lily's paperwork. The AKC certificates that show her pedigree, the rabies vaccination certificates, and receipts for the supplies I bought upon first bringing her home—for the bowls and the bed I laid out for her in my empty house the night before we first met, for the little place mat that said *woof* that sat under her supper dish for our first meal together, for the crate she hated sleeping in. Near the back of the folder I find what I'm looking for. The papers from her back surgery. I can't go back to Doogie. I have to make one last-ditch effort and reach out to the people who took her in when I last thought she might die. I pull out the invoice for six thousand dollars. *Did I really pay six thousand dollars?* It seems like forever ago. On the invoice are two numbers, one for emergencies and one for nonemergencies. I hold the invoice in my hands for a good five minutes, crumpling and sweating on the middle of it, completely unsure of which number to dial.

I peek around the corner into the kitchen; Lily is lying on her side in her own bed, home base, exactly as I placed her a good thirty minutes ago. I retreat into the bedroom and shut the door and hold the invoice for another five minutes. I reach for my cell phone, still on the charger next to the bed, and dial the number for nonemergencies. It seems wrong, but I can't bring myself to dial the other. The numbers are too jagged.

"Animal Surgical and Emergency Center. Is this an emergency, or can you hold?" A woman's voice. Cheerful.

I look at the invoice and again at my phone. Didn't I dial the nonemergency number? I did.

"I can hold."

The longer I hold, the longer it's not real. The longer I don't have to assign words to the purpose for my call. Yes, I can hold. Put me on hold forever. I'll live here, set up camp in your phone bank. It has to be better than this. It has to be better than where I am.

There is no hold music. Just a faint yet deafening hum. It could be the blood in my ears, in the swollen capillaries that feed my ear canals.

"Thank you for holding."

My tongue is thick. "I can hold." I'm vaguely aware this is the wrong thing to say.

But it is the right thing to say.

"How can I help you?"

I inhale. I exhale.

"My dog. She has a . . . mass." I don't say *octopus*. "It's on her brain. It causes her seizures. She's on medication. They're not going to operate. We've decided not to operate. I think she has dementia. I don't think she can stand up. I don't think she's there anymore. I think this is the end."

I've wadded the invoice into a ball in my sweaty hand. It reminds me of a trick my granny taught me when I was a boy that involved crinkling the paper wrapper of a straw, then wetting it with a drop of water and watching it expand and writhe like a worm. I could almost perform the same trick with this scrunched paper and my sweat. Almost.

My granny is gone.

My childhood is gone.

Magic is gone.

I inhale. I exhale. Again.

I make two false attempts at speaking, each time my voice cracking between words.

My words are gone.

I bite my tongue hard and it finally enables me to speak.

"Who do I speak with about youth . . . ?"

Confusion on the other end. "About youth?"

I compress my diaphragm and force the word out. "Euthanasia."

10 A.M.

The woman on the phone asked when we would be in and all I could manage was "today." I sit on the floor next to Lily and I transfer her gently into my lap.

"What do you want, Tiny Mouse? If you could have anything."

Lily does her best to cock one eye, but you can tell that she's in pain. After a beat she gingerly licks her chops.

"You probably want chicken and rice, don't you, Bean? Well, chicken and rice is for when you're sick, and you're not sick, you're perfect. You're just in pain, is all, and the pain is almost over, so you can have whatever you want. Something even better."

Lily nods, and her chin flops over my knee.

"Anything. You name it."

There are heavy weights pressing down on my lungs. It's almost impossible to draw breath. And when I do the oxygen is leaden with a barbed pain.

"I know!" I'm barely holding back tears. "Peanut butter. How about peanut butter?" I vaguely remember aboard *Fishful Think-ing* asking her what she would like first upon returning home. Peanut butter was the answer. "You always liked that best."

Lily doesn't protest, so I slowly get up and carry her to the cabinet and I get the peanut butter and this time we sit down at the kitchen table. Carefully, I remove the lid. The jar is almost new, and I hold it under her nose and it takes a long time be-fore she reacts, but then she finally recognizes the sweet scent of peanuts and sugar and oil. Slowly she lifts her head. Slowly she starts licking the air. Slowly I move the jar to her chops so that she makes contact with her prize.

"Take all that you can. You can have the whole jar if you want."

She makes contact with the peanut butter, but she's so weak she doesn't ingest much of it. Essence of peanut butter. I put a little on my finger and let her have that. I remember the feel of her tongue when she was young. Soft and rough all at once. How she would get in these trances licking my hand and how they would go on endlessly until I rebooted her like a computer that had crashed.

Twelve and a half years ago.

Lily finishes the peanut butter on my finger and returns to the jar, where she continues to lap at it until she doesn't any-more. Then she puts her head down and makes moist smacking sounds, but eventually those stop, too.

"Good girl," I say.

Jenny and I once talked about how we manage to live despite the knowledge that we are all going to die. What's the point of it all? Why bother getting up in the morning when faced with such futility? Or is it the promise of death that inspires life? That we must grab what we can while there is still time. Is it the not knowing if today is the day that keeps us going?

But what if this is the day? What if the hour is here?

How do you stand?

How do you breathe?

How do you go on?

11 A.M.

I get dressed in clothes that I would normally never wear outside the house, but I don't care. I wrap Lily in a blanket in case she becomes incontinent again. We stand in the kitchen, and I wonder if she knows this is the last time she'll see it. If she knows this, if she understands, she doesn't make a big deal of it. I, on the other hand, can't help it. This was her home for ten of her twelve-plus years.

There on the floor lies her empty bed. There in the bed is her paw-print blanket. There in front of the sink is the morning sunny patch she likes to lie in. There is the rack where we keep the pots and pans, the one that would swallow red ball, the one I'd find her stuck beneath trying her best to retrieve it, just haunches and a wagging tail. There is the vinyl breakfast booth; an understudy for her bed that was occasionally drafted for afternoon naps. There is the closet door that hides the garbage can, the door she would bat with her paw when she thought I'd been hasty in throwing decent food away. There is the drawer that houses her toys, the one she would give expectant looks to when she wanted to play. There was the pen that confined her for twelve weeks as she slowly recovered from surgery. There is the metal tin that holds her puppy chow and there on the floor is her bowl that twice a day gets filled. There is the back door she would guard with the menacing bark of a German shepherd whenever anyone came near. There is the mixer I used to make the batter that became her home-baked birthday cookies. There is the stove she would hit with a clang after her eyesight was gone. There is the corner she would stand and bark into once dementia had set in.

There is red ball sitting untouched on the floor.

Frozen.

Lifeless.

Still.

Noon

We enter the animal hospital through the sliding doors and it's the same as I remember and the woman behind the desk asks if she can help us (she doesn't ask if we can hold) and I stammer, "I called earlier," and she nods and flags down a passing coworker by putting her hands on her shoulders.

She whispers to her friend.

The second woman ushers us into an examining room and tells us the doctor will be in shortly. When she leaves she closes the door behind us, sealing us in.

I sit with Lily on the only chair. It's cold.

The clock on the wall has no second hand and I look at it for what feels like three minutes before I see the minute hand move once.

It's quiet. Not much is going on in the middle of a Thursday.

Thursday is the day that my dog Lily and I set aside to talk about boys we think are cute.

"It's Thursday, Bean. On Thursdays we talk about boys."

Lily does the thing where she lifts an eyebrow, but otherwise remains perfectly still.

"How about we go old school: young Paul Newman, or young Paul McCartney?"

Lily sighs.

Q: *What sound or noise do you love?*
A: Puppies sighing.

My voice cracks.

"I gotta tell you." I tip my head back to keep my tears from falling on Lily. "I don't think there was anyone more handsome than a young Paul Newman."

Footsteps outside the door. *Please don't come in. Please go away and leave us be. Please go away forever.*

They pass.

"*Butch Cassidy. Cool Hand Luke.* Brick in *Cat on a Hot Tin Roof.*"

The clock ticks off another minute. And then several more.

I want to run, but my feet are encased in cement, glued to the floor, the lower half of my body paralyzed, like Lily's was when last we sat in this hospital.

More footsteps. They come to a halt.

A hand on the doorknob.

The opening door.

A woman in a white lab coat enters. She smiles warmly, but not too warmly. She already knows what's happening.

"Who do we have here?" she asks.

I pinch my finger until it hurts. "This is Lily."

The woman produces a stool from underneath the examining table, wheels it beside us, and takes a seat.

"What's this on Lily's head?" She places three fingers under Lily's chin and raises her head very gently to get a better look.

"That's the octo—" I start to say, but stop. *Enough is enough.* "That's her tumor."

The veterinarian takes a pocket light and shines it in Lily's eyes. There is no real response.

"Is she blind?"

"Yes. The tumor has taken her eyesight. And just about everything else."

She runs her other hand gently over the mass and slowly lets Lily's head rest again in my lap.

"She has seizures. Bad seizures. And I think dementia. And this morning she looked at me like she was . . . done." This is the last I can say before I have to fight to speak, to do battle for each individual word. "I want you to take her. I want you to take her and to fix her. I want you to tell me you can make everything okay. To make this all go away. And, short of that, if you can't do that, if you can't produce a miracle, I want you to tell me I'm making the right decision."

There's a panic attack looming. I can feel it. The right decision. The wrong decision. The happy memories. The sad reality. Good. Bad. Up. Down. Win. Lose. Life. Death.

The doctor holds Lily's head in her hands and covers her ears.

"You're making the compassionate decision."

There will be no miracles.

There will be no tomorrows.

I nod like my head weighs a hundred pounds and make some sort of noise. Pain mixed with acknowledgment mixed with consent.

Again. "It's the compassionate decision."

My eyes blur.

I'm underwater.

Fishful Thinking has capsized.

I am drowning.

"How does this work?" I already know that I don't want the answer.

"I'm going to take Lily and fit her with a small catheter in her leg so we can easily inject the drugs intravenously. There will be two. The first will render her unconscious. She will be asleep, but still alive. You can have a moment with her to say good-bye. And then when you say, we will inject the second drug to cause cardiac arrest. Once we inject that second drug, it should be over within thirty seconds or so."

"Two drugs," I say.

The woman reaches for Lily, but I don't let go.

"Right now we're just going to find a vein and fit her with a catheter so things will go as smoothly as possible."

She reaches for Lily again, and this time I loosen my grip. She promises to be back in a few moments.

I'm alone in the room and for the first time I can stand. I walk in three tight circles the way Lily does before lying down. Except I don't lie down. I pound my thighs with my fists.

I need to feel pain. Physical pain.

I slam my arm against the metal examining table in an effort to break something. The pain splinters up to my shoulder and it feels good. So good I do it again.

But I don't need to break anything.

My heart is broken enough.

Time stops.

Time passes.

The woman returns, this time with an assistant. The assistant offers a half-smile but otherwise does her best to be invisible.

The veterinarian places Lily on the table. She's still wrapped in my blanket. Her leg is exposed. I can see the catheter. It is taped in place with plastic.

I kneel down in front of Lily so that we are face-to-face.

"Hi, Monkey. Hi, Tiny Mouse."

Lily chuffs a few deep breaths.

"There is a wind coming," I cue her.

Silence.

There is no Cate Blanchett. There is no response. She can no longer command the wind, sir. She no longer has the hurricane inside of her.

Lily makes one last effort to stand, and that's when I really lose it.

We can still run. We can still break out of here. We can still choose life.

But what kind of life would it be?

Instead, I shower Lily's face with kisses.

"So many adventures we had. And I loved *every* one."

Lily's head droops and I kiss her again.

The assistant holds her back legs and I hold her front.

I nod at the veterinarian.

"Okay. I'm going to inject the first drug. The anesthesia. She's just going to fall asleep."

Sleep well, my beautiful slinkster dog.

The anesthesia is fast.

For a few seconds, nothing. But then Lily's eyes open wide as she feels the whoosh of the drug inside her. Then her eyes grow heavy.

She blinks once, maybe twice.

She staggers left.

We slowly lower her to the table, where she falls gently asleep.

"Let me know when you're ready and I will inject the second drug."

"*Wait!*" I snap.

I'm not ready.

OH GOD WHAT HAVE I DONE?

Why is this happening?

It's Thursday.

Thursdays are the days my dog Lily and I set aside to talk about boys we think are cute. I look at the tape on the catheter, the bandage holding it in place.

Rip the Band-Aid. Quick. It's the only way.

"Okay." I can feel the letters vomit off my tongue.

O.

K.

A.

Y.

I watch the vet insert the syringe into the catheter and inject the second drug. And then the adventures come flooding back:

The puppy farm.

The gentle untying of the shoelace.

THIS! IS! MY! HOME! NOW!

Our first night together.

Running on the beach.

Sadie and Sophie and Sophie Dee.

Shared ice-cream cones.

Thanksgivings.

Tofurky.

Car rides.

Laughter.

Eye rain.
Chicken and rice.
Paralysis.
Surgery.
Christmases.
Walks.
Dog parks.
Squirrel chasing.
Naps.
Snuggling.
Fishful Thinking.
The adventure at sea.
Gentle kisses.
Manic kisses.
More eye rain.
So much eye rain.
Red ball.

The veterinarian holds a stethoscope up to Lily's chest, listening for her heartbeat.

All dogs go to heaven.

"Your mother's name is Witchie-Poo." I stroke Lily behind her ears in the way that used to calm her. "Look for her."

OH FUCK IT HURTS.

I barely whisper. "She will take care of you."

I look up at the vet, pleading. Inject me. Give me the poison, too. At least enough to make my heart stop breaking. Anything. Just please make it stop.

After ten more seconds, the vet pulls her stethoscope away. She doesn't need to say anything.

Lily is gone.

"I'm so sorry for your loss." She puts her hand on my shoulder while motioning for her assistant. "Take all the time with her you need."

I don't even notice them leave.

Time passes. I don't know how much. I'm aware I'm alone in the room with Lily and that is the only thing I'm aware of. I kiss the tip of her nose.

"Oh, god, please forgive me."

I'm sitting on the floor with my legs tucked to my chest and I'm rocking back and forth.

The tiniest bit of tongue hangs out of Lily's mouth. So pink. So still. So lifeless.

So many tears. I can't remember ever in my life crying this hard.

This is some sort of mistake. It has to be.

I slide my hand under the blanket and place it on Lily's chest. She's still warm, but her chest does not rise and fall like it does in even her deepest sleeps. I keep it there long enough to make sure, but after some time even I'm forced to concede that her heart has stopped.

I put my head down and sob, as there's nothing much else to do. My brain detaches from my heart and creates independent thoughts. It wonders how long I should stay in here so people don't think that I'm callous. It wonders how long I should not stay in here, how long before people will think that I'm creepy. It tells me to remember every detail of this. That it's important to catalog. So I do.

The clock.

The white walls.

The blanket.

The cold empty chair and the rolling stool.

The metal table.

How hard the floor feels.

How hard my face feels.

Lily.

Her tongue.

The octopus.

The octopus! I look at the octopus and he lies there with his eight arms fallen limp and his one visible eye rolled back in his stupid head.

You did this. You could have left, but you didn't. I hope you rot in hell.

There's no point in saying it out loud. He can't hear me.

The octopus is dead, too.

I pull the blanket over Lily's head just enough to cover the octopus, so that it is just her and me, like it had always been.

"I will love you forever. For the rest of my days and even all of the days after that."

With one last look, I pull the blanket up high enough to cover her completely. It takes me a minute to stand, but when I do I walk out of the room and, without looking back, I close the door behind me.

1 P.M.

I sit in the car for a long time not knowing what to do or where to go. Eventually, I pull out my phone and call Trent.

"Lily died."

"Come to my house. I'll leave work right now."

Somehow, I drive to Trent's house. Once, in college, I had to drive home to Maine from Boston during the throes of a migraine headache, and when I got home I had no memory of how I got there. This drive is like that. Except the migraine is heartbreak.

Trent greets me at the front door and pulls me into a hug and we both cry and I say "pills" and he already has them laid out for me. I let a Valium dissolve under my tongue and I kneel down to pet Weezie. Sweet, sweet Weezie. She just wants to play, but I can't.

I help myself to two shots of this Russian vodka from a bottle I gave Trent for his birthday. We first enjoyed this vodka at the restaurant Red Medicine, a neo-Vietnamese joint that we had sought out because the *LA Times* named it the "bad boy" of the Los Angeles dining scene, and it goes down smooth and it is just that: medicine. I don't know if it's the vodka or the Valium that takes hold first, but the weight lifts from my lungs just enough so that I can breathe.

Trent asks me how it all went, and I tell him as much as I can but it isn't much. Weezie is nipping at my heels but I just can't throw this rope chew she wants me to throw for her and my head gets very fuzzy. I collapse on Trent's sofa and he puts on the TV and we both sit down to watch, but before either of us knows it I'm asleep.

2 P.M.

The waters lap softly at the sides of *Fishful Thinking*, lulling us into a rhythmic hypnosis. As anxious as we are to get home, I've killed the engines just now so we can drift in the quiet and take in the great beauty that surrounds us. The blue of the cloudless sky matches the blue of the water and the air is soft and the sun from the east makes a sparkling golden path for us to follow home. There is total silence except for the gentle sounds of the waters kissing the hull. Since we're stopped, the octopus sinks and the weight of his corpse raises the hull just enough so that it feels like we're sailing to the heavens, or at the very least wherever Sandy and Danny flew off to when they left Rydell High at the end of the movie *Grease*.

Lily is by my side.

I'm almost startled to see her and I start crying, and since the octopus is dead, Lily looks like her old self, her younger self—there's a lightness to the way she moves, and I hold her head in both hands and scratch behind her ears and just say "oh, my baby" over and over again.

"What?" Lily asks, confused.

I say the only thing I can think to say. "You're here."

I lift her off her perch in the deckhouse and we stroll out to the bow and lean over the front of the ship.

"Isn't it beautiful?"

"It is," Lily agrees.

Lily places her front paws on the edge of the boat and stands on her hind legs for a better look. Her tail starts wagging in perfect synchronization with the lapping water, her inner metronome setting the beat with slow metrical ticks, and I remember what happiness feels like.

I stand back just to drink it all in. If I had the ability to press a button and pause time and live in one moment forever, this is the moment I would choose.

A breeze picks up from the northeast, and Lily's ears rise in the wind like the outboard flaps on airplane wings at takeoff.

"What do you see, Monkey?"

Lily takes in the expanse between us and the horizon. There's a softness to everything, and it really does feel like we're flying, not floating.

"Everything," she replies.

"We're going home now. To return to our lives. How do you feel about that?"

Lily remains silent, transfixed by the sun's reflection on the water. I wait a moment for her to respond.

"Puppy?"

Lily gives me something of a nod, I think, but she still doesn't really answer me, and this strikes me as odd. My question hangs limply in the air, uncomfortably, like an unreturned *I love you*. Why wouldn't she be ready to get back to our lives? To return to the quiet stability of our everyday togetherness? Does she know of something unpleasant waiting for us on shore?

Suddenly, red ball falls from the sky and lands on the deck with a deafening thwack. Startled, Lily and I both jump. Red ball bounces in a high arc and lands again closer to the deckhouse. Lily springs into action as it bounces in a series of increasingly smaller arcs toward the stern. She catches the ball in her mouth just before it bounces over the rear of the boat and into the water where the octopus anchors us down. She trots proudly with her catch back toward the bow and plays with it near my feet.

It's clear now, the source of her distraction—she never responds to me when she senses red ball is near. My insides settle and I watch her play as life ambles toward normalcy. It is the perfect moment, a perfect marriage of stillness and life, of beauty and harmony, of aloneness and togetherness. Red ball glides smoothly across the deck of *Fishful Thinking* and Lily chases it with ease and I've never felt more calm.

But it doesn't last.

Out of the corner of my eye I see fire in the sky, like a comet, coming toward us with increasing velocity.

"What the . . ." I manage, as the comet grows nearer.

A second red ball lands on the deck with a wallop and bounces high above us. Lily turns to watch it rebound, confused as to what to do. She looks at the one red ball already trapped under her paw, and then back at the other as it settles near the rear of the ship.

I catch Lily's look of confusion just before the third and fourth red balls hit. A shadow falls over the boat, and we both look at the sky as hundreds of red balls blot out the sun. They rain down upon us with increasing ferocity, making a deafening racket. Lily is frozen, terrified, as am I. She might have once dreamed of something like this, but the reality of it is horrifying.

We scramble for the cover of the deckhouse, but the red balls come too fast and I quickly lose Lily in a heap of rubber. I claw and scrape to get to her, to unearth her from the sea of red, but the balls pile up too fast. The ones that hit the water do so with a horrible splash and kick ocean spray into my face. I desperately wipe the salt from my eyes as the balls multiply around my chest and there's a tightness and I can't breathe and the last thing I remember is screaming *"Lily!"* and then everything goes dark.

3 P.M.

Trent's hand is on my shoulder and I look at him and there is no pain, just the presence of my friend, and for one brief second I feel okay until everything comes rushing back and it's like someone has their hands around my heart and is squeezing.

"You were screaming," he says.

"I was?" I was.

"Yeah."

The TV is still on and Trent has started watching *Friday Night Lights*, a favorite of mine that I've been trying to get him to watch for years since he's from Texas and loves football. I'm from Maine and I hate football, and I still love the show. We watch together silently. The show is so good, the drugs are still doing their thing, and part of me is transported to west Texas—but only a small part. There is too much pain anchoring me to Trent's couch.

At the end of the first episode, when quarterback Jason Street goes down, Coach Taylor gives the first of his trademark speeches. Something about life being so very fragile. Something about us all being vulnerable. Something about how, at some point in our lives, we will fall. "We will all fall."

I've never played football or any kind of team sport. I've never sat through a coach's halftime pep talk. I've never been in the room with someone rallying the troops to turn the tide of the fight. But hearing Coach Taylor speak, I prop myself up on my elbows. I am forty-two. This is the halftime of my life, and my team is losing. I've never been more in need of this speech.

He continues about how what we have can be taken from us. Even what we have that is special. And when it is taken, we will be tested.

I'm captivated by this speech, and even though I've heard it before, even though I own it on Blu-ray, I'm also hearing it for the very first time. It is in this pain that we are tested. Since I am in this pain, the pain of having what is special taken from me, I look inside myself and I don't like what I see: a man who is broken and alone. I think of all the time Lily and I spent together, just the two of us—the talks about boys, the Monopoly, the movies, the pizza nights—and I wonder how much of it was real. Dogs don't eat pizza; dogs don't play Monopoly. I know this on some level, but everything feels so true. How much of it was an elaborate construct to mask my own loneliness? How much of it was built to convince myself the attempts I made at real life—therapy, dating—were not just that: attempts?

Somewhere, sometime, I stopped really living. I stopped really trying. And I don't understand why. I had done all the right things. I had Lily. I had Jeffrey. I had a family.

And then I didn't.

I don't understand how my life got so empty, or why the octopus came, or why everyone eventually goes away.

4 P.M.

Trent orders pizza, and when it comes I try to eat, but the first bite makes me retch and I think I'm going to throw up but I overcome it and manage to keep it down. The red peppers and tomatoes and olives and cheese mix with the bile that rises in my throat and everything tastes awful. And yet I keep eating. Every bite delivers a stomach pain so sharp that for one glorious nanosecond it overcomes the one in my heart. There are three empty Pacifico bottles in front of me on the coffee table, which I don't remember drinking. I look over at Trent and I can tell he's happy that I'm eating. I guess the idea of someone overdosing on booze and pills on his couch (if one could overdose on a Valium, two shots of vodka, and three Pacificos) is not one he relishes.

"Good pizza?" he asks.

I raise a slice to him like I'm offering a toast.

Why didn't I run? Why didn't I scoop Lily up in that blanket and take her home? If I had we would be there now, together. It's the question I can't get out of my head. Why? Didn't? I? Run?

Weezie sits expectantly, hungrily, in front of Trent and I forget again if dogs do or don't eat pizza.

"I don't know what I'll do when it's Weezie's time," Trent says. I know he says this because he's experiencing some of my pain, coupling it with imagined future pain of his own, trying to understand. Plus the not knowing what to say that all of us experience in the face of grief. And I appreciate it, I do. But it's not Weezie's time. She is here. Unscathed. Alive. He also has Matt. What do I have?

The distribution of loss is inequitable. And I don't want him not to have Weezie. And I don't want him not to have Matt. I love my friend, and I want him to have every happiness. So I say this as a realization only. Not as a desire to redistribute loss or to make it more equitable. The distribution of loss is inequitable. That's just the way it is. That's just the way the world works. There's no one handing it out. There's no one making sure everyone gets a fair share.

So many adventures we had. And I loved every one.

Had.

Past tense.

Did Lily know this as her eyes grew heavy? That the adventures were over? Or did she feel the heaviness of sleep as the onset of a satisfying rest, one that would allow her to be fresh for new adventures ahead? Was it exciting or terrifying? Or did she see nothing at all?

I think of Kal and rub the tattoo on my arm. *To die would be an awfully big adventure.* But it's not true. Life is the real adventure. Having the hurricane inside you is the true adventure. And then I think not of Cate Blanchett as Queen Elizabeth I, but of Mel Gibson as William Wallace. Everyone dies. Not everyone really lives. And then of Mel Gibson in the movie *Ransom*: *Give me back my son!*

The pizza makes me listless, and I lie down again. I'm vaguely aware of Trent taking my plate so that Weezie won't eat the crust I've left untouched. Pizza bones, my dad called them.

Bones.

Remains.

Ashes to ashes.

Dust to dust.

I try to focus on getting back to *Fishful Thinking*, on getting back to Lily, on rescuing her from the meteor storm of red balls. I will try harder this time to get to her, to save her. I will grab her and we will run. The fact that we are on a boat surrounded by water and there is no place to run to is of little consequence. This time we will run.

Except when sleep comes, I do not dream of Lily.

5 P.M.

What are these?" Trent is holding pamphlets.

"I don't know." I sit upright and lean on some throw pillows. I've never seen them before. The pamphlets. The room is vaguely spinning and the TV is still playing *Friday Night Lights* and this time I don't need to be reminded what happened; I wake up already knowing.

Trent thumbs through them before saying, "Oh." He places them on the coffee table.

"What?"

"Nothing. You can read these later."

I reach forward and my abs hurt in the way they do when I've been working out a lot, except I can't remember the last time I've seen the inside of a gym. Weeks ago, maybe. When I pick up the pamphlets, I immediately regret it. Pet mortuary. Pet crematory. Pet burial grounds. Words jump out at me and assault my eyes. Respectful handling. Individual cremation. Selecting an urn. Bereavement counseling. Fine products. Compassionate care. Each phrase is a new stab at my heart.

Trent takes them from me.

"Where did you get those?" I ask—I accuse.

"They were here on the table."

Someone must have put them in my hands before I left the animal hospital, but I have no memory of it. Did I drive here with them clutched in my hands? I have no memory of that, either.

"I'll put them over here with the letter."

"There's a letter?"

"You can read it later. You don't need to read it now."

Dear Sir,

We were able to remove the octopus after all. Your dog is fine. Please come pick her up at your earliest convenience. She is excited to see you!

Yours in science,

The Animal Hospital

"What does it say." I don't ask; this is an order for him to tell me. There is no reading it later. I need to know. I need to know what the letter says now.

Trent sighs. He opens the letter, which is folded in thirds. He scans it until he gets to the end. "You have until Monday to decide what you want to have done with Lily." He reads me the options. If I choose individual cremation, I can shop for an urn, bring her home. If I choose group cremation, they will dispose of the cremains for me. There are other packages for burial. One includes a "precious clay paw-print keepsake."

All of this tests my beliefs. I don't believe in God; I don't believe in an afterlife. I do believe you live and you die. I do believe death is eternal nothingness. I do believe the body is just a shell. I do believe Lily is no longer there. There is no deciding what to do with Lily; there is no more Lily. There is deciding what to do with her body.

None of this frightens me.

Or does it?

I don't need Lily's remains to remember her by.

I don't need an urn to remind me of her love.

I don't need a precious clay paw-print keepsake to remind me that life is fragile, temporary, short.

Or do I? Do I need them so that I know I loved her? Do I need them to know that *she* loved me? Can I stomach the idea, years from now, of not knowing where her body is?

Stop all the clocks. Cut off the telephone. Prevent the dog from barking with a juicy bone.

It hits me.

Lily's body is in some freezer, stacked with the bodies of other unfortunate dogs. That's how they can still make a precious clay paw-print keepsake.

Trent puts the pamphlets with my keys on the dining room table.

I don't have to read them now.

9 P.M.

My phone is ringing and it's Jeffrey and I don't want to answer it. Before I got in the car I sent him a text: *Lily passed away. I was with her at the end. I'm not able to talk about it yet, but I thought you should know.* And then a second text: *Thank you for being an important part of her life.*

I'm not able to talk about it yet.

My phone is ringing.

It's Jeffrey.

I grip the steering wheel with both hands and concentrate on the freeway and the lane ahead of me. I think back to our relationship and my saying explicitly, *these are the things that if you do them they will hurt me*, and his uncanny ability to just do those things anyway. *I'm not able to talk about it yet.* Talking about it would hurt me. So what do you do if you're Jeffrey? You call to talk about it.

Just as I decide not to talk to him, to let the call go to voice-mail knowing I may never listen to the message, my fingers betray me and answer.

"Hi."

"Hi." It's been a long time since I've heard his voice. It sounds familiar, yet foreign. "You're driving?"

"Home. From Trent's."

"I didn't think you should have to drive home alone."

It's the Bluetooth feature on this car, new since our breakup. His voice spills from the stereo speakers, surrounding me on all sides. It's . . . unnerving. There's a long, empty pause before I say, "Thank you." And then, "Where are you?"

"I'm home."

I laugh.

"Why is that funny?"

Why is it funny? "I don't even know where home is for you now." How could I not know where he lives? I can picture a few of his things, things that used to be ours. But I can't picture them in the context of any space.

"Do you want, like, an address?"

I'm suddenly panicked that he might invite me over. "That's okay. I'm driving."

Silence.

"She was a good girl."

Another long pause.

"The best," I agree.

I pass the exits for Vineland, Ventura, and Lankershim before we speak again.

"What happened to us?" Jeffrey asks.

Is this the right time to be honest? I don't have anything left in me to be otherwise. "You weren't as faithful as I needed you to be."

Jeffrey swallows.

"You never seemed fully invested." He says it without anger or retaliation. We are just stating facts.

Fireworks burst over the Universal Studios theme park, their last embers raining over the freeway, just as our statements now are the dwindling cinders of explosive arguments we had long ago.

"I know." That much is on me.

Another silence you could drive a truck through.

"We had a really good run for a while," Jeffrey says.

"I think so, too."

As I pull the car to the right to prepare to exit on Highland, I tell Jeffrey I have to go.

"Take care of yourself, Ted." The way he says it, I can tell it's the last time we'll ever speak.

"You, too, Jeffrey." It feels weird that we use our names— names are for people who are less acquainted than we are. My finger hovers, paralyzed for the briefest of seconds, before I disconnect the call. Ted and Jeffrey. We are strangers again.

I open my sunroof and crank the radio. "Cecilia" by Simon and Garfunkel is playing, but in my head *Cecilia* sounds too close to *Lily* and I change the station to something else, something that means nothing, something I don't recognize. Something angry at life.

Pulling up to my house is such a normal activity that I almost think the whole day hasn't happened. I wonder what I was doing at Trent's; I wonder why Jeffrey had called. Lily is fine. She's waiting for me, asleep in her bed in the kitchen. It may take her a minute to perk up when I walk in the door. She's been a terrible watchdog these past few years. But she will wake up. She will wake up when I walk in the door.

As long as I sit in the car this is true.

Once I go inside this is not true.

As long as I sit in the car this is true.

I've so convinced myself that, when I do work up the courage to go inside, I stand in the dark, unwilling to turn on the lights, to do anything that might shatter my delusion. Finally, when the darkness becomes deafening, I whisper.

"Lily?"

Silence.

Of course there is no answer.

I got out of the car.

11 P.M.

There's an empty bottle of vodka in the freezer and I don't know why it's there or why there's not a full bottle. I toss it into the recycling bin. Then I take the unopened bottle of vodka from the cabinet and the remaining beer in the refrigerator and I dump them down the drain. I do this before undertaking the somber task of putting Lily's bed out of sight in the closet. I take her paw-print blanket and hold it up to my face, inhaling deeply, before folding it neatly and placing it on top of the laundry. I lift her food and water dishes off the floor. I don't even wash them, I just empty them and put them in a drawer. There's a stray piece of kibble hidden under her food bowl.

Unfinished business.

My bed is unmade. In the middle is a nest of towels where Lily slept her last night. I strip the bed, and under the towels I find an empty trash bag laid out over the sheets. I don't remember putting it there, or even having the thought to do so. I flip the mattress, even though it's dry, and make the bed with clean sheets.

Slowly, I'm erasing the events of the day.

I take a hot shower and stand for a long time under the spray. I'm aware that I'm washing her off me, removing her from the spots where we last touched. I turn off all the cold water until the hot water scalds, and when I can't stand the pain any longer I turn the cold knob until the water becomes temperate again.

When I get out of the shower I forget to even dry off and I just stand there next to the open window in the thick July air looking out into the darkness of the backyard. Tomorrow is Friday—therapy with Jenny. How will I speak of this with her?

On Fridays we play Monopoly.

I find some shorts on the floor, flop down onto the sofa, and turn on the TV. I look down at my legs and they are splayed in a way that creates a nook for Lily—the one she would always step into, turning around three times and then falling asleep in, her chin slung over the bend in my knee. This is how I sit now. I never sat like this before. This is how I sit now. Lily has fundamentally changed me.

What was the point of grieving early? That's what I will ask Jenny. If the point was to alleviate the grief I feel now—to make it malleable, to spread it thinner in a more manageable fashion—grieving early had utterly failed. If I was detaching weeks ago, shouldn't it be easier to fully detach today?

There will be two drugs.

I want to go back to that space in between them. After the first, where she is no longer in pain, just floating on a peaceful cloud of sleep. Before the second, where her heart still beats and her chest still rises and falls and that little bit of pink tongue is still tucked safely inside her closed jaw.

Midnight encroaches and I want to stop the clocks. Tomorrow will be the first day that Lily never saw. There's an overwhelming desire to run away.

The octopus came when I was away. All this time I have felt at fault, the one to blame, but suddenly I am overcome with a wave of anger at Lily. She used to bark at the mailman, bark at the wind, bark at every passing car. She used to race to the front door to scare away potential attackers, her silly body rigid with readiness, her nose pressed through the wooden blinds to smell danger, her bark that of a much larger dog. She used to dash to the door whenever I got home. She used to be diligent when things would go bump in the night. But somewhere along the line, she aged. She got older, and harder of hearing and maybe lazy or just impaired. Whatever the cause, she let her guard down. She failed to protect us.

That is when the octopus came.

She is the one at fault.

She is the one to blame.

Or maybe the octopus tricked her into submission. He was that wily. He could have come prepared. He could have come unannounced. The octopus, after all, is a master of camouflage.

It's impossible to focus my anger.

Why did I think we would be together forever? Lily never made that promise. Dogs don't live as long as people. In my head, I knew this. But to think that there would come a day when we would part was to take the joy out of a day we had together. A day together at the beach. A day together taking naps and walks. A day together chasing squirrels.

My body fights with my mind for rest. My eyes grow heavy and yet still resist sleep, but I don't know why. I need sleep. Desperately. Maybe I fear the return to *Fishful Thinking* now that I know it does not end how I thought it did. Now that the journey does not return us home.

I finally break free of my repose and wander aimlessly through the house, turning off switches wherever there is light.

When I get to the kitchen I find red ball staring at me from the linoleum floor, and my eyes water again. I lean down to retrieve it. It's impossibly fixed to the floor, like the sword in the stone. It takes a long time to move it but, like Arthur, I do, and I tuck it in the drawer with her food.

I turn off the kitchen light.

She was twelve and a half in actual years, which is eighty-seven in dog years.

I'm forty-two, which is two hundred and ninety-four.

We had twelve brilliant years together. That's eighty-four in dog years.

That's a lifetime, even if dog years pass too quickly.

A heart is judged not by how much you love, but by how much you are loved by others.

There will be two drugs. *The second will stop her heart.*

Good night, my sweet puppy.
Good night, Monkey.
Good night, Silly Goose.
Good night, Tiny Mouse.
Good night, Bean.
Good night, Lily.

You were fiercely loved.

Three Hearts

August

I'm already parked when it occurs to me I'm not sure which of the two Starbucks is the one we agreed upon. It's now two minutes until three, the time we planned to meet, and so I should probably hope for the closer of the two, even though the farther would be a much better choice for a first date. At least there we could sit outside. How can there be two Starbucks in one location? One is inside a Barnes & Noble, that's how. The Starbucks of books. I text him quickly and start in the direction of both Starbucks, and when he texts back he asks *How do you feel about frozen yogurt instead?* I write back *Sure*, and head to the farther Starbucks, since it's closer to the frozen yogurt place, even though now it's probably more complicated than ever, the plan about where to meet.

It's been a month to the day since Lily died.

Until today I have been doing okay. I took my mother up on her offer to come home. I timed my visit with Meredith's, and we all spent a few lazy days enjoying the Maine summer, and no one pressured me to talk or to laugh if I didn't want to. Upon my return, I threw myself into other things—work, exercise (a lot of running—running to? running from?), catching up with friends. Dating, sort of. There have been a few dates; all firsts, no seconds—no real interest on my part. (Afternoon dates, all of them, so that it's not a big deal when I don't drink.) All of this is not to say there weren't a few dark days, even lonelier nights, and a few horrifying nightmares, but I powered through somehow, kept marching forward. It seemed critical, rejoining the world—I have been away too long.

I'd been dreading today, the one-month anniversary of Lily's passing, but I hadn't expected it to land with such a numbing clonk. I probably only made this date knowing I would need the distraction. Not that I didn't find his pictures attractive. Not that I didn't enjoy our email exchange. I think I'm attracted to his name: Byron. A poet's name. Romantic. I've read a lot of Lord Byron of late; he had a Newfoundland, named Boatswain, who was the inspiration for one of his more famous works, "Epitaph to a Dog." *Near this Spot are deposited the Remains of one who possessed Beauty without Vanity, Strength without Insolence, Courage without Ferocity, and all the virtues of Man without his Vices.* Boatswain, it seems, was a lot like Lily.

It felt like some sort of sign, my date's name being Byron. He would understand me and the depths of my pain. He would speak in poetry, real emotional verse, and not pablum and platitudes. But I don't really know what I'm doing as I march toward the farther of the two Starbucks, the one closer to the yogurt place.

Living, I suppose. Breathing. It seems I'm almost ready to do those things again. Not just go through the motions, but attempt them for real.

I weave through L.A.'s famous Farmers Market (which is really more of an outdoor food court) and now I'm a few minutes late and the place is packed and there's still the uncertainty about where to meet when I look down and realize I'm wearing yellow pants. Yellow pants. Really? Sometimes I don't know what I'm thinking. They're rolled at the cuff and paired with a navy polo and it looks like maybe I just valeted my yacht and I'm certain to come off as an asshole. I think about canceling, or at least delaying so I can go home and change, but the effort that would require is unappealing and this date is mostly for distraction, and when I round the last stall (someone selling enormous eggplants, more round than oblong), I see him casually leaning against a wall and something inside my body says there you are.

There you are.

I don't understand them, these words, because they seem too deep and too soulful to attach to the Farmers Market, this Starbucks or that, a frozen yogurt place, or confusion over where to meet a stranger. They're straining to define a feeling of stunning comfort that drips over me, as if a water balloon burst over my head on the hottest of summer days. My knees don't buckle, my heart doesn't skip, but I'm awash in the warmth of a Valium-like hug. Except I haven't taken a Valium. Not since the night of Lily's death. Yet here is this warm hug that makes me feel safe with this person, this Byron the maybe-poet, and I want it to stop. This—whatever this feeling is—can't be a real feeling, this can't be a tangible connection. This is just a man leaning against a stall that sells giant eggplants. But I no longer have time to worry about what this feeling is, whether I should or shouldn't be here, or should or shouldn't be wearing yellow pants, because there are only maybe three perfect seconds where I see him and he has yet to spot me. Three perfect seconds to enjoy the calm that has so long eluded me.

There you are.

And then he casually lifts his head and turns my way and uses one foot to push himself off the wall he is leaning against. We lock eyes and he smiles with recognition and there's a disarming kindness to his face and suddenly I'm standing in front of him.

"There you are." It comes out of my mouth before I can stop it and it's all I can do to steer the words in a more playfully casual direction so he isn't saddled with the importance I've placed on them. I think it comes off okay, but, as I know from my time at sea, sometimes big ships turn slowly.

Byron chuckles and gives a little pump of his fist. "YES! IT'S! ALL! HAPPENING! FOR! US!"

I want to stop in my tracks, but I'm already leaning in for a hug and he comes the rest of the way and the warm embrace of seeing him standing there is now an actual embrace and it is no less sincere.

He must feel me gripping him tightly because he asks, "Is everything okay?"

"No. Yes. Everything is great. It's just . . ." I play it back in my head, what he said, the way in which he said it and the enthusiasm that had only a month ago gone silent. "You reminded me of someone, is all."

"Hopefully in a good way."

I smile, but it takes just a minute to speak. "In the best possible way."

I don't break the hug first, but maybe at the same time. This is a step. Jenny will be proud. I look in his eyes, which I expect to be brown like Lily's, but instead are deep blue like the waters lapping calmly against the outboard sides of *Fishful Thinking*.

"Is frozen yogurt okay?"

"Frozen yogurt is perfect."

We sit across from each other with our yogurt, which is a better choice in the August sun than coffee. His is plain and mine is pomegranate. I'm surprised that he looks both exactly like and nothing like his pictures. The way he moves, the way he smiles, it makes him more handsome than anything a still photograph could capture. We run through the usual first-date banter and I start to tell one of my stories and even though it comes off okay, when I finish I tell myself to stop it.

This one is worth being present for.

He is from New Orleans. He used to be a TV news reporter in Las Vegas and I wonder how that is because his hair curls and it moves in the breeze and he kind of looks like the poet his name suggests and nothing like a TV news reporter, at least any that I've seen. He's an uncle like I am an uncle. He's close with his mother, but not his father. He's sad about the death of Whitney Houston.

He loves dogs.

"Have you ever been in love?" Byron asks.

I pause and think of Lily, even though I know that's not what he means. I answer yes because, even if there had never been a Lily, it's true. I even go so far as to try to mask the pain of it. "You?"

He looks sheepishly at his feet. "I don't think so." And then he adds a hopeful "Not yet."

I recognize in his face the look of someone who has been on a lot of these . . . *dates*, and I admire his ability to remain hopeful.

"How long was your last relationship?" he asks.

"Six years."

"How did it end?"

I pause.

"I mean, if you don't mind me asking."

"I don't mind," I say. "I ended it."

"Why?" And then with a chuckle, "I have a tendency to be direct."

I look at him and weigh the advantages of several lines before deciding the best way to answer directness is by being direct in return. "Because I thought I deserved to be treated better."

"GOOD! FOR! YOU!"

I look around at the crowd and wonder if someone is playing a cruel practical joke. Like I might see the octopus in human form five tables away, sipping an iced latte and saluting me with one of his tentacles. But the octopus is dead; I know that. And I don't think this is a joke—I think this is who this guy really is.

"When did you know it was over?" he asks.

"In the days leading up to the election when marriage equality was on the ballot in California, he talked about us getting married. I had such a visceral reaction to tying my life to his that I thought about casting my vote to make gay marriage illegal, denying all gay Californians their basic civil rights, just to avoid an uncomfortable conversation at home."

Byron laughs.

"I guess that's when I knew it was over." I put my hand on his forearm. I don't know why I do this—and it's not exactly natural, although it's not unnatural—except that I really want to touch his skin. It's smooth, and tanned just a little bit, and feels like summer—like something familiar and warm and good. Like my skin did on the first days aboard *Fishful Thinking*, before it salted and burned and peeled. "We broke up three years after that." I sit back in my chair and give a sly smile. Relationships are complex, and sometimes you can't really explain them to an outside party. "I can't believe I just told you that."

"YES! YOU! ARE! LIVING! YOUR! FULL! LIFE!"

A third time. I'm not imagining it.

There you are.

This time my heart does skip a beat. I look down at his arm and we're still touching and he has made no attempt to retract his arm or retreat.

All my surroundings—the red Formica tabletop, the pink yogurt, the blue sky, the green vegetables in the market—they all come alive in vibrant Technicolor as the sun peers from behind a cloud. I am living my full life.

"Honesty in all things," Byron adds, lifting his cup of yogurt for a toast of sorts.

I pull my hand away from him and the instant my hand is back by my side I miss the warmth of his arm, the warmth of him. *Honesty in all things.* I should put my hand back. That's where it wants to be. That's Lily's lesson to me. Be present in the moment. Give spontaneous affection.

I'm suddenly aware I haven't spoken in a bit. "Did you know that an octopus has three hearts?" As soon as it comes out of my mouth I realize I sound like that kid from *Jerry Maguire. Did you know the human head weighs eight pounds?* I hope my question comes off even a fraction as endearing.

"No," Byron says with a glint in his eye that reads as curiosity—at least I hope that it does, but even if it doesn't I'm too into the inertia of the trivia to stop it.

"It's true. One heart called the systemic heart that functions much like the left side of the human heart, distributing blood throughout the body. Then two smaller branchial hearts, near the gills, that act like the right side of our hearts to pump the blood back."

"What made you think of that?"

I smile. It may be entirely inappropriate first-date conversation, but at least it doesn't bore me in the telling. I look up at the winsome August sky, marred only by the contrails of a passing jet and a vaguely dachshund-shaped cloud above the horizon. I don't believe in fate. I don't believe in love at first sight. I don't believe in angels. I don't believe there's a heaven and that our loved ones are looking down on us. But the sun is so warm and the breeze is so cool and the company is so perfect and the whole afternoon so intoxicating it's hard not to hear Lily's voice dancing in the gentle wind.

ONE! MONTH! IS! LONG! ENOUGH! TO! BE! SAD!

I want to argue with Lily—one month is not long enough. But in dog months that's seven months, over two hundred days. But none of it matters; to her even one day of my sadness was one day too many. I pick up my spoon and swirl it around the bottom of my empty yogurt dish and think more of Lord Byron's poem. *But the poor Dog, in life the firmest friend, The first to welcome, foremost to defend.* I corral the melted puddle of pomegranate yogurt into one side of the dish with a coordinated series of scrapes.

"I recently lost someone close to me." A few last drags of the spoon in my empty dish before I put it down and turn my full attention to Byron. "I don't know. I feel her here today. With us. You, me, her—three hearts. Like an octopus." I shrug.

If I were him I would run. What a ridiculously creepy thing to say. I would run and I would not stop until I was home in my bed with a gallon of ice cream deleting my profile from every dating site I belonged to.

Maybe it's because it's not rehearsed. Maybe it's because it's as weird a thing to say as it is genuine. Maybe it's because this is finally the man for me. Byron stands and offers me his hand.

"Let's take a walk and you can tell me about her."

The gentle untying of a shoelace.

It takes me a minute to decide if I can do this, and I decide that I can, and I throw our yogurt dishes away and I put my hand in his and it's soft and warm and instead of awkward fumbling, our hands clasp together like magnets and metal, like we've been hand-in-hand all along. And we are touching again.

"We could grab something to drink at this place up ahead," I suggest.

"Is it okay if it's iced tea?" Byron asks. "I don't really drink."

If only he knew how perfect that would be. "Iced tea sounds great."

Byron smiles. His eyes are still blue, this time like the sky. The sky with the dachshund cloud. I remember one of the more spectacular sunsets aboard *Fishful Thinking*, when I sheepishly confided in Lily that I would like to fall in love again. How the words tripped heavily off my tongue with guilt. How even saying them out loud suggested a time after Lily. And I remember her simple response.

"You will," Lily said.

We start walking.

I start talking.

"We met on a farm in the country when she was just twelve weeks old. She was gentle and kind and this lady called her a runt. Her father was called Caesar and her mother's name was Witchie-Poo."

Byron squeezes my hand twice with waggish delight.

I begin the story of Lily.

BEGIN! THE! STORY! OF! ME!

Acknowledgments

I understand that most everyone thinks they have the world's greatest dog, and I'd be hard-pressed to make the case that Lily was the greatest dog of all time. She never rescued anyone from a house fire, she was never separated from me in a way that required her to miraculously journey hundreds of miles home, and a passing skateboard could send her cowering indoors for hours. And yet she taught me everything I know about patience, kindness, strength, and unconditional love. For that, I am forever in her debt. Lily, you were, quite simply, the greatest to me.

Thank you first to Rob Weisbach, agent, advocate, visionary, and treasured friend. Even though I'm the Taurus, you've been nothing shy of bullish in your enthusiasm for and devotion to this book and making it an unqualified success.

My editor, Karyn Marcus, was a champion of this book before she even acquired it. We've laughed together, labored together, procrastinated together, celebrated together, cried together, watched YouTube videos of Cate Blanchett together—and hand in hand we made this book better. Together.

Here I should just print Simon & Schuster's main directory, as everyone worked overtime to make a publishing house feel like home. Instead I'll single out Marysue Rucci for her early embrace of this first-time author, and thank Carolyn Reidy, Jonathan Karp, Richard Rhorer, Wendy Sheanin, Cary Goldstein, Marie Florio, Megan Hogan, Sydney Morris, Julia Prosser, and Stephen Bedford for their hard work and for making me feel part of a team.

If this book has a fairy godmother, she is Molly Lindley Pisani. Molly, your contributions are too numerous to list here, but I won't ever forget them. You made magic happen. Bibbidi-bobbidi-book.

Thank you everyone who read an early draft and provided invaluable feedback: Trent Vernon, Wende Crowley, Katherine Lippa, Marcy Natkin, Susan Wiernusz, Laura Rowley, Brianna Sinon Rowley, April Wexler, Travis McCann, Lindsey McCann, Jill Bernstein, and Kristin Peterson. Additionally, this book has many friends, and they include Derrick Abrenica, Sven Davison, Malina Saval, Harlan Gulko, Sam Rowley, Evan Roberts, Cara Hancock Slifka, Steve Lekowicz, Ryan Quinn, Kyle Cummings, Elissa Dauria, and Barry Babok.

My entire life, my parents, Norman Rowley and Barbara Sonia, have given me nothing short of their full support, encouragement, enthusiasm, and love. They championed this book and embraced its weirdness, even when it was tough to read. I thank you both.

Tilda, you had big shoes to fill. Thank you for being exactly who you are.

Evelyn, Emmett, Harper, Elias, and Graham, being your uncle is one of the great joys of my life. Please don't ever stop loving books, as they will take you everywhere.

Acknowledgments

Finally, a heartfelt thank-you to Byron Lane, who read a short story entitled "The Octopus" and said, "I love it! Now go write chapter two." You were my first reader and my last. Your insight, passion, honesty, ardent margin notes, and gung ho enthusiasm simply gave this book life. All the lessons Lily taught me about love? I hope to spend a lifetime living them with you.

About the Author

Steven Rowley has worked as a freelance writer, newspaper columnist, and screenwriter. Originally from Portland, Maine, he is a graduate of Emerson College. He currently resides in Los Angeles with his boyfriend and their dog. *Lily and the Octopus*, his first novel, has been translated into more than fifteen languages. Follow him on Twitter and Instagram @mrstevenrowley.

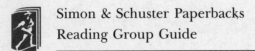
Lily and the Octopus

STEVEN ROWLEY

Introduction

*T*his reading group guide for Lily and the Octopus *includes discussion questions, ideas for enhancing your book club, and a* Q&A *with author* **Steven Rowley**. *The suggested questions are intended to help your reading group find new and interesting angles and topics for your discussion. We hope that these ideas will enrich your conversation and increase your enjoyment of the book.*

Topics and Questions for Discussion

1. Ted agonizes over the fact that Lily's octopus has gone unnoticed by both of them for so long. Discuss how he internalizes his grief, transforming it into guilt. How would you react in his shoes?

2. The book is divided into eight sections, each with an octopus-related theme. What other octopus imagery and symbolism did you find in the book?

3. Ted hates "living in the not knowing" (p. 17). How does this aversion to uncertainty affect his personal relationships? Do you think this attitude changes over the course of the novel?

4. There is a level of trust shared between Ted and Lily that does not seem to extend to the humans in his life. Discuss how trust requires a kind of courage that humans find difficult to muster. Is it possible to replicate the unconditional love of a dog? Why or why not?

5. Ted notes that Lily has been the closest witness to his life. Discuss why this is clarifying for him. How can new perspectives become powerful?

6. Throughout the novel, we learn that omens can be just as bad as they are good. What happens when Ted goes looking for more omens? Where do they lead him?

7. What role does forgiveness play in this novel? Who does Ted ultimately make peace with, and at what point?

8. Lily admits that she has not held on to a single bad memory. In fact, she does not have many memories at all. Still, she adores Ted's stories. Discuss how memories can become their own forms of storytelling. What does Ted learn from distilling their shared history?

9. The vet has warned Ted that as she gets older, Lily may start to encounter Enclosed World Syndrome. How is this syndrome mirrored in Ted's own life? Do you recognize the phenomenon?

10. Ted catches a glimpse of himself in the glass door by the pool and recognizes the octopus. Discuss the meaning of this scene. Why do you think this conflation of identity occurs in his mind's eye?

11. The tattoo artist, Kal, claims to enjoy the permanence of his work. Ted is skeptical that permanence even exists. Did you see anything in the novel that you felt to be permanent? If so, what was it?

12. One idea that Ted *is* partial to is karma. Karma implies a sense of causality and order to the universe. Do you think that his opinion evolves as Lily gets sicker?

13. Discuss the scene in which Ted finally acknowledges that the octopus is, in fact, a tumor. What has changed? Did he kill the octopus? What is the significance of this semantic twist?

14. Lily loves her red ball. Ted even goes so far as to suggest that hers is not a life without it. Discuss the symbolism of the ball, especially in Ted's dream when he loses Lily in a storm of them.

15. What does Ted see in Byron? Do you see a happy future for the two of them?

Enhance Your Book Club

1. Ted takes solace in the J. M. Barrie quote "To die would be an awfully big adventure," and the book calls upon Rudyard Kipling for its two epigraphs. Did you read *Peter Pan* or *The Jungle Book*? Discuss your memorable childhood reading experiences and whether you would go so far as to tattoo a favorite line on your body.

2. W. H. Auden's "Funeral Blues" is a beautiful poem of all-encompassing grief. Pull up a copy and read it aloud together. Compare and contrast the lines that resonate with each of you, sharing any memories that they evoke along the way.

3. In honor of Lily and Ted's last great adventure, take a group trip to the local aquarium or science center to consider the octopus or any of its underwater friends in their natural habitat. (Take care to remember that they are not all evil!)

4. Everyone needs a good pep talk once in a while. Treat yourselves to an episode of *Friday Night Lights* and soak in Coach Taylor's inspiring words.

A Conversation with Steven Rowley

Lily and the Octopus came about when you began jotting down memories of your own dear dachshund. Was this writing experience cathartic for you? Did it surprise you in any way?

It was indeed cathartic. Six months after my dog died of cancer, I wrote what became the first chapter of *Lily and the Octopus* as a short story to help process my grief. I didn't expect it to go anywhere; I was just doing what writers often do—putting feelings down on paper to get them out of my heart and my head. I shared the story with my boyfriend, who encouraged me to keep writing. Still, I felt the story was so deeply personal (and disconcertingly weird) that I wasn't sure it would connect with anyone who didn't know me or didn't know my dog. What has been surprising (and deeply humbling) is the way the book has resonated with so many readers—dog lovers and non-dog lovers alike. I tried to write Lily's story with unflinching emotional honesty, and the connection that people seem to feel, despite the magical realism, is a testament to the power of the truth.

You have also worked as a screenwriter. What do you think are the main differences between the two mediums? Do you have a preference?

When I decided to write *Lily and the Octopus* as a novel, I removed my screenwriter's cap and threw myself into the medium entirely, and it was incredibly freeing. Not once did I have to think about something being too expensive to build, too hard to cast, or too impossible to film. My only limits were those imposed by my own imagination. Talking dog as a main character? Sure. Octopus stuck to dog's head? Why not! Expansive battle at sea? Yes, please. I've always enjoyed writing dialogue, which lends itself to screenwriting. In the course of writing this book, I became really taken with crafting prose and the pace and depth at which you can really explore what's going on inside a character's head. Screenwriters have to externalize the internal, show what's going on through action and dialogue, and that can be difficult.

As a screenwriter, you're part of a team—one of many people who bring a story to life. Novelist is a much more solitary occupation. Collaboration can be fruitful, but it is often not the writer's vision that makes it to the screen. Likewise, a novel doesn't make it to the shelves without a real team of people who believe in the story, but for me it has been so rewarding to create something that itself was the final work and have my vision honored.

If *Lily and the Octopus* were adapted for film, who would be your ideal cast?

There are particular actors I imagine in the role of Ted, actors who have an inherent sadness to them and can convey a lot by doing very little. A certain stillness is important. Ewan

McGregor and Jake Gyllenhaal are two actors who I think are wildly underappreciated. Paul Rudd, I think, has untapped dramatic range. Jude Law. I keep naming incredibly handsome actors. Hmm. The voice of the octopus as I was writing was always Eddie Izzard's—and I mean that as the highest compliment. I am a huge fan and cannot imagine a more polished, brilliant, or formidable foe. I don't picture a film version where Lily actually speaks, as so many of her conversations with Ted are imagined. But I can't imagine a happier process than sitting with a casting director in a room full of dachshunds of all ages.

The narrative puts a lot of weight on naming and nicknames. Lily has an abundance of them, while Ted is mainly relegated to "that guy." There is also a poignant moment in which Ted and Jeffrey become only that to each other. Discuss the power of naming as it plays out in both the novel and real life.

One of my favorite moments in the book comes when Trent calls Ted Theodore, even though his full name is Edward. I think that one shorthand sums up their relationship perfectly and tells you everything you need to know about their friendship. Naming characters is hard for me, because I do indeed believe that names carry a lot of weight. Sometimes a name has the proper rhythm or length and it simply sounds right. I have three siblings whereas Ted has only one, so the three-syllable name given to Ted's sister, Meredith, allowed me to honor them. Lily in real life stemmed from Little Weiner Dog, and Lily became its own term of endearment. I do think it feels formal and stilted when people who are very close call each other by name, particularly those in romantic relationships. Ted was the last to be named. For the longest time he was simply "The Narrator," but people too often conflated him with me. I wanted him to have his own identity, and there is a huggable quality about the teddy bear that I hoped the reader would also feel for Ted. The last name I ripped straight from Melville. Flask was the third mate aboard the Pequod in *Moby-Dick* and was a man who seemed to regard the whale's very existence as a personal affront.

Ted considers Lily to be his best friend, but he also has a very strong human support system—Trent, Meredith, his mother. Where did you get the inspiration for these characters? Do you think that Ted appreciates them in the same way that he appreciates Lily?

I wanted Ted to be as isolated from people as possible in order to enhance and spotlight the special relationship he has with Lily; he has one parent, one sibling, one friend. They are an excellent support system in that they will always be there for him, even if at times his first instinct is to keep them at arm's length or to push them away. And I do think he appreciates the people in his life, but not in the same way as he does Lily— simply because she is there. Dogs don't let you keep them at a distance. They will doggedly push their way into your life, like it or not. It's also hard to craft a separate persona to present to a dog, the way humans often present somewhat different or edited personas to the various people in their lives. Dogs generally see the whole you and love unconditionally. I think there's a part of Ted that thinks the love he has from people is somehow conditional, and that prevents him from fully letting go.

The book takes place in Ted's early forties, a stereotypical time for midlife crises. Indeed, Ted muses that "this is the

halftime of my life, and my team is losing." Tell us how you would approach a "halftime" in your own life. What helps you get perspective after a fumble or two?

I thought it was important for Ted to be well-worn, a little weathered with a heartbreak or two under his belt, but too young to be pinned against the ropes or to tap out and not fight again. To me, that's your early forties. Or maybe it's as simple as I was in my early forties when I wrote the first draft of the book. In either case, turning forty is a bellwether moment for many people. My forties have been the first time I have fully felt like the person I was meant to be. It's with that confidence and sense of self that I pick myself up after fumbles now. It's so much easier to get back up and stand tall when you really know who you are.

The ocean—both the LA coast and the open sea—figures heavily throughout the novel. It is almost a character in its own right. Do you have a personal connection to the water? And—as a Maine native and California transplant—do you prefer the Atlantic or the Pacific?

The ocean has played a huge role in my life. I grew up in Portland, Maine, and have lived most of my adult life in Los Angeles. I've never lived far from the ocean, and I think I would panic if I had to. The word *landlocked* sends shivers down my spine. I've contemplated my life's big decisions—moving across the country, coming out, ending relationships—while sitting on a beach or looking over a cliff staring at the sea. That said, I think everyone who loves the ocean also has a healthy fear of the ocean, or at least a respect for its sheer size, deep mysteries, intelligent life, and awesome power. The octopus is an octopus in part because

I wanted the novel's antagonist to come from the ocean. To be both of this world and not.

For everything but swimming—for its seafood, for its rocky shoreline, for its moody vistas—I prefer the Atlantic Ocean. There's nothing like your first love.

You are clearly an avid Kipling fan. Who are your favorite literary beasts in (and out of) the canon? What do you think made them so memorable?

I love Kipling's *The Jungle Book*, although I forget when I was introduced to his work. It may have been as a Cub Scout. I know that growing up I had a short story version of "Rikki-Tikki-Tavi." The Kipling quotes from "The Law of the Jungle" that serve as the book's two epigraphs were quotes that I jotted down early in the writing process and referred back to throughout. I love thinking of Ted and Lily as a pack, and there's something comforting about laws, even violent ones, providing structure in the vast jungle that is life; laws that are defined and understood from the outset. Death is a part of life. The earlier one understands this, the more fully one can live. Opening the book with a quote from *The Jungle Book* helps underscore the fable elements of *Lily and the Octopus*. I also am a huge fan of blurring lines between prose and poetry, building a rhythm and cadence through word choice, sentence length, repetition, and other literary devices that Kipling excels at.

Other writers who have inspired me include John Steinbeck, Michael Chabon, Donna Tartt, Jonathan Franzen, Richard Russo, Joan Didion, and Francesca Lia Block, whose book *Weetzie Bat* (another prose poem) was handed to me at a critical moment in my life.

Other than the uncanny physical similarities, why choose an octopus? What kind of research did you do on the species, and what is your favorite piece of trivia?

I chose an octopus because they are smart, wily, and slimy. They can learn, adapt, and even (according to numerous scientists) play. I needed a foe that would needle Ted, toy with him, study his weaknesses, and adjust, just as cancer mutates in the body. It helped the story that they are in many ways the physical opposite of dogs, especially dachshunds. A hairless invertebrate that lives in the sea is nothing like a furry dog that is all spine and lives on the land. I did an incredible amount of research on octopuses, and gave each of the book's eight sections an octopus theme. There are so many fascinating facts about them it's hard to pick a favorite; in writing the book it was hard to shake their having three hearts. Once I learned that piece of trivia, I knew the entire book would be driving toward that end.

While the octopus as villain fit the needs of this story, I want to be clear that they are magnificent creatures and are in no way inherently evil. I am quite in awe of them, really!

Do you think Ted and Byron will adopt another dog? Will it be a dachshund?

I do think that Ted and Byron will adopt a dog, but I don't think it will be a dachshund. I think Lily is irreplaceable to Ted, and just as Byron is very different from Jeffrey, a new dog will be different from Lily. No judgment here toward others who feel differently, but limiting oneself to one breed always struck me as odd. As does the idea of there being another dachshund named Lily 2. I imagine that Ted and Byron would adopt a dog from an area shelter—just as I would encourage readers of *Lily and the Octopus* in the market for a dog to do.